Terroir

Sheila Scobba Banning

Winter Goose
Publishing

Winter Goose Publishing
2701 Del Paso Road, 130-92
Sacramento, CA 95835

www.wintergoosepublishing.com
Contact Information: info@wintergoosepublishing.com

Terroir

COPYRIGHT © 2013 Sheila Scobba Banning

First Edition, August 2013
ISBN: 978-0-9894792-3-3

Cover Art by Winter Goose Publishing
Typeset by Michelle Lovi

Published in the United States of America

Dedicated to all who live passionately
and love with abandon . . .
and everyone who tries

Becca N

Enjoy this with a glass
of fine wine. You & I shall
are a fine vintage, too.

Chad

Chapter 1

Mermaid Tears:
a bright wine with surprising intensity, it opens with wild strawberry
and black cherry, then cranberry, plum, and lavender.
Mature tannins with a hint of damp cedar
and violets on the long, silky finish.

Suzanne cradled the grape cluster in her hands as if receiving alms. She caressed the soft mauve globes with her thumbs, careful not to press too hard and break the skin. The purple was coming on fast, harvest whispering sweet nothings in her ear. This was Suzanne's favorite time of year, that back-to-school sense of transition and new beginnings that she never quite outgrew. The fall butterflies of expectation were even more pronounced since she started making wine, because crush wasn't something you could write on the calendar in ink a year ahead of time. Choosing the start day was as much art as science, turning berries to wine the alchemy of the modern age. She angled the cluster to catch the light. It could be a week, maybe a bit longer. The weather had been perfect this season, with both growers and critics already anticipating one of the great vintages. The late September heat had escalated ripening, but nothing to raise alarms. Suzanne had refrained from public comment, but she was certain this year's wine would be the best thing she had ever done, not just in her winemaking, but in her whole life.

In the decade since she began bottling wine from her own tiny vineyard, her pinot noir had developed a cult following. She knew better than to take the attention too seriously, though. Suzanne had started out working for some of the biggest names on the Sonoma Coast and in the Santa Lucia Highlands, experiencing firsthand the fickle nature of the celebrity pinot world. Quality always mattered, but by itself it didn't make you a star. It was all the other little pieces, the points and the reviewers, and the right mention at the right time that made Suzanne roll her eyes. If pressed to confess, however, she would admit to a tiny bit of smug satisfaction whenever she ran into one of the early skeptics after her wines started selling out immediately after release and provoking bidding wars on eBay.

There's an adage among pinotphiles and producers alike that anybody can make a mediocre pinot noir, but almost no one can make an exceptional one. Pinot noir grapes require more delicate handling than other varietals; the skin is thin and the fruit especially sensitive to its environment. The vines do best when the sunshine they need is moderated by cool evenings for a long slow ripening. Suzanne's favorite clones thrived on rocky moonscape slopes with good drainage that didn't look like they would support life of any sort, let alone nourish something both delicate and complex. Her favorite people were like that, too. Complicated, layered, maybe even difficult, but containing treasure well worth the effort. It wasn't that she didn't appreciate people who were exactly what they seemed to be, whose full range was visible practically on first meeting. In fact, she had married a man like that. But whether it was a universal human attribute or some peculiar taste of her own, Suzanne placed a higher value on the things that required more effort.

Dragging her hand lightly through the gravelly dirt beneath the vines, Suzanne left a pattern like a Zen garden. She rubbed her fingertips together and brought them to her nose, feeling the chalky slip and releasing the mineral scent that subtly infused her berries. The microclimate variations of the Santa Cruz Mountains had become well-known to Suzanne when she was a college student. She had spent every weekend she could hiking or driving through hot ridges, shady valleys, and everything between. She loved to watch the fog spill over the peaks from a distance like a bubble bath overflowing, and it wasn't long before she could taste the difference in the air on the East slope and the West slope. When she happened upon a bright hardscrabble hillside next to a dry creek bed where foggy fingers reached in from the sea every night until you could almost smell the salt on the breeze, she liquidated the inheritance from her mother's estate, took out a big loan, and literally put down roots. Even as she made wine for other growers, any time off she could squeeze out of her schedule was spent digging post holes and planting vines.

Brushing hair off her face with the back of her hand, Suzanne stretched and surveyed the property. *Her* property. It was barely ten acres, a smidge of dirt that wouldn't even qualify as a farm in the Midwest. Where she grew up, a single crop could cover hundreds of acres, fields of green or chartreuse or gold stretching to the horizon. Her family had not been farm people, though, and the closest she got to agriculture was walking beans in the summers when she was old enough to want money but too young to get a job. One of the neighbors would contract for a bean field, and she would join her older friends pacing up and down the loamy row hacking out weeds with a hoe and feeling dirt trickle down the sides of her tennis shoes. The fragrance given off by the vanquished weeds was like freshly mown grass with a hint of something tangy beneath. The chlorophyl notes combined with the scent of the black alluvial soil as it warmed to produce an almost opiate sense of calm. Even as they laughed and joked back and forth, racing to the end of the row then having to go back to catch the thistles they had missed in their haste, there was something comforting in the rhythm and pattern. It was hard sweaty work for minimal pay, though, with work beginning at dawn each day and ending just past midday. Suzanne abandoned it as soon as she was old enough to get a "real" job. No one who knew her growing up would have imagined Suzanne making her living from the land, least of all her.

Suzanne held up a hand to shield her eyes against the last orange flares from the setting sun. She could not see the ocean from the vineyard hillside, but she could sense its presence all the same. The ocean was what brought her west, a call to live on the edge of the world next to the tides pulsing like the heartbeat of the planet. She had seen it once when she was little, the only family vacation she had had, and that sealed her fate. Maybe it was because she had grown-up on a landlocked plain, or maybe it was the phantom memory of that early trip, but she faced the sea many times each day as if turning toward her own personal Mecca.

"Miss Suzanne?"

She started, then turned to the voice. "Carlos! I didn't hear you. Como gatito," She laughed, but her vineyard manager barely smiled.

"Mr. Will, he asked me to give you this."

Carlos removed his hat with one hand and held out a thick official-looking envelope with the other. They both stared at it, orphaned in the space between them. Suzanne knew what it had to be and could not lift her arm to take it from him anymore than she could look away from it. Finally he said, "He asked me to give it to you. Myself. To be sure you got it."

Embarrassed for putting Carlos in an awkward position, Suzanne willed her hand up to grasp the heavy cream paper. Once it was in her hand, the spell was reversed and she could no longer look at it at all.

"Lo siento mucho, Carlos. Of course; thank you."

She arranged what she hoped was a not-too-big smile on her face as she looked into the eyes of her manager. His gaze immediately dropped to the ground. He turned away for a moment, toward the sundial shadows of the distant pines, then back to Suzanne, mouth open as if about to speak. Instead, he nodded, put his hat back on, and started down the hill.

"Ten days!" he shouted his prediction over his shoulder without looking back. Suzanne knew he meant the start of harvest, but it had the ominous ring of a verdict. Or maybe a curse. She inhaled deeply and held the air in her lungs as if hoping for narcotic effect from the damp sea breath, then sighed and walked to the end of the row, pausing to inspect the vines that were the foundation of her signature wine.

A great pinot might include any number of variations on a theme of red and black fruit, spice, herbs, and earthiness. Blackberries, plums, mushrooms, cedar, all sorts of things could come into play. The silky mouth feel was mandatory, and Suzanne thought a long finish was, too; but the nuances of the flavor profile in an exceptional wine could have a surprisingly broad range. What constitutes a truly great pinot noir is personal and very subjective, like the definition of great sex. There may be some baseline requirements, but beyond that, it is all about personal taste in pleasure. But like transcendent sex, once you have experienced a spectacular wine, that becomes the standard by which you judge everything else. You might appreciate the variations, but you pursue that initial sensation unless and until you have another singular experience to surpass it.

Suzanne loved the caramelized sugar on the nose that some of the Saints, as she called them, offered. The best of the pinots from Santa Rita, Santa Maria, and Santa Lucia often had that hint of burnt sweetness on opening which she found irresistibly seductive. Next she wanted bright red strawberries and raspberries, maybe black cherry or plum in the middle with a hint of lavender or leather emerging just before the lingering finish she relished.

That was her goal when she started, to create a wine she would love to drink and to share that pleasure with others. She chose the six clones she planted for what she had learned from her work in other wineries and from what she expected the soil to give to the berries. The first tasting from her first barrel made her laugh out loud. The nose was floral and the dominant flavor was cherry. There was a hint of honeysuckle and almond and an enticing, not quite long enough finish. It wasn't really what she was aiming for, but it had a delight all its own. As she swirled the wine in her glass, holding it up to the light to check the color, her husband walked in.

"Look at those legs!"

"Mine or the wine?" Suzanne stood on tiptoe with one hand on her hip as if posing and they both laughed.

"You're such a tease." Will grabbed her from behind and she leaned into him.

"Not compared to this." She took a sip from the glass and tilted her head back as if for a kiss. When Will's lips touched hers, she blew the wine softly into his mouth like a sigh.

"You're right," he said, "that's a much bigger tease."

On bottling, the wine retained all the bright fruit and floral notes while gaining a little depth. The finish was a bit longer, but it was still over before you were ready. Suzanne named the wine Cherie Amour and talked an artist friend into embellishing the sketch she had done for the label: a winking redhead in tap pants and marabou slippers posed like a vintage pinup girl.

After the second bottling of Cherie Amour, Suzanne tore out a small section of the vineyard and replaced the vines with two different clones. It took three years to get enough fruit to use, and another two to produce the wine she was looking for, with the profits from Cherie going right back into the new production. She didn't expect to get the caramelized sugar nose she loved out of the Santa Cruz Mountains soil, no matter what clones she used, but she did manage to capture a hint of something reminiscent of cotton candy with a soft wildflower scent like the throat of a woman wearing expensively understated perfume. The color in the glass was a little darker than pinots from other regions, but held up to the light it still glowed a brilliant ruby deep in its heart. The wine opened with red berries, then shifted so slightly to cranberry then plum, it was like trying to find the color boundaries on a piece of hand-dyed silk. A hint of damp wood and violets lingered after the finish, leaving the drinker with a sense of wistfulness almost like nostalgia. Suzanne noticed that the first tasters began mourning the end of the glass as soon as they took their first sip, as if longing to hold onto something they knew would never last.

When Will tasted the new wine he said, "This is the one, Suzanny! Even with three hundred cases, even if you only get one, this is it. We're entering all the big competitions and we're going to put you out in front of all the media coverage." He had been in sales before they met, and he managed all of the business side of the Suzanne Mathews Vineyard. He had accomplished the unexpected feat of turning a profit on the first commercial release of Cherie Amour and had developed a broad network of restaurant and wine shop contacts since. Will refinanced the property and negotiated a deal on a few more acres adjacent to the new clones so they could expand enough to increase production. Because the most intense flavors come from berries that are not overcrowded on the vine, the only way to get more fruit without compromising quality is to plant more vines.

Suzanne named the new wine Mermaid Tears for the maritime dew that cooled the vines and for the ethereal qualities she could only hope she would be able to reproduce. She did a series of sketches to capture what she wanted before she was ready to sit down with Craig, the artist, and design the new label. Against a pale background the color of fog, a mermaid balanced on a rock, leaning toward the sea, a hint of a smile on her lips that never reached her eyes. The scales of her tail were an iridescent but understated green-gold hue that caught the light with a rippling effect like water, and on her cheek was a single tear in the same metallic color, visible only from certain angles.

At the small release party for the vineyard family, Suzanne toasted her friends and staff by first swirling the wine in her glass then holding it up to the light so they could watch the slow stream of rivulets back down to the surface.

"Real Mermaid Tears!" She smiled and drank with them, thinking she might never again think of that simple phenomenon of alcohol evaporating faster than water as "legs." When she finished, Will unveiled an oversized poster of the label he had commissioned as a surprise for Suzanne. In large format, the mermaid's firm jaw, upturned nose and pale eyes bore an unexpected resemblance to Suzanne which had gone unnoticed at the scale of the label drawing. The artist raised his glass and winked at her when it was pointed out.

"Okay, Craig, was that your idea or Will's?"

"Honey, *everything* is my idea! Besides, I didn't change anything; you just couldn't see it before."

Suzanne refilled his empty glass and inspected the bottle label before turning back to the poster. "I'm not really the mermaid type."

Craig raised an eyebrow. "Pining for the sea? Yearning for something you've never had as if it's lost? That fits you like a latex glove."

"Maybe luring sailors to their destruction." She lifted her glass and clinked it against his.

"That too, Susie-Q." Craig gave her a quick squeeze, then turned to Will as he approached. "Beware the siren song, my friend." Will laughed at the punch line without benefit of the set up.

When Will had laid out his aggressive plan to launch Mermaid Tears, Suzanne was thrilled to have him share her joy in creating the wine. She loved his enthusiasm despite her instinctive reluctance to be marketed as if she were a product, too. Will connected with people in a way she never had, though, and she trusted his savvy.

They had met at a winemaker dinner, discovering within a couple minutes that they had overlapped at UC Davis. Even if it hadn't been a huge campus, Suzanne was pretty sure they would not have run in the same circles. As a transfer student, she had already missed out on two years of socializing, and when she switched her major from chemistry to viticulture, she added one full year and two summers to her academic tenure. When she wasn't studying, she was going to the mountains, more often than not by herself. Will had been a frat boy with good grades but even better parties. He thrived on interaction, his personality giving him a natural affinity for sales. If he sometimes talked more than he listened, she didn't mind. Will was full of good stories. He was also younger than she was, not enough to raise eyebrows, though he joked about being her boy-toy, anyway.

Suzanne was initially leery of being grilled by some hostile talk show host trying to cultivate a following by manufacturing controversy, but she found that most interviewers were people who loved wine. She came to enjoy the interviews and appearances because the meetings felt more like a conversation with friends than a publicity stunt. The only thing she refused was a morning show that ended up conflicting with crush when the grapes were ready a week earlier than she had projected. Will wasn't happy about her canceling, assuring her that her absence at the vineyard for one day wouldn't ruin the wine. She bristled at his cavalier attitude. He was pushing her for Woman Winemaker of the Year and had called in a lot of favors to get her the appearance, insisting that she was the one in need of attitude adjustment. In the end, though, he took her place and discovered he was one of those people the camera loved. He came to love it, in return, taking on more and more of the media appearances and event pourings.

Suzanne stood at the end of the row staring at the rose bush just beyond. The envelope felt unnatural in her hand, parched and outsized. She had a sudden urge to fling it into the thorny flowers, but she resisted. Roses were traditional vineyard plantings, originally they probably did serve as diagnostics for disease, the canary in the coal mine for winegrowers. Now that so much scientific testing and sampling could be done, their presence was mostly ornamental. Will was not much of a gardener, rarely ventured into the vineyard, but he had asked her to include this deep red variety in the border after they were married. These were the roses he had given her when he proposed, "Forever Yours."

She slid her finger into the corner and under the flap, her hesitation lending an almost erotic slowness to the opening process. Suzanne scanned the pages, more numb than anything, until she got to the end. Halfway through the last page she stopped and went back to read the whole thing again from the beginning. She folded the pages with shaking hands and crammed them back into the envelope, then shoved the envelope into her back pocket. She crouched and lifted another cluster of berries so close to ready she thought Carlos's prediction would surely be late. She ran her thumb lightly over the grapes, then plucked one with her other hand and popped it into her mouth. At the explosion of tart-sweet juice as she bit down, she burst into tears. Sobs convulsed her body, a shaking so furious it felt like the ground, itself, was moving. Northern California was scored with fault lines, San Andreas, Hayward, others whose names she couldn't remember. That at any given moment the tectonic plates might slip and everything around you shudder to the ground was a risk everyone assumed when they decided to live in the state. People tended to forget, though, or they ignored the hazards. Even when you know the rift is there, as long as things are stable, you're willing to pretend they always will be. Until the earth tears open and there is nothing left to you but the struggle to survive. The fault line in her relationship had turned out to be far more destructive than any earthquake.

She heard the yipping of a coyote one hill over and tried to pull herself together. The last edge of twilight was holding off the night, and Suzanne accepted that she had to go back to the house. At least she knew she would be there alone. She took a ragged breath and looked down at the grapes in her hand. Squeezing them in her fist until the juice ran like blood between her fingers sending stain lines down her wrist to soak the soil, she said aloud, "I will tear every one of these vines out with my bare hands before I will let that bastard take my winery!"

Chapter 2

Appellation:
a legally defined and protected geographical area
used to identify where the grapes for a wine were grown

"How can anyone else, even my husband, have a right to *my* name?"

Suzanne delivered the question like something between an accusation and a prayer. Her lawyer leaned across the desk and squeezed her forearm.

"I'm sorry, Suzanne. When you restructured and incorporated the winery, it became the company name, not yours." His voice was a rich baritone, slow and soothing. "I mean, of course you still have your own name, but 'Suzanne Mathews Winery' is now a marital asset subject to all property division regulations."

She tried not to cry. That was the part she hated the most, the crying in front of people, sometimes at the slightest provocation. Suzanne thought some emotions were meant to be private; she hadn't even cried at her mother's funeral. Now, though, she could feel a constant prickling in her eyes, and she couldn't always disguise it as allergies. She thought if someone came up with a drug that prevented tears the way antiperspirants prevent sweat, people would rush to hand over their cash, and she would be first in line. As much as Suzanne despised public breakdowns, a tiny little bit of her believed she deserved the humiliation for being so stupid in the first place.

Most winemakers aren't in it for the money, which is a very good thing. Except for the big commercial vineyards or the family wineries that have been around for generations, winemaking more closely resembles the arts than any business. Like writers or painters, some vintners can make a living with their wine, some supplement with another job, and a rare few become wealthy beyond imagining. The impulse to create is as much a labor of love as a drive to achieve, and success has many standards of measure. Suzanne wouldn't claim she didn't care about the money, but it just wasn't as interesting to her as the sensory elements of fragrance and taste and color. Patterns in clouds and weather and organic compounds captured her attention in ways a simple spreadsheet never could. All the financial and legal structures Will put in place before the second release of Mermaid Tears had seemed above reproach. Suzanne read them before she signed them, so did Jeff, her attorney. It allowed the winery to expand slightly and increase production as quickly as possible. The restructuring was exactly the right thing to do financially, as long as you believe you will be married forever. And who doesn't want to believe that?

Suzanne closed her eyes and swallowed, concentrating on breathing slowly.

"You must think I'm a complete idiot."

Jeff reached into his desk drawer and handed her a tissue. She accepted it as insurance against a future loss of control.

"No, Suzanne, I don't. You and Will were already full partners in the winery. Even if you could have held the land, proper, separate from the rest of the company holdings like the buildings and equipment, Will would likely be able to make a claim against it based on the work he's done. And then there was the adjacent parcel purchase, which he initiated. One could argue that without the business management, the equipment leasing, marketing, and especially the sales, you wouldn't have a winery at all, just another backyard vanity project. And without the land as part of the deal, you would never have secured the loan for the new property, root stock and clones. You didn't make a stupid decision, you took a calculated risk."

Calculated risk was Suzanne's forte, or so she used to think. Moving to California, becoming a winemaker, building her own vineyard and winery, to some people those might have all appeared to be giant leaps of faith, but Suzanne had done her research. Her greatest asset was her own determination and tenacity, and she considered any endeavor which relied on personal effort to be much lower risk than it looked on paper. Of course, the expansion of the winery had been a joint effort with her husband. She had calculated that risk as if their partnership were as dependable as her solo performance.

"What do I do now?"

"You get another lawyer." Jeff took a business card from the folder in front of him and slid it across the desk to Suzanne. "Hanna Jackson is the best divorce attorney I know. Her reputation as a pit bull is so widespread that most opposing counsel settle out of court."

Suzanne picked up the card and studied it. "Are you sure you can't do this?"

The lawyer shook his head. "You need someone who knows family law. Hanna is the best thing I can do for you."

The Shoreline exit came and went, but Suzanne kept driving. She hadn't heard back from the lawyer Jeff had recommended, and somehow just leaving a message without having a conversation or setting an appointment had amplified her ambivalence about that night's event. She was never late for a pouring, especially not when it was high profile, but while she refused to concede the face of the winery to Will by bowing out, the thought of spending the evening beside him maintaining a cheerful professional facade made her want to vomit. The toxic mix of feelings left her stranded in her closet for an hour, trying to choose an outfit that would make her look good enough for compliments but not so good she seemed desperate. Never had she delegated so much responsibility to a bunch of silk and wool. It made her feel silly and frivolous, and she blamed Will for that unnatural batch of emotions, too.

Grinding her teeth, she took 85 and looped back around on city streets to get to the Computer History Museum, consciously delaying her arrival while still driving toward the event. She drove past the valet parking attendant and wound through the parking lot to find a space far in the back. Suzanne knew she was behaving like a child dragging her feet on the way to a dentist appointment, but she did it anyway. There was a cigar bar set up on the back patio, so she was able to enter the building without walking all the way to the front. She was sure that Teri, the SMW promotions coordinator, would have picked up the table packet and all the name badges even before Will arrived, but she thought she should check in with the event staff, anyway.

The Computer History Museum acquired and preserved artifacts and stories from the dawn of computing through the rapidly changing present. Art collections might be grouped by century, and the schools and movements might vary by decade, but with computers, the change was measured in years and sometimes months. This presented a particular challenge to the computing historian trying to gather everything without being fully aware of how it might eventually fit into the larger picture. When Suzanne had first walked through the exhibit of the Timeline of Computing, she was reminded of watching the movie *Blade Runner* again twenty years after it was released. Most of the technology companies whose presence had been projected into that imaginary future in the form of giant neon signs didn't even exist anymore.

The evening's event was an invitation-only fundraiser featuring wines with a connection to technology. Silicon Valley had a long and incestuous relationship with the wine industry. Many an entrepreneur from the '80s had planted his dividends in vineyards either as an investment or as a lifestyle. The scientific mind had a natural affinity for the matrix of knowledge required to produce a good wine, and for those used to find-ing solutions to problems that didn't yet exist, the transition from lines of code to rows of vines was easy to make. Suzanne loved wide-ranging conversations with people who could keep up, with or without segues, and she always felt at home with groups of engineers. In the midst of this group of retired venture capitalists and CEOs, though, she was an inter-loper. Her first and biggest fan, a man who had loved her way with wine when she was making it for someone else and who bought futures in her first release before even she knew what it would be like, was on the Board of Directors for the Museum. Suzanne Mathews Winery was part of the occasion only because her friend Gerard had requested it.

As she navigated the crowd surrounding the Babbage Difference Engine to find her assigned place, she passed the featured table in the main room, Clos de la Tech. If there were a more direct line between com-puters and wine, Suzanne didn't know what it would be. Every bottle even had a chip built into the label. T.J. Rodgers, the man who had founded and continued to run Cypress Semiconductor, was such an avid fan of Burgundy he decided to produce the best version possible in California. Suzanne had tasted the first vintage in 1996, made from vines planted on the acre of land around his Woodside home. The research he had done on the best French Burgundies he wished to surpass rather than replicate was impressive, his attention to detail amazing. At the point where she was just about to strike out on her own, Suzanne was inspired by his thoroughness and tenacity, but even more by his complete disregard for whether people thought it was merely self-indulgence. The wall of tuxedoes surrounding the table made it impossible to see who was pouring, but Suzanne knew she couldn't delay her arrival any longer anyway.

Teri spotted her and popped out from behind the table to give her a hug and hand her a name badge lanyard.

"Everyone really likes the wine!"

Suzanne noticed that her voice was pitched a little higher than usual, but whether from excitement or nervousness, she couldn't say. She could hear Will's voice behind them.

"We created this blend especially for tonight. It includes our own fruit as well as grapes from some of our friends in the Santa Cruz Mountains and just a touch from Oregon."

The words "we" and "our" made Suzanne's jaw tighten, so that when she turned, her expression was less like smiling than baring her teeth.

"And here's the winemaker, herself!" Will introduced her with a flourish, redirecting the attention of the handful of people, and hers as well. If he had caught her expression before handing off the patter, he gave no indication.

Seeing a familiar face in the crowd, her smile relaxed into something warmer and less feral.

"There are six sub-regions in the Santa Cruz Mountain appellation, and I chose fruit representing each of those areas, as well as some from the Willamette Valley. Not only do they have a way with pinot up there, but any homage to technology has to have at least a nod to the Pacific Northwest."

The group chuckled at the obvious Microsoft reference.

"The acidity comes from the Skyline and Saratoga grapes, the big fruit and touch of sweetness are from the foothills with rhubarb and plum borrowed from Ben Lomand, the subtle notes of rose hips, lilac, and blueberry are courtesy of the Corralitos vines, and the hints of smoky dark chocolate come from the Summit." Suzanne poured a couple ounces of wine into a big-bowled pinot noir glass and swirled it, holding it up to the light as she spoke and encouraging the small crowd to do the same. "I played with the blend to balance the masculine tannins with layers of red and black fruit followed by a long, silky finish. I wanted the wine to tell a story, with a bright opening, a complicated middle, and an end that goes on and on." She paused. "Like everyone's best hope for a startup."

They laughed louder at that line, and a voice called out from the side, "And what about the name? Is that some sort of guerrilla marketing for

Apple?"

Suzanne recognized Gerard's voice, and turned toward him, laughing. "No, Gerard. IPinOt is a smash up of pinot and initial public offering—three accented syllables, not two." She poured wine into the glass he held toward her like a character from Oliver Twist. "Sometimes an *I* is just an *I*."

Two hours flew by in a stream of conversations as the members circulated, each dialogue or mini-lecture punctuated by sips of wine and a few crackers. Suzanne had the buoyant sense of completion that comes when you hit the last page of a final exam; you're not done yet, but the end is in sight.

"Let me introduce you."

Suzanne heard the rise in Will's voice and turned.

"Suzanne, this is Trevor Constantine. He's with BDP on Sandhill." Will delivered the name as if he were announcing royalty, but his hand rested on the man's shoulder.

"So this is the woman behind the wine." Constantine's hair was buffed to a high sheen, and his tailored suit conjured visions of brandy and cigars in a club she would never be invited to join. He had arranged his features into the perfect expression of amused condescension for so many years his face had frozen that way, proving everyone's mother right. "Will speaks so highly of you; it's a pleasure to finally meet."

Suzanne ground her teeth into a smile until her jaw hurt and extended her hand. "We've met."

Constantine's eyebrows shot up in exaggerated surprise as he took her hand in his right and then covered it with his left. "I'm sure I would have remembered you!"

"We were on the same panel a couple years ago, a newspaper feature on local business. I don't think I made much of an impression." She remembered Constantine's boorish behavior, interrupting, talking over other people, basically behaving as if he were the only one in the room worth listening to.

He frowned. "Clearly my loss."

Because she had slid her thumb as far into his grip as possible in case he was the knuckle-crusher he appeared to be, Suzanne found herself trapped in the overly-familiar clasp. "How do you know Will?"

He shot Will a look of genuine, if guarded, surprise before responding. "We're fraternity brothers. Of course, I was at SC."

Suzanne faked a sneeze and extracted her hand. "Excuse me. Nice to meet you. Again. Mr. Constantine."

"Trevor," he interrupted.

"Trevor." She smiled without showing teeth. "If you'll pardon me, I need to check the bottle count."

His smug suggestion of a smile made the carnivorous gleam in his eyes all the more disconcerting. "I look forward to seeing you again, Suzanne. Very soon."

Suzanne conferred with Teri as Will walked off with Constantine. She did want to check the numbers for the night, even if she didn't really need to do it right then. She stepped out from behind the table again as a bearded man in a smoking jacket approached. She discussed the wine with him briefly, then handed him off to Teri to place an order. The thing she loved most about CHM events was the characters that populated them. Entrepreneurial engineers uncoupled themselves from other people's expectations in refreshing and unexpected ways.

She was leaning on the table smiling, when Will returned and opened a new bottle.

"What did you think of Trevor?" Will held out the bottle to pour the first taste for her.

Suzanne felt her nose wrinkle involuntarily. "The same thing I thought the first time I met him."

Will looked pained. "Why are you making this so hard?"

"Does it really matter what I think? Our circles don't overlap enough for it to come up. But there's a reason Bridge Development Partners is known as the Big Dick Parade."

Will didn't respond, turning instead to rearrange the glasses on the table and fidget with the bottle display. After a minute or two, he turned back to face Suzanne and lifted his glass to touch hers.

"Tonight wasn't so bad, was it, Suzanny?"

"Don't call me that." The use of his personal nickname as if they were still on intimate terms made all the anger and shock and humiliation come flooding back. She wanted to slap the lopsided one-dimpled smile she used to find charming off his face.

"But I always . . ." He looked confused, then moved on. "I mean, doesn't this show that we can still work together, that we can separate our personal lives from our professional ones?"

Suzanne reached to the side to set her glass down on the table without breaking eye contact. She missed the edge and the glass shattered on the floor, opening a bubble of silence in which her rising voice sounded like a shriek.

"Professional? Like trying to steal the winery out from under me as if I'm just some stockholder and not the name on the bottle? Or is that the personal part?"

She saw the look on Teri's face and realized everyone within twenty feet had heard her. She closed her eyes for a moment, holding her breath. When she opened her eyes again, she pitched her voice so low that only Will could hear.

"Get out."

Whatever he heard in her voice, he didn't try to argue, but his flushed face betrayed his feelings. He spun on his heel, grabbed his bag from behind the table, and vanished into the crowd.

She offered Teri a tiny smile filled with as much reassurance as she could muster, then turned toward the front of the building under the scrutiny of the curious onlookers, held both hands up beside her mouth and shouted, "Cleanup on aisle nine!"

The tension was broken and the volume of the party drone returned to its pre-social disaster level. Suzanne shook off Gerard's questioning look when he came to see if she was okay and feigned interest in the people she spoke to until the event shut down. She usually helped pack up after a pouring, but she didn't think she could maintain the facade any longer.

"You go," Teri said. "Between pouring and people buying, we went through all but half a case. There isn't much to do."

She paused, and Suzanne braced herself for some expression of sympathy that would open the floodgates instead of offering comfort, but something in Suzanne's face must have stopped her, because Teri dropped her eyes and started clearing the table.

"Thanks, Teri. I really appreciate it."

Suzanne knew she shouldn't be driving, not because she had been drinking, but because her vision was so blurred by tears she could barely see the road signs. A deer appeared in the headlights as she made the turn to climb the hill toward the house. She slammed on the brakes, then wrestled with the wheel to correct the skid. The residual adrenaline rush left her nauseated and still shaking as she unlocked the door. She dropped her keys into a shallow ceramic dish sitting on the table by the door. The flat bowl was glazed in shades of teal and aquamarine with flecks of gray and fuchsia, and it had a mermaid as a handle. The dish had been made by a local potter whose animal-themed work included a line of soy sauce dishes with fish handles. She had requested a series of pieces after the first release of Mermaid Tears and now mermaids cropped up at Craft Faires all up and down the Peninsula. Usually it made her smile, but tonight it was just another reminder of what she had to lose.

The light on the answering machine was blinking insistently, a signal she had never learned to ignore. Suzanne knew a lot of people who spurned land lines entirely, but the cell service in the hills just wasn't reliable enough for her to make that leap. There were three messages; the first from Carlos confirming that he would have a crew in the bottom rows of the northwest corner in the morning to begin harvest, the second was from her nephew. She paused that one and replayed it, frowning at the terse "Suzanne, call me when you get this." With only a handful of years between them, she and Donnie had been close as children, but the difference between three and eight was much less than the distance between ten and fifteen. Suzanne had left home for college before Donnie entered high school, and their contact was reduced to the occasional phone call. She checked her watch. It was two hours later in Minneapolis, and Donnie hadn't said anything specific. He could wait. She skipped to the third message.

"You bitch! Your way or . . ."

Suzanne dropped the phone as if her hand had been scalded. She didn't need to listen to the message, because she recognized the shrill voice on the machine. It belonged to her friend, Laura, the woman who had replaced her in Will's affections.

Chapter 3

Crush:
extracting juice from grapes for wine;
sometimes used as a synonym for harvest

Suzanne's sleep was scattered across the night in restless bits that left her more exhausted than when she lay down. She stood wrapped in a blanket at the window facing the hills, sipping a cup of strong French Roast as the gradual illumination of sunrise washed the landscape first in pale gold that contrasted with the dark blues of night, then brighter orange that brought out swathes of green, and finally a full light spectrum. The shadows she had been watching shift in the dark were filled with color by the rising sun and became her crew moving between the rows. She recognized the choreography even at a distance, and the opening-night butterflies of crush lifted her mood.

Harvest was equal parts relief, euphoria, sweat, and panic, much like a theatrical opening. Unlike live theater, though, that initial rush of performance in winemaking had time for correction, more like filmmaking. Editing decisions could be made after the juice was in the barrel, after the land and the climate and the nuances of the year's weather had given to the fruit what it could. Once the fruit was off the vine, the future lay in the hands of the winemaker. While many of those who produced burgundian-style pinot noir believed that post-harvest intervention should be kept to a minimum, that, too, was a winemaker decision. Action suited Suzanne far more than moping. She fished the card Jeff had given her out of her purse and left another message for Hanna Jackson, then pulled on some jeans and a sweatshirt and went out to join Carlos and the crew until she could get an appointment.

Hanna Jackson did not look like a pit bull, she looked like a model. Suzanne took in her expertly layered hair, dark silk suit that whispered when she moved, and simple diamond earrings and swore she heard the sound of a cash register drawer open and close.

"Jeff is a great guy." The lawyer had a low, almost sultry voice. "I hope I can help you come out of your divorce with as little loss as possible."

"He said you're the best."

The corners of her mouth lifted, but she did not smile. "I'm good, but I can't rewrite the community property laws. We have a lot of work to do. Did you bring the recording?"

Suzanne gave her the handheld recorder she had used to copy the message and Hanna Jackson played it back.

"You bitch! Your way or the highway, right? Feelings be damned! How dare you humiliate Will in front of the very people most likely to invest in the winery? It's not like you won't benefit, too. Even if you can't feel anything, you can still hurt him, you know. Just leave him alone!"

The lawyer played the message three times, pausing, to make notes as needed, then continued writing after the recording clicked off. She looked up at Suzanne.

"Well, as threats go, that's pretty vague, but we might be able to use it. What does the reference to investing in the winery mean?"

Suzanne sighed and shook her head. "I don't know. We're a family business, an estate winery. We grow our own grapes, harvest, ferment, barrel, and bottle on the property. I hired my vineyard manager after our third year, and we have a small field crew as well as a marketing and administrative assistant. It's a family business." Suzanne realized she was repeating herself and stopped. "Will had talked about bringing in investor partners, expanding, but that was over a year ago. I told him I wasn't interested in giving up control, and that was the end of it."

Hanna Jackson raised an eyebrow and Suzanne felt her cheeks flush.

"The letter from his attorney is in the packet of materials I requested? Good. We will likely need to hire a forensic accountant to examine the winery financials. If we can demonstrate any fraud, misrepresentation, or coercion at the time you reorganized and added his name to the original property, we will have grounds to reclassify that parcel as an asset acquired prior to marriage."

Suzanne nodded, but she wasn't hopeful. She had wanted Will to share everything, wanted them to be equal partners.

"And the woman on the phone . . ." the lawyer checked her notes, "she is your husband's lover?"

Hearing it put so bluntly made her wince, even if it was accurate.

Suzanne nodded. "She's my friend. Was my friend. That's how they met." She also had no idea why Laura said she had no feelings. She did not deny that as a scientist, logic and reason mattered most to her, but she was an artist, too, moved deeply by many things. Laura, of all people, should know that. The bitter taste of the false accusation lingered.

"Okay. We may need more background on her and your husband both if we pursue the threat option." She typed something into her blackberry, paused while she read, then typed again. "So we're back to the primary question. What is your goal?"

Suzanne was watching her internal visions of grape clusters in baskets being dumped into a trailer and hauled down to the shed, stems being pulled from the fruit on the table. She wanted to be back at the vineyard, had naively thought she could just give all the data to the lawyer and walk away, back to her real life, to wait for some answer, the result.

"My goal?" She frowned.

"Do you want to protect your assets? Do you want to destroy your husband? Do you want the fastest possible resolution? Do you want to save the marriage?"

Suzanne snorted at that. "I guess I would like it to be over quickly, but the only thing that really matters is my winery. Whatever it takes to prevent him from taking over, that's my goal."

She did not flinch under the lawyer's scrutiny, and after a few moments, Hanna nodded.

"You can leave your deposit with my secretary. I'll be in touch."

The number of zeros on the check seemed more like mortgage payments or French oak barrels than fee for services. A deposit on fee for services, actually, an amount that seemed huge as she looked at it, but which she knew might be a mere fraction of what she would have to pay eventually. Suzanne looked at the check and felt a momentary kinship with the captain of the Titanic. She had never been asked to put a value on her life before, not really, but Hanna's question forced her to define her priorities. Her winery, her wine, was not just the most important thing in her life, it *was* her life. Maybe that was something neither Will nor Laura understood about her, but they were going to find out.

Suzanne had met Laura at a blood drive after hurricane Katrina. Laura was a perky little blonde like a nurse right out of sitcom central casting, but she obviously loved her job and radiated a soothing competence beyond her years. Waves of new donors poured into all the blood banks as they did following any disaster, and the normal intake and screening process was compounded by the anxiety of the inexperienced. Laura was funny and relaxed and put everyone at ease, whether they were turned down as donors or nervous about needles or lightheaded after donating. Suzanne noticed she was also the one the other nurses called over if they found a difficult vein: small, deep, or angled. Laura would make the stick in one try with no flinching by the donor.

Because Suzanne had never given blood, she had no idea what to expect. The initial questionnaire covered things like travel to the UK and Africa, military service, sex with men who had had sex with other men, and history of diseases with long names she had never heard of. When she was called into the interview room and Laura asked her the questions again one by one, she burst out laughing when asked if in the last twelve months she had had sex with anyone who had ever accepted drugs or money for sex.

"I'm sorry." Suzanne made a visible effort to stifle her laughter. "It's just that when I was filling it out I pictured calling my husband and asking him."

Without changing her expression, Laura had picked up the phone on the desk and offered it to Suzanne, which set her off again.

"That's not exactly textbook, so don't tell," Laura winked and smiled. "It's been a long day."

While Suzanne was on the reclining donation chair with a tube running from her arm to the bag being machine-rocked on the floor beside her, Laura offered a conspiratorial smirk as she passed. It was several donations and many months before they discovered a shared love of spicy food, margaritas, and live theater that led to real friendship, but that first pint of blood had been the start.

Suzanne signed the receipt for the deposit and folded her copy into her purse. From a pint of blood to a pound of flesh. She couldn't wait to get back to the vineyard.

Carlos was emptying baskets and cleaning up when Suzanne got back to the winery.

"We finished the first three rows, Miss Suzanne, except for a few vines on the end. The color seemed not quite what it should, so we tested again and Brix was not yet twenty-four."

"I'm not surprised. This was the earliest harvest start we've had. It could be a few days for the next set. Tomorrow we'll check pH and Brix on the ends and in the middle of every row." She picked up a stack of baskets and carried them over to the barn that housed the barrels. Her stomach complained loudly enough to cause Carlos to look over at her. She shrugged. "I missed lunch. Nothing serious."

As Suzanne turned to enter the vineyard, Carlos spoke. "Miss Suzanne?"

She turned, hearing something in his voice but seeing no other evidence of concern.

"Some of the men have asked me . . . they have heard . . ."

Suzanne knew from experience that to rush Carlos or even to acknowledge the tentative inquiry in any way before he was finished would put an end to the conversation. Carlos had a strong sense of propriety in business relationships, maintaining boundaries that he breached rarely and even then with a pronounced reticence. For him to approach her about something personal meant it was important.

Carlos removed his hat, whacked it hard against his leg to knock off the field dust, then examined it closely as he spoke.

"There is talk of big changes. Perhaps there will be no more work after this season."

"What?" Suzanne wasn't surprised that there were rumors about her separation from Will and what might happen, but why would the crew think they'd be out? Unless it had to do with the mysterious investors from Laura's message. If they didn't know who would be in charge, how could they count on having jobs? "I don't know what you've heard, Carlos, but as long as I am here, you will be, too. And I'm not going anywhere."

Carlos nodded and shook her extended hand, then turned back to the barn to finish cleaning up. Suzanne looked up at the leafy bands running up the hillside, but she was too enervated to walk the vineyard now. It was time to talk to Will.

No argument precipitated the separation, no acrimony or accusations; it evolved organically in the way of all drastic change that is really the accumulation of subtle unacknowledged variation. A tiny black spot of emotional distance and indifference grew and spread until it consumed all the good times and shared memories and even the white heat of desire. What was left was a kind of cordial camaraderie like that between coworkers who had dated once but remained friends. There was never really anything wrong, so it never occurred to Suzanne that something needed to be fixed.

After all the attention generated by the first vintage of Mermaid Tears, Will had leased a condo near the California Avenue Train station in Palo Alto so they wouldn't have to drive back to the house after the increasing number of late night events on the Peninsula. It was convenient to have a place where one or both of them could spend a night or two, though Will logged the most hours in the little studio. Over time, a few nights a month became a few nights every week, and then one day Will told her he was moving all his things into the condo. What surprised Suzanne the most was the fact that she wasn't surprised at all.

The complex was painted in Southwestern earth tones, natural but lively. Suzanne parked on the street and tried to organized her thoughts. Her cell phone rang, and she sent the call to voice mail without looking at it. She didn't want to be distracted, needed to focus so the conversation would not be derailed by an irrational emotional overreaction—or a rational one, for that matter. She looked up at the window, wondering if Will had seen the car pull up. The last time they had been here together was after a big event in San Francisco. It had been exhilarating to have the wine receive the kind of attention it did from giants in the industry. They had smuggled a bottle onto the last southbound train and finished it before they reached their stop on the slow late-night milk run. When Will kissed her with a lingering invitation, she had responded by escalating so that by the time they made it into the condo, half their clothes were already undone and they could barely be bothered to close the door.

The last time they had been here together was also the last time they had been intimate. The early sexual foundation of their relationship had become little more than memory. The electrical sizzle of attraction remained as an undercurrent in their relationship, but the opportunities they would have seized in the first years of their relationship began to pass without consideration. Suzanne grew tired of being the one to initiate sex, particularly after Will started to decline more than respond. She found that when her desire was not reflected back, it became something else all together.

Climbing the stairs to the second floor, she rifled through her purse for the key, then stopped. She had had the locks changed on the house after she got the divorce papers; he had probably done the same here. Even if he hadn't, she thought the all-access pass to each other's lives had expired. Suzanne pictured Carlos and his crew, took a deep breath, and knocked on the door.

Will's first response to everyone was to hug them or shake their hand. Suzanne could see his effort to stop himself from embracing her. They stood awkwardly in the doorway for a moment before he stepped back and gestured for her to enter.

Not much had changed, but the place had a lived-in feel that it hadn't had when they were using it only sporadically. Suzanne caught herself scanning the room for telltale feminine details and was embarrassed but unrepentant.

"I'm sorry about the Computer History Museum." Suzanne hoped a peace offering would establish a civil tone for the conversation.

"You should be."

"What?"

"You should be sorry." Will stood with his arms crossed and his eyebrows raised. "Throwing your wine glass on the floor and yelling at me was juvenile and beneath you, but dismissing me like I'm some sort of lackey was unacceptable."

"That was an accident! The wine glass, I mean. How could you think I threw it? What am I, five? I'm sorry for making a scene, but it never would have happened if you had just kept your mouth shut!" Suzanne couldn't believe Will thought she had broken the glass intentionally in a fit of pique, thought she might be capable of a tantrum like that without provocation. "If you're so keen on separating personal from business, why did you even bring it up? Did that really seem like a good place to talk?"

"I wasn't trying to start a detailed post-mortem on our relationship. It was just an observation. You're the one who made a big deal out of it."

They glared at each other across the coffee table, both posed as if their righteous indignation were superhero cloaks. So much for civility, Suzanne thought.

"I didn't come to argue, I came to talk about the crew."

Will looked puzzled. "What about the crew?"

"We started harvest." When Suzanne saw Will nodding his head in a get-to-the-part-I-don't-know rhythm, she wanted to smack him. "Naturally there are a lot of rumors going around, and the men don't know what's going to happen."

"Who does?"

"This isn't a joke. They're worried about their jobs. They think new management might mean a new labor pool."

Will grew quiet. Suzanne watched his reaction intently, but he did not make eye contact.

"I told Carlos they don't have anything to worry about," she said.

There was a drawn out silence during which Suzanne watched Will watching a spider on the ceiling as he composed his thoughts. His jaw muscles twitched, either in anger or tension, and his eyes narrowed slightly. He hadn't changed that much in the years they had been married. His hair was a little thinner and silvered at the sides, but it was the same slightly tousled preppy cut. The crows feet that now framed his eyes gave him an air of experience that made him better looking, if anything. Suzanne doubted the same assessment could be made of her own well-earned lines.

"Did I lie to Carlos?"

Will's eyes snapped to hers at the word "lie". "Saying something that turns out not to be true is not the same thing as lying."

Suzanne waited.

"I do not foresee changes to the staffing at this point."

She considered Will's carefully chosen words as if they were a mouthful of wine, trying to tease out some deeper meaning.

"You know, Suzann—" he bit off the name abruptly to keep from adding the last syllable of her pet name, lending a strange stutter to the pronunciation, "if you had ever read the proposal, you would know all this."

"You mean that lovely letter you made poor Carlos deliver? Oh, I read that in excruciating detail."

Red splotches marked Will's cheeks. "I'm talking about the packet I gave you over a year ago. The business plan you dismissed out of hand without even pretending to review."

Suzanne grew queasy with dawning comprehension. "I didn't need to read it because I already told you it wasn't an option."

Will offered a thin-lipped smile so tight it looked painful. "There's where you're wrong. It *was* an option and now it *is* going to happen."

"How can you do this? Why would you want to destroy everything I've built?"

"You've built? *You've* built? I was there, too! If you even once considered that anyone besides you could have a good idea, maybe you would have seen what a great opportunity this is."

"I didn't say it was a bad idea in general, just bad for *us*. But your self-esteem issues aren't my problem, and I am not going to apologize for being good at what I do!"

Suzanne took a step toward Will then stopped, fists clenched at her sides. She didn't recall ever wanting to hit someone until the last few weeks, and now it happened disconcertingly often.

Her cell phone rang, and just as if a round had ended in a prize fight, they both stepped back and turned away from each other. Suzanne checked the number before she sent it to voice mail. It was her nephew again.

"I have to return this call." Suzanne jumped at the opportunity to get away from the conversation, away from Will. She was halfway around the room on her way to the door even as she made her transparent excuse to leave.

"We aren't done here." Will had lowered the volume, but his voice was still tinted with anger.

Suzanne paused in the doorway. "Yes, I think we are. There may be more that needs to be said on this subject, but we are *so* done."

Striding up and down California Avenue, too agitated to drive home, Suzanne finally landed at La Bodeguita del Medio, taking a small cafe table on the sidewalk. She sat drinking the signature mojito while waiting for her ropa vieja to arrive, the comfort of food and drink a balm for her battle with Will.

He had pursued his proposal to bring in investors, build a fancy tasting room, expand the winery and the Suzanne Mathews "brand" through events and merchandise even though she had said no. And he had taken her refusal as not just a rejection of the idea, but a rejection of him. She had always felt a touch of condescending disdain for people who had nasty acrimonious divorces where hundreds of thousands of dollars in legal expenses were accumulated while haggling over who got the dog and whether she got to keep the egg poacher his great aunt gave them as a wedding present. Suzanne thought those people were immature, that they had lost perspective on a relationship that must have had some good in it, too. But now Will wanted to put her name on t-shirts and napkins and god only knew what else with no regard for the only thing that mattered—the wine. And worse than that, he wanted to sell the rights to make decisions about her wine to total strangers. She didn't feel so smug anymore.

The mojito smoothed the rough edges of her emotional state, and Suzanne tore into the perfectly spiced shredded skirt steak as soon as it was put in front of her. She waved off the waiter's offer of another mojito and asked for water instead. When she'd wolfed down most of her dinner, she leaned back in the chair and pulled out her cell phone.

"Suzanne! I've been trying to reach you."

"I know, Donnie, I'm sorry. We just started harvest and life is . . . complicated." She didn't see any reason to go into her pending divorce when her nephew was making a polite social call. "How are you?"

"It's Mom," he said as if she hadn't said anything. "She has cancer. The doctors said it's a matter of weeks, maybe days."

His voice broke. Suzanne could hear him struggling for control, but found she had been silenced by the news, too. She listened to his breathing until he regained his voice.

"You need to come home."

Chapter 4

Rootstock:
vines developed to be resistant to pests and disease;
fruit-bearing vines (scions) are grafted onto rootstock

Suzanne's arrival in Minneapolis was accompanied by a brisk breeze and a hard blue sky. The drive to her sister's house would have been a little shorter from Des Moines, but there were no direct flights from any Bay Area airport, and all the saved driving time and then some would have been spent changing planes in Denver or Dallas or Chicago. Suzanne refused to take a flight routed through Chicago because flying past her destination then doubling back just because it was convenient for the airline had always offended her sensibilities.

"I'm here." Suzanne strode down the concourse with her cell phone to her ear and her roller bag trailing behind her. She hesitated at the Caribou coffee counter, Minnesota's version of Starbucks, but she didn't have enough hands.

"Thanks for coming. Mom didn't want to say anything, but I just . . ."

"It's okay, Donnie. I'm glad you told me. I'll call you after I've seen her. Maybe tomorrow."

"I'll be down on the weekend. We can talk more then—just a minute." Donnie held a muffled conversation with someone else, then came back on the line. "Sorry. Anyway, I feel like I should prepare you for seeing mom, but she's not really that different. Thinner, but still her, you know?"

Suzanne smiled. "I know."

Donnie had offered to pick her up, even though it would be a six hour round trip, but she needed the long drive alone even more than she needed the rental car. She loaded her suitcase into the back seat, put her purse on the passenger seat, took the wheel of the electric-blue PT Cruiser that appeared to be the compact car of choice at all the airport car rental companies, and pointed it south.

October suffers from mood swings in many locations, but in Iowa it cries out for medication. An Indian Summer day in the eighties might be followed by the first snow of the season. A string of temperate days with no more than twenty degrees of variation between high and low might be broken by a sudden violent thunderstorm more suited to spring than fall. The hot air from the tropics and the cold fronts from the North clash over the prairie states in a recurrent epic battle that never ends and cannot be won. The conflict may be more severe in the turbulent days of May and June, but by October the innocent civilians are so war-weary that every change seems apocalyptic.

The trees flashed past in shades of scarlet and pumpkin and marigold. Suzanne was cheered by the pallet even as she watched for her turn off the highway. Northern California trees put on an autumn show, but nothing quite so extravagant as this display. It was like the lilacs. Someone had worked diligently to create a strain of lilac that would grow in the Mediterranean climate of the Bay Area, but it did not succeed in reproducing the perfume of those few weeks every year of her childhood when the lilacs bloomed and scented the whole world.

Suzanne was surprised by how clearly she remembered the way, even after so many years. The scenery was eerily familiar, and she could see the ghosts of the old buildings in the houses and chain stores that had replaced them. Time had passed here, but very slowly. She made her turn and stopped at a red light that held her for nonexistent traffic on the cross-street. The sense of being in a place both alien and familiar was like grocery shopping while stoned. The loud crunching of the gravel in the driveway eliminated the possibility of driving around the block one more time. Her arrival had been announced.

The front yard was in transition from dying lawn to cemetery. A couple tombstones had been mounted halfway to the sidewalk, and half a dozen more were stacked by the porch. Cobwebs stretched across the front of the house from eaves to steps, and Suzanne wasn't entirely sure whether they were the result of neglect or her sister's enthusiasm for Halloween.

Suzanne pulled the luggage out of the back seat and locked the car. The house she grew up in looked the same—only smaller. Two stories, white paint with green trim cracking under the eaves, screens on the window for summer except for the one at the top of the stairs where the storm window had been painted shut decades ago. A tsunami of memories engulfed her, and she squeezed her eyes shut to keep from being swept away.

The three steps up to the kitchen door were warped, and the paint clung in strips of pigment jerky. The side entrance had been the main entrance even when she was living there, and that was where she went now. Suzanne raised her hand to knock, then smiled and tried the knob. Her sister never locked the door. She pulled it open, but years of retraining prevented her from walking into anyone's house with neither invitation nor announcement.

"Anybody home?"

The kitchen was empty, but the ashtray on the table was full and the coffeemaker light was on, a half pot of coffee simmering into caffeine sludge. From the front of the house came a raspy shout.

"Who wants to know?"

Suzanne stepped inside and closed the door behind her, instantly engulfed by the smell of burning tobacco and stale smoke. She didn't know many people who smoked anymore, at least not cigarettes, and nobody in California had been allowed to smoke indoors for decades. Her exposure to hazy clubs and nicotine clouds was so far back in the past that the atmosphere in the house left her a little lightheaded.

"If I told you it was the neighborhood rapist, would you start locking the door?" Suzanne carried her bag with her as she followed the sound of the voice and the trail of smoke into the dining room, which was also empty.

"Hell, no! I'd tell you to hurry up—I haven't got forever!"

Janice's laughter dissolved into a gurgling cough. Suzanne strode through the dining room into the living room where her sister sat red-faced and not breathing, frozen mid-cough. When her breath finally caught and everything seemed to be functioning normally, Janice took a last drag on her cigarette and stubbed it out in the full ashtray next to an open can of Budweiser. Suzanne's expression must have betrayed her thoughts, because Janice rolled her eyes.

"What? Cigarettes are going to kill me? I've got maybe six weeks, tops. For the cigarettes to kill me first, you'd have to beat me to death with a carton!"

Suzanne missed a beat before responding. "I'm sure I'll be willing to oblige long before we get to six weeks. I was more concerned that the stench might make the house unsellable."

"No matter. The equity's all gone anyway. I'd like to say I threw it away on drugs and hookers," she gestured to the assortment of prescription bottles clustered on the coffee table behind the ashtray, "but I ran out before I got to the hookers."

The sisters sized each other up in silence. Janice had always been heavy, but now her skin fit loosely, as if she were melting from within. Her face was slightly jaundiced, and her eyes were bloodshot, but whether from the beer or the meds or the disease, Suzanne couldn't be sure. She wore a gaudy yellow and turquoise scarf on her head, wrapped and tied at the side like a flamboyant pirate. Her fingernails were bitten to the quick. Suzanne could guess what Janice saw: hair that used to be chestnut now streaked silver, the family blue eyes rimmed red by tears and fatigue, arms turned ropy and brown from hours of outdoor lifting. Or maybe she just saw her little sister.

"What the hell are you doing here, anyway?" Janice broke the quiet as she lit another cigarette. "Wait, I know," she dropped her lighter on the table and blew out a burst of smoke, "Donnie! That boy never could keep a secret."

Suzanne shrugged. "Everybody's got a price."

An enormous calico cat, mostly white with a few patches of orange and a black tail and ears jumped up beside Janice and flopped over against her. She scratched it under the chin and it lifted its face, eyes squeezed shut, and purred loudly. "Well, you came this far, you might as well stay." Janice gestured toward the stairway with her can of beer. "You can have your old room."

There was a spot of black just under the cat's nose that looked like a large beauty mark or an off-center Hitler mustache. Suzanne looked closely at the cat and said, "Is that Molly?"

"Yeah. She's not dead yet, either."

Suzanne leaned over to pet the cat, then turned to climb the stairs to the second floor bedrooms. Before she reached the landing, her sister yelled, "I let the local girl scouts redecorate a couple years ago for one of their badges."

It wasn't warning enough. The room was filled with lace-edged pillows, folded quilts, and knickknacks like geese with hats, tiny spoons, and antique kitchen tools. Suzanne didn't know whether to laugh or gag. She put her bag down on the trunk at the foot of the bed and looked at the cluster of black and white photos in oval frames on the wall beside the dresser. She recognized her great-grandparents' wedding picture, her grandmother as a child standing beside a pony and a teen-aged Janice holding a baby wearing what looked like a tie-dyed dress. The other two photos she had never seen, but she knew who they were: a young girl with a half smile and eyes so pale they looked a little eerie and a solemn boy beside a striped cat almost as big as he was. Suzanne ran her finger over the girl's frame, reflecting the same one-sided smile.

That little girl became a beautiful woman, or at least that's how

Suzanne remembered her mother. Jasmine perfume and a loose topknot of unchanging honey-gold hair defined her, along with a white uniform worn with low heels. Her eyes always seemed to be looking through you to what was next, but Suzanne understood without asking that that was the way of single parents. Suzanne's image of her father suited that serious little boy: a collage of other people's stories glued together with bits of actual memories. She remembered a Ferris wheel ride that must have been at the County Fair, and sitting on his lap to watch fireworks on the Fourth of July so his musky aftershave clung to her and scented her dreams. The rest of what few real memories she had included blinking lights and tubes, hushed voices, and the stinging scent of disinfectant.

She looked more closely at the photograph of Janice. Her eyes were full of mischief, challenging the camera. The baby was Suzanne. The photo looked like it could have been Halloween because of the outfit, but she was pretty sure it wasn't. Suzanne remembered an Easter when Janice bought a frilly white dress covered with yellow daisies for Suzanne to wear. It came with a white straw hat and matching purse that had silk flowers with fuzzy yellow pompoms as centers. Janice had treated Suzanne like a big doll all through her early childhood, dressing her up, taking her everywhere. They had been far enough apart in age that strangers sometimes assumed they were mother and daughter. After Donnie was born and Suzanne started kindergarten, though, their lives began to move in different directions.

The room was stuffy and smelled of potpourri long past its prime. Suzanne crossed the room to the window and shoved upward on the frame until the breeze swept in, fluttering the edge of the curtain. She looked down on the backyard, the old clothesline was still there, now rusted into a rural sculpture to complement the battered eggbeater and flat iron on the shelf above the dresser. Beyond the scarlet maples at the edge of the property there were no mountains on the horizon, no froth of fog spilling in for the night, no vines climbing a hillside like neatly typed rows of *T*s.

Suzanne had briefed Carlos in a rush before driving to the airport that morning, repeatedly telling him to call her if anything about harvest seemed even remotely unusual until she sounded paranoid and neurotic even to herself. Between crush and Will's legal assault, she felt irresponsible leaving the winery, but she knew she would have felt something much worse if she had failed to respond to Donnie's request. Suzanne thought of her relationship with her sister as a close one, but though they exchanged frequent e-mails and talked on the phone a couple times a month, it had been at least five years since they had seen each other. The miles and years had accumulated into another kind of distance that had gone unrecognized until her nephew's phone call.

Suzanne rinsed off the film of travel in the bathroom down the hall, then went back downstairs and sat in the chair across from Janice.

"You should have told me."

"Why? What were you going to do that all the surgeons and specialists couldn't?"

Suzanne looked at Janice's scarf. "I could have been with you, taken you to chemo."

Janice threw back her head and laughed until she brought on another coughing fit. When she cleared her lungs and got her breath back, she pulled off the scarf to reveal a soft stubble of gray hair. She ran her hand over the top of her head like ruffling the fur on a puppy. "I shaved it."

"I know."

Janice shook her head. "No, I mean I *only* shaved it. No chemo for me. Apparently the pancreas doesn't like to give bad news until it's too late to change it into good news. But all the ladies in my cancer support group had breast or ovarian tumors and they all had chemo."

"You shaved your head . . . in solidarity?"

Janice shrugged. "Well, it sounds sort of silly when you say it like that, but at the time I thought it was a noble gesture." This time they both laughed.

Janice drained her can of beer. "The eyebrows and eyelashes should have been your first clue. See? I've still got mine; they're not colored on."

Suzanne shook her head. "Okay, maybe you didn't need me for chemo support, but you still should have told me sooner."

"Sooner? I didn't tell you at all!"

The tone had shifted. Janice wasn't vehement, but she also wasn't joking. At a loss for words and everything else, Suzanne watched her fold and wrap and retie her scarf with the same jaunty side knot as before, then stand slowly and pick up her empty can.

As Janice turned to walk to the kitchen, Suzanne found her voice, "Why?"

Janice sighed. "Maybe I just didn't want an audience. You barely share my life with me; why should you share my death?"

Suzanne felt like she had been slapped, and the shock must have shown on her face.

"I haven't known that long," Janice said in a softer voice, "I probably would have told you eventually." She left the room, calling from the kitchen, "I've got plans tonight; my weekly dinner date. You're welcome to join us."

Suzanne considered staying home or going out alone, but finally went upstairs. Whenever she traveled, she carried a bottle of Mermaid Tears with her like a talisman or security blanket. She dug down through the clothes to find the bubble wrap sleeve in the middle of her suitcase. Whatever else happened tonight, at least she would drink well. She heard a car drive up to the house and stop, followed by the *thunk* and creek of someone walking up the steps. As she reached the landing going downstairs, the door opened and closed and a low rumbling voice she hadn't heard since college said, "Hello, gorgeous! You ready?" Her knees buckled a little even though he obviously wasn't talking to her. Mark Jorgenson, the one she left behind, the one who still made guest appearances in sweaty dreams and starred in sticky fantasies, was their dinner date.

When she walked into the kitchen, Mark's face froze, his jaw dropped, then he ran through a series of expressions from disbelief to delight. He looked exactly like she felt.

Janice said, "Guess who's coming to dinner?"

Suzanne said, "Of all the gin joints in all the towns in all the world, he had to walk into mine."

Mark covered the distance between them before she finished speaking and engulfed her in a hug. Her body molded to him as if no time had passed, and the scent at the nape of his neck, all salt and spice and unadorned flesh, made her shiver in the instant before they broke the embrace.

"I think that was supposed to be my line," he said.

He looked exactly the same, heavy-lidded espresso eyes, dimples carved into his cheeks, hair a cluster of thick curls like a Renaissance cherub. She blinked, and then she could see where time had left its tracks. The crinkles at the corners of his eyes were there even when he didn't smile, and his dimples had been etched in permanent lines. The curls were a wiry gray now, and they started further back on his forehead.

"You were too slow," Suzanne said.

Mark held the door for the two women to walk out. "That always was my problem."

The restaurant was one of three in town that didn't have a "drive-thru" window. It was a family restaurant with unfulfilled aspirations of white table cloths and candlelight. The menu was steaks and pork chops and chicken and for those looking for something healthy, fish that had been frozen, breaded, and deep fried. There was a bit of tension when Suzanne put her bottle of wine on the table and the waitress looked shocked and said, "No outside food." After Mark went to speak to the manager, though, a corkage fee was negotiated and the wine was opened.

The conversation on the short drive to dinner had consisted of aborted attempts to find a topic of mutual interest interspersed with stretches of awkward silence. After they had all ordered, Suzanne asked, "How long have you two been going out?"

They both started laughing after "going out".

She scowled at them. "You know what I mean. When did this weekly dinner outing get started?"

The waitress returned with the open Mermaid Tears and three glasses. She poured a splash into Suzanne's glass and waited while she tasted the wine, then filled Janice's glass nearly to the rim before Suzanne stopped her.

"If you don't mind, I'd like to pour for my friends." She smiled her best it's-not-you-it's-me smile and poured half a glass for Mark and for herself. She caught herself waiting for his reaction to the wine.

When he didn't say anything after tasting it, she said, "What do you think?"

He said, "I think I don't know enough about wine to offer an opinion to an expert." Then he smiled. "But I like it."

Suzanne returned his smile and lifted her glass. "May the road rise up to meet you, may the sun shine warm upon your head," she nodded to Janice who continued.

"May the wind be always at your back, and may you—" Suzanne chimed in with, "be in Heaven half an hour before the devil knows you're dead!"

All three drank and Mark said, "Isn't it supposed to end with something about God holding you in the palm of his hand?"

The women laughed. "Not the way we learned it," said Janice.

Suzanne added. "I learned it from her, so leave me out of the debate. Now, back to your dinners . . ."

Mark reached over to squeeze Janice's wrist, and his face softened as if all history of sorrow had been momentarily erased. In that moment, Suzanne saw the boy she had known in school and wanted like nothing and no one before or since.

"Janice joined the cancer support group on Mom's last day," he said.

"Literally. Mom didn't have cancer, but it was the only support group for chronically ill and terminal patients. Her kidneys were shot, she could barely see, and her arteries were as close to completely blocked as they could be and still function. She was too sick for bypass surgery or angioplasty, and her veins were so bad she had to have an insulin pump installed."

"I'm sorry," Suzanne said. "I remember the time she went to the hospital when we were freshmen."

Mark nodded. "She was really careful after that, kept the diabetes in check, but eventually it just wore her down. Anyway, the way I heard it, the ladies went around the circle talking about their treatments and their fears and their complaints of the week, but when it got to be Janice's turn, she said, 'I just got the diagnosis and I'm already dead. No treatment, no recovery rates, no nothing, so you bunch of whiners have no idea how lucky you are.' They all laughed until they cried. Mom hadn't laughed in a long time."

Mark paused as their salads were delivered and Suzanne refilled their glasses.

"After the meeting, Janice was waiting with Mom when I got there to pick her up. They were reminiscing, talking about how Janice gave me my first taste of ice cream when she was babysitting. Mom looked sort of wistful and said she hadn't had a Buster Bar since she was diagnosed when I was three."

Janice broke into Mark's explanation. "And I said, 'Because they're bad for you? Might kill you?'"

Mark continued. "Mom looked from Janice to me and said, 'Let's go.' So the three of us drove to the Dairy Queen." He drained his wine glass and put it down. "That night Mom's heart gave out. She went to the hospital, but since she had a DNR . . . ."

Mark pushed his plate aside. "Anyway, that was how it started."

"Yup. I killed his mom and he bought me dinner," Janice said.

"That's *not* what happened." Mark shook his head. "I wanted to thank Janice for making Mom's last day the best one she'd had in longer than

I could remember. The dinner helped us both, I think, so we decided to do it again." He raised his empty glass to Janice. "And the rest is history."

Janice lifted her glass in return. "Just like me!"

The two of them chuckled and clinked glasses, but Suzanne found her throat closed and her vision blurred. The arrival of the entrees brought a welcome distraction. Suzanne poured the last of the wine.

"This is opening up nicely; in a couple years it should be spectacular," Suzanne said.

"How can you tell it's going to get better?" Janice asked.

"Partly it's the tannins, the slight astringency that will soften as it ages, partly it's the character of the fruit. Like the way you can sometimes tell just from meeting someone that they are going to get better the longer you know them."

Janice rolled her eyes. "Can you explain it without being so anthropomorphic?"

Suzanne shrugged. "Yes, but it wouldn't be as accurate, and I know you wouldn't want me to lower my standards."

Janice snorted. "Yeah, that would be wrong."

Suzanne nodded. "Besides, it works the other way, too, with wine. Just like people, sometimes the ones with the most promising beginnings end up disappointing you in the end."

Mark watched them like a tennis match then laughed. "Are you guys always like this?"

This time they both shrugged.

The waitress appeared beside the table to clear the empty bottle, but Mark waved her off. "I'd like to keep it." He picked up the bottle and examined it closely, then looked up abruptly. "It's you!"

Suzanne could feel the heat rise in her cheeks. "That wasn't intentional, at least not on my part."

"I think I like you as a mermaid."

"Maybe your 'place' should have been by the ocean instead of the river," Janice said.

"What?" Mark and Suzanne asked in unison.

"The song. 'Suzanne takes you down to her place by the river . . .' you know, Judy Collins?"

"Oh." Suzanne wondered if Janice's faculties were slipping a bit, and apparently Janice could still read her every expression.

"I've got cancer, not Alzheimer's! That's where your name *came* from. Actually, not the song so much as the poem. I was in a Leonard Cohen phase for a while in high school, so I named you after my favorite poem."

"You played it so often, I always thought of it as my song, like it was written for me," Suzanne said. "I didn't realize it was the other way around."

"You got to pick her name?" Mark was grinning like a kid.

"Yup. Mom retained veto power, but she let me choose. I think it was the consolation prize for inflicting a baby sister on me halfway through high school." Janice took a sip from her still-full glass of wine and raised her eyebrows at Suzanne. "You're welcome."

Suzanne raised her own glass, looked into her sister's eyes and saw their mother.

"Thanks," she said, "for everything."

Chapter 5

Clones:

a genetic subdivision within the pinot noir varietal,
each offering distinct contributions of aroma and flavor

The scent of frying bacon disrupted Suzanne's dream, teased her awake while the effects of the fading dream lingered, its sexual efficacy evident from the twisted comforter between her legs. Suzanne did not credit dreams with larger meanings or predictive powers, so while she often had erotic dreams involving friends or casual acquaintances, she thought nothing more of them. The brain stored information in chemical electrical signals, peptide thunderstorms that flashed the same patterns whether the eyes were open and observing or closed and remembering. This dream, though, this one seemed so real she slid her hand across the other side of the bed just to be sure it was empty. Part fantasy, part memory, the dream of Mark had been so vivid she could still feel his fingers on her spine, his tongue on her nipples . . .

She closed her eyes and let the fantasy consume her again, this time consciously. The tension built quickly, and she tensed her thighs around the bedding, moved against it as she pressed one hand between her legs and bit the back of her other wrist to keep from crying out. She could tell from the quick climax that her dreamland encounter had worked at least once already in the real world, too.

Suzanne rolled to her back and stared at the ceiling. There was a border of ivy and violets running along the top of the walls. It was not that bad compared to the assorted waterfowl in bonnets which she had pivoted in place before going to bed so they wouldn't be watching her all night. Of course, that meant her view upon waking was a chorus of tails. That seemed to be a theme in her life just now, a horse's ass in her vineyard, a goose's ass in her childhood bedroom. She couldn't help wondering which branching path she had chosen to end up with this particular view. She hadn't been able to reach Carlos the night before, and she had panicked just a little, even though she knew cell service was spotty and it had only been one day. One day during harvest. She had never missed a day of harvest, not only at SMW, but for any of her previous employers. And here she was, "home," where she wasn't wanted nor apparently even needed, instead of *home*, where she wanted and needed to be. The problem was, she did need to be here, too, even if Janice didn't think so.

Suzanne squeezed her eyes tight and held a pillow over her face for a moment of muffled scream therapy before leaping out of bed and hurrying to the shower.

"Scrambled or scrambled?" Janice asked as Suzanne walked into the kitchen and sat down at the kitchen table. A heaping plate of crispy bacon and another plate of toast sat in the middle of the table. The ashtray was clean but for half a dozen butts and the fresh coffee smelled good.

"Could I have scrambled instead?" Suzanne took the empty mug from the table and filled it from the pot. Today's scarf, still tied in a rakish pirate fashion, was a riot of orange, purple, chartreuse, and fuchsia that made yesterday's pattern seem dull by comparison. "What time do you get up?"

Janice scraped eggs out of the pan and onto a plate which she handed to Suzanne. "Most days between six and six thirty. I don't always get dressed so early, but I have group today." She turned off the stove and sat down across from Suzanne with a cup of coffee. "You can take me and feel useful."

Suzanne scooped up a forkful of eggs to cover the sting she felt from the end of the statement and said, "You're so high maintenance."

"Yeah. I get that a lot." She rinsed out the pan and flipped it upside down in the drainer next to the sink. "No rush. We've got fifteen minutes."

Suzanne checked her cell phone for messages, but no hopeful icons appeared. "Do I have time to check my e-mail?"

"Sure." Janice stubbed out her cigarette and lit another. "Just don't answer it all. And don't screw up anything on my desktop."

There were forty-seven messages, none of them from Carlos or Will. She wasn't surprised about Carlos, since he would resort to e-mail only when all else failed, but Will said he would keep her posted, swore he would leave an update. His voice had been tight when she had called him after their argument, his tone when he heard her voice guarded. But when she told him she had to go, that Janice was sick, he was all lower-register soothing phrases, offering genuine concern that was almost comforting. Today, though, today there was no word, and the sort of silence that offers comfort was not what lay between them. Even though she had complete confidence in Carlos and his crew, she didn't trust Will to stay out of their way. She began to wonder if his offer to update her had been an excuse to hang around harvest, something he never did before.

"You ready?" Janice stood in the doorway with a big purple Laurel Burch bag that looked like a survivor from the eighties slung over her shoulder. The gold and multicolored cat on the front had lost an eye and part of a leg to the skirmishes of time, and the woven handle was frayed with battle-fatigue.

Suzanne logged out of her account without responding and went to get her keys. It was only six thirty in California, the crew would not have been out for long, and Will probably wasn't even up. He would probably go up later, rely on Carlos to do what was needed, e-mail after he checked in at the winery. Probably. For all the role that probabilities had played in her life, all the literal and metaphorical calculations she had made, Suzanne decided "probably" offered little solace.

Halfway through the short drive to the hospital, Suzanne realized she had been so caught up in obsessing about harvest and Will that she had given only cursory responses and noises of acknowledgment to Janice with the sort of half-attention you give to toddlers talking about dinosaurs and old people reminiscing. She made a conscious effort to focus as Janice talked about Donnie.

"Is he still seeing that girl? What was her name, Katie?" Suzanne heard herself say "girl" knowing that Katie was no more than five years younger than she was, about Donnie's age, but here, girl could be used for any woman without seeming derogatory in any way.

"I don't know, maybe you should tell me. Seems like you've got an in."

Suzanne turned to give Janice a more thorough appraisal, but there didn't seem to be more on her face than in the comment. "He said he's coming this weekend, right? I just got the one phone call—you see him all the time."

"Not as much as you think." Janice turned toward Suzanne, the lines around her eyes and lips more pronounced in the harsh floodlight of morning. "He's not dealing well with his Kobayashi Maru test."

"Ah." As a child, Suzanne had watched Star Trek reruns with Janice until she could chew the scenery along with her favorite episodes. Janice's teenaged lust was directed at Captain Kirk, and she teased Suzanne mercilessly about her preference for Mr. Spock. When the movies started coming out years later, they would talk about them over the phone. *The Wrath of Khan* had been their favorite, partly because of the revelation that Captain Kirk had reprogrammed a test called the Kobayashi Maru—he didn't believe in the no-win situation. "I like to think there are always . . . possibilities," Suzanne quoted.

Janice smiled in recognition. "Yeah. But Donnie never was much one for thinking outside the box. And he doesn't know what to do with what's *in*side this particular box."

"How we deal with death is at least as important as how we deal with life," Suzanne quoted the movie again. She frowned as she pulled into the parking lot of the hospital where the group met. "Is that why he called me?"

Janice gave her a look that carried an uncomfortable amount of pity. "Probably. Not that you wouldn't have heard eventually, but he's been panicking more recently." She looked down, fiddling with her seatbelt and purse as she prepared to get out of the car. "And when he panics he stays away." She slid out of the car without making eye-contact, then turned before slamming the door closed to say, "I'll be done in two hours."

She walked away with a slightly lopsided gait Suzanne didn't recall and walked into the hospital without looking back. Suzanne thought that was so like Janice, never looking back, always moving on, like a cruise ship. Or maybe a battle cruiser was more apt—slow to turn but hard to sink.

"Just coffee, please. Black." Everything was within a ten-minute drive, so Suzanne had decided to wait out the meeting somewhere with coffee and cell service. She found the former, but the latter was less satisfying. She texted Will and called all the lines. She finally got the machine for the winery with the standard message in her own voice about the unpredictable timing of return calls during harvest. She just said, "Call me!" and hung up, wondering if the sensation of talking to herself was more accurate than she knew. Maybe nobody else was listening. Her rising panic at her inability to contact the winery made her think about Janice and what she had said about Donnie. If Donnie couldn't handle death, maybe she had been summoned as his guilt-relief without full-disclosure, an emotional buffer that could be viewed as a good deed if you squinted hard and spun it right. She was dialing his number when a voice interrupted her.

"Is this seat taken?"

Everything stopped. All the restaurant sounds, all the questions in her head, her finger on the phone, even her heart, she was sure. "It is now."

Mark sat down across from her and gestured for coffee and something else in cafe semaphore that drew a nod from the waitress. "This must be my lucky day."

"I must look pretty desperate if you think that's all it takes to get lucky."

Mark was momentarily taken aback, then he burst out laughing. "I forgot that *everything* can be a double entendre—and you're the master."

Suzanne offered a little smirk. "I prefer 'mistress'."

Mark just shook his head in response as his coffee and giant cinnamon roll arrived. "Did you bring your whip?"

"Nope, riding crop."

Hands up in surrender, Mark said, "I told you I never could keep up with you."

"I thought you said you were too slow," Suzanne smiled, "and I don't remember that being the case at all."

Mark stirred milk into his coffee and smiled down at it as if more in private memory than in response to her comment. When he looked up he said, "You had your phone out; did I interrupt something?"

"Janice just told me that Donnie hasn't been quite the ever-present caregiver I had been led to believe. Not that I fault him for that," she added quickly when Mark frowned, "it's just that I'm wondering if he called me against his mother's wishes to be his surrogate."

Pulling a chunk off the side of his cinnamon roll and popping it into his mouth, Mark looked directly into her eyes as he chewed slowly and swallowed. She could hear the clinking of his spoon as he stirred his coffee and smell the vanilla in the frosting as he bit down through the sugary glaze, but she saw only him. She found herself salivating, and his unblinking gaze made her squirm in a way that was not the least bit uncomfortable.

"What if he did?"

Suzanne opened her mouth, then closed it again.

"What if he did?" Mark repeated. "Everyone deals with grief differently; death doesn't come with a handbook."

"Who are you and what have you done with my friend?" She remembered Mark as a romantic, a dreamer. He had been full of plans and schemes and bright prospects, but their attraction and been physical and chemical more than intellectual. When she had told him she was going to move to California and asked him to come, too, he had hesitated. That was all she needed to know.

"A lot happens in twenty years, Suzanne." His phone buzzed and he checked it, then crumpled his napkin and stood. "I'm sorry, I have to go."

Suzanne realized she wasn't even sure what he did now. Janice had said something about insurance, but could that be right? Insurance? When he reached for his wallet, Suzanne waved him off.

"I'll get this."

"Okay, on one condition. I get the next one."

"Sold," Suzanne said. "How about Saturday?"

Mark leaned on the table. "How about dinner?"

"It's a date!" Suzanne was a little surprised she had pinned him down in the first place, more surprised that he raised the stakes.

"I sure hope so."

Suzanne watched him walk away feeling like he was both completely familiar and a total mystery.

While Janice napped, Suzanne took her grocery list to Hy-Vee and did the shopping. She filled the cart with fruits and vegetables and assorted cheeses for herself along with the eggs, bread, coffee, and beer that Janice needed. She felt like a teenager with a fake ID when she asked for cigarettes at the check stand where they were locked up behind the counter. The clerk's raised eyebrows when she asked for four cartons made her feel even worse, but the surprise seemed to be more about the cost than the quantity. As drug habits went, tobacco might be even more expensive than the illegal alternatives.

Instead of going directly back to the house, Suzanne drove around town taking in the fall colors and playing scenes from her past. The jungle gym at her elementary school could not have been more than five feet tall, yet she remembered the thrill of finally reaching the top was as if she had scaled Everest. She had run home after Brownies to tell her mother, and for just a moment, her mother had seemed truly happy. The hint of sadness around her eyes, the slight tilt of the head as if she were listening to distant music were gone in that instant, back in the next. Every prize Suzanne won for years after that, every achievement and award was calculated to make her mother smile. By the time it stopped working, she found that accomplishment had become its own reward.

At the edge of town past the grain elevator was the cemetery where her parents were buried. It was shady in the afternoon light and full of leaves jostling in the breeze. What she remembered of her father's funeral was the stark contrast to her flashes of hospital memories before. There was bright sun and the smell of freshly mown grass, and Suzanne had chased a butterfly around an obelisk. She had thought of it as a park, a magical outing, and she begged Janice to take her there every day. Sometimes Janice would say yes and even pack a little lunch for them. Suzanne inhaled sharply, struck by sudden insight, and she braked hard. She watched the leaves blow from the trees and tried to splice her scattered memories into a coherent film. They had picnicked in the cemetery because she had thought of it as a playground; Janice had taken her to the place where the father *she* actually knew and had a relationship with was buried. And they never told their mother.

Suzanne drove slowly through the looping cemetery road long

enough to see the light shift and the shadows lengthen before she pulled out onto the main road and drove home.

When she pulled into the driveway, she saw the rest of the tombstones had been positioned, though the rotting corpses and crows were heaped by the porch. Tattered rags waved from skeletal arms like banners in battle. One of the porch windows had the silhouette of the classic arched-back Halloween cat and the bedroom window above it on the second floor held the bulky shape of Molly. Suzanne carried the groceries into the kitchen and found Janice standing over a Styrofoam headstone with a paintbrush.

"What do you think?"

She lifted the piece and flipped it around for Suzanne to read.

R.I.P.
Janice Mathews
195? - Any Time Now

Suzanne started unloading her purchases into the refrigerator. "Morbid. And perfectly in character."

"Good!" Janice added a skull and crossbones at the top with a flourish and carried her marker outside to place with the rest of the graveyard.

"I hope you chose a good plot," Suzanne said when Janice returned. The hesitation in her sister's gait was more pronounced and the nap hadn't seemed to refresh her much, her exhaustion had become something permanent and systemic in a way Suzanne had never witnessed in anyone.

"Right under the tree with a big floodlight." Janice hacked and wheezed and grasped the back of the chair in front of her until she caught her breath. Then she looked for her cigarettes and got a beer out of the refrigerator. She held up the bottle of Anchor Steam and gave Suzanne a skeptical look.

Suzanne shrugged. "I thought I'd get something that I would drink, too."

"Snob."

"Not having dulled my taste buds with decades of tar and nicotine does not make me a snob."

Janice raised the bottle again in a toast of surrender. "Touché." She opened the bottle and drank as she began untangling a string of bat lights. "I'm way behind on Halloween. I usually have everything up as soon as September's over, but I'm a little slower this year. You can help me hang lights tomorrow, and I think we could use more cobwebs. I'm gonna skip the fog machine and just get some dry ice from Bret in the meat department."

Suzanne hadn't thought it possible for Janice to love Halloween any more than she remembered, but it seemed she was wrong. "Fog machine?"

"What's a graveyard without creepy mist?"

"I went to the cemetery today." Neither of them spoke for several minutes, and Suzanne started working on another string of lights before continuing. "Did it bother you back then, taking me there to play?"

Janice examined the label on her beer and her lips twitched into a smile and out again. "You were so happy there, so separate from everything that had happened, it made me happy, too. A lot of people say you should celebrate a person's life instead of mourning their death, but nobody does it. That's what it felt like we were doing. I think Daddy would have liked it, too."

Before Suzanne could say anything else, Janice said, "Oh, I forgot to tell you, some guy with an accent called for you. Carlo, maybe?"

Suzanne dropped the strand of lights in her hands and grabbed Janice's sleeve. "Carlos called? When? What did he say?"

Janice looked from the hand clutching her blouse to Suzanne's face and back again. "He just said to call."

Suzanne ran outside and dialed the winery.

The machine picked up and Suzanne blinked back tears. "Pick up, Carlos, pick up, damn it!"

"Miss Suzanne?"

The tears spilled over in relief. "Carlos, thank god! Sorry I'm so testy, lo siento. I just haven't gone this long without an update . . ."

"Miss Suzanne," Carlos interrupted her. "Mr. Will, he told us today to pick everything. Pick it all now."

An icy calm filled Suzanne and dried her eyes. Why was Will telling them anything? "Are the grapes ready?"

She read volumes into the silence, waiting for Carlos to choose his words and knowing that his hesitation had nothing to do with his English skills.

"The blocks we picked today were."

Suzanne waited, digging her nails into her palm to keep from saying anything.

"The other sections . . . they are in a range of Brix other wineries would harvest."

"Is the sugar level over twenty-three point seven?"

"No, Miss Suzanne. I told Mr. Will that we do not pick before twenty-three point seven and that twenty-four point five is better."

"And the physiological ripeness, Carlos? The stems and seeds? Can we do whole cluster?" She took a breath to stop herself and cut to the chase. "Do the grapes taste the way they should? The stems?" It wasn't the same as tasting them herself, but Carlos was the only one who came close to knowing what she wanted.

"No." He did not hesitate. "There is at least one day, maybe more."

Suzanne felt lightheaded and nauseated. What was Will trying to do? Was this why he had seemed so understanding when she told him about Janice? Because he saw an opportunity? But for what? Is this why he hadn't called as promised? She closed her eyes for a moment, then inhaled and exhaled, counting silently to calm herself and focus.

The twilight was falling fast, and across the street a boy raked leaves in a race against the dark. The bonfires of her childhood complete with roasted marshmallows were no doubt forbidden now. She squinted into the gloom, reviewing her options. There was no flight she could get from anywhere that would get her back before morning, no time to find a private jet ride at any cost. She didn't know why Will was so eager to rush the harvest, and right now she didn't care; she just needed to buy time for Carlos and the crew. She needed to buy time for her grapes.

"Carlos," she paused, mentally running her options. "I plan to reorganize the barrel room and shed when I return. We've talked about that, right? After crush? Why don't you get a jump on that tonight. Clear the corner with the smudge pots and stack them out in front under the eaves along with the emergency lanterns, would you?"

"Miss Suzanne?"

She could hear the confusion in his voice.

"Yes, Carlos?"

"Mr. Will . . . he said not to bother you. Because of your sister."

Suzanne felt her face grow hot. That bastard! "Calling me was the right thing to do, Carlos. Muchas gracias. I'm sorry I can't be there right now, but everything will be okay. Will won't know that you called. You are staying at the winery tonight?"

"Si. I will be here until you return."

"Good. Be sure you get that cleaning started before you lock up. And Carlos?" Suzanne hesitated, unsure how much she could say without saying too much. "Take care of my vines."

Suzanne ended the call and pulled up Craig's number from her phone book. "I need a favor."

"I don't even get a hello? Since when are you all wham-bam thank you ma'am?"

The teasing and his obvious pleasure at hearing her voice made her wish all the more that she was back in California. "Sorry, Craig. There isn't much time and you're the only one I can ask, the only one I trust."

He picked up her desperation and dropped the slightly salacious banter that was his usual tone. "Anything for you. Tell me what you need."

"I want you to set fire to my vineyard."

Chapter 6

Brix:

degrees Brix is the unit representative
of the sugar content of an aqueous solution;
sugar converts to alcohol during fermentation

"Nothing big," Suzanne reassured the silence at the other end of the phone line. "I just need you to torch one of the rose bushes."

"Let me retract that 'anything you want'—I think you have me confused with Arsonists R Us." Craig sounded somewhere between appalled and terrified, as if he wanted to believe she was joking but was pretty sure she wasn't.

"Will told Carlos to have the crew pick everything. The grapes aren't ready."

"And setting fire to them will help because . . . ?"

Suzanne detected a subtle shift in tone away from outright panic so she pressed on. "Not the vines, a rose bush or maybe two at the ends of rows already picked. Not big enough to get out of hand, but a little petty vandalism that ought to slow harvest by a day."

"Is it just me, or does that seem like a big risk just to buy one day? Oakland Hills, Witch Creek, Bonnie Doone, for heaven's sake! Do these names not mean anything to you?" Craig's voice was strained. "Starting fires in California during fire season is not considered *petty*."

"I know it sounds crazy . . ."

"Oh, ya think?"

". . . but it isn't as risky as it sounds." Suzanne ignored Craig's interruption. "Look, Carlos is staying at the vineyard, there's plenty of water in the tank and in the pond, and the ground should be cleared around the finished rows. I didn't tell Carlos anything so he couldn't be blamed, but I know he'll put out the fire."

Craig sighed. "You can't know that for sure."

She heard the resignation in his voice and knew he was almost there. "Okay, let's improve the odds. Pull the file with the original sketches for the Mermaid label. I'll tell Carlos that you'll be dropping off artwork for me to review before the next bottling. You then have a reason to be there, don't have to run, and can alert Carlos if he doesn't see the fire right away."

"Why are you changing the label?" He sounded hurt.

Suzanne rolled her eyes, grateful her friend couldn't see her, considering what she was asking him to do. "I didn't say I *am* changing the label, Craig. I'm just giving you an excuse. An alibi?"

"Oh."

"But I actually might want to alter the design this year. Will is claiming the right to develop products and peripheral lines under the Suzanne Mathews Winery name, and he's bringing in outside investors to do it. Everything we have is community property. I don't know what's going to happen. I don't even know why he's giving Carlos any orders at all, let alone about harvest. This might be my last vintage."

The silence at the other end of the line told her she'd won.

"Craig?"

"If anything goes wrong, I am totally ratting you out."

"Fair enough. I'd rather go to jail than see this harvest screwed up." As soon as she said it, she realized it was true.

"You will so owe me for this."

"Anything you want."

Craig couldn't resist the opening. "A lap dance with Gavin Newsome?"

Suzanne smiled, relieved to have set her plan in motion. "Gavin Newsome is a little out of my league, but if I could arrange a lap dance with the former mayor of San Francisco, I might have to keep that for myself."

"That's okay," Craig said, "I'll settle for sloppy seconds."

The day faded to black as Suzanne discussed the details with Craig, repeatedly reassuring him when doubt crept back into his voice. Lights came on in the houses all around, and she shivered in the cool night air. They walked through the plan, the timing, what to wear, where to park to avoid Carlos seeing him before he could set the fire, how to use the smudge pots and kerosene, the row options, and where all the water sources were.

When she walked back into the kitchen, Suzanne saw that one more strand of lights had been untangled, and the rest were still piled on the table. She walked into the living room where she found Janice snoring softly, slumped on the couch with her chin on her chest. Two empty beer bottles stood next to the ashtray where a cigarette had burned down to the filter. Suzanne reached over and stubbed it out. With her features relaxed in sleep, Janice looked older and sicker. It was her waking animation that leant the appearance of vitality, but in repose, the jaundiced cheeks and sunken eyes made Suzanne want to check her pulse. Half a peanut butter and jelly sandwich with one bite gone balanced precariously on the arm of the couch. Suzanne moved it to the table beside the beer bottles, and went back to the kitchen.

She found plates and knives where they had always been, marveling at the memory buried so long it had become instinct. She sliced cheddar cheese and a tart green apple and fanned them out on the plate, then added some almonds on the side. It would be hours before she would hear from Craig—or from Carlos, for that matter. She was almost too nervous to eat, but she knew she needed to. Suzanne had given Carlos the house number in case he couldn't reach her cell, but he had called it first. She put a rectangle of cheese on a piece of apple and chewed slowly. Of course, Carlos knew her sister was sick, knew why she went back. He would assume that she would be home, with her sister, because that's where he would be if it were his family.

Suzanne went back to work on the last strand of bat lights while she ate, wishing she had brought another bottle of wine. She sent bottles to Janice every year, but if she had saved any, they were well-hidden. Suzanne squinted at the little pantry at the back of the kitchen on the other side of the stove from the dining room entry. Her eyes opened wide and she stood abruptly. Of course!

At the back of the pantry was a door with a glass knob and chipped paint that could be used to determine its age like counting the rings on a tree. Suzanne yanked on the knob, but the door had swelled and stuck at the top. She braced her feet and leaned back, jiggling the door and making incremental headway. It looked like something from a slasher movie where many teenagers died horribly. "Don't open the door!" she said under her breath, laughing. It finally gave way, and a rush of cold musty air blasted her. She waved her hand around just inside the door as if shooing flies until she found the string dangling from the ceiling.

A bare bulb cast a dim cone of light on the wooden stairs leading down into the cellar. Suzanne tested the banister and gingerly shifted her weight from one stair to the next as she descended, making sure it would hold before she moved on and brushing aside thick spider webs as she went. She thought if Janice could direct trick-or-treaters down here instead of the front door, she wouldn't have to decorate. The floor and walls were dirt, it was almost more crawl space than basement in the sense people thought of them now. Houses in California were built without basements until land became so valuable that underground garages and fully finished extra levels became common. In Iowa, though, there had always been basements or cellars, insulating buffers against the elements used for storing food and waiting out tornados.

Suzanne remembered huddling around a candle with Janice and baby Donnie listening to a battery operated radio one summer evening when a storm front had made a sudden turn to the north. The tornado watch was upgraded to a warning as the green-tinged sky crackled with lightning and the smell of ozone filled the air. Their mom had called from the hospital where she worked to make sure they were going to the basement. After Janice stopped babysitting, Suzanne made those trips to the basement, one or two every summer, mostly on her own.

The small space was filled with boxes and a few rusted folding chairs stacked against one wall. Suzanne closed her eyes and inhaled deeply, the fragrance of the damp black earth as reminiscent of cabernet as of shelter from a storm. Suzanne moved to one of the stacks of boxes and knelt beside it. It had her logo on it. She dusted off a box at the back and squinted at the label. It was the first winery she had worked for. The boxes were all unopened. She stood, shaking her head, and took the cleanest two-pack box from the top of the stack beside her and went back upstairs.

Suzanne pulled the light cord and slammed the door almost as one motion as she hurried out of the pantry with the box. She nearly collided with Janice who dropped her bottle of beer to the floor with a crash, her gasp of shock building into another of the now familiar but still disconcerting coughing fits. Suzanne put the box on the counter and grabbed the roll of paper towels, which she used to clean up the broken glass and splattered beer while casting quick sidelong glances at her sister. Janice wasn't wearing a scarf, and the silvery peach fuzz made her seem more vulnerable. Suzanne knew CPR, she knew the Heimlich maneuver, she knew all sorts of first aid treatments for everything from bleeding wounds to broken bones, but she had never learned the protocol for when there was nothing you could do.

By the time Janice caught her breath, Suzanne had dumped the wet paper towels studded with brown shards into the trash.

"What are you trying to do, kill me? Oh—too late." Janice lit a cigarette and gestured toward the refrigerator. "While you're over there, get me a new beer, would you?"

Suzanne retrieved an Anchor Steam and opened it before handing it over. "I was just inspecting your wine cellar. Is it okay if I open this?"

"Open anything you like. I'm not much of a wine drinker. Though you probably figured that out."

"Have you even tasted anything I've sent you? Ever? Why didn't you tell me to stop sending it?" Suzanne wasn't angry as much as bemused. She dug through the junk drawer, which didn't look as if it had ever been cleaned out and probably still had things in the far back that she had put there as a child, found a pair of scissors and opened the box.

"I gave away a few bottles here and there as gifts, gave some to Donnie after he moved to the Twin Cities and started drinking the stuff." Janice shrugged and went back to organizing the decorations on the table. "Even if I didn't drink it, it was kind of nice to get the packages. Nice to have the UPS guy ask about my 'family' winery."

Suzanne was touched by Janice's unspoken pride in their connection, in her work, even if it wasn't something she specifically valued. She smiled and pulled off the cardboard top that protected the wine bottles during shipping and always reminded her of a jet pack. The box held a bottle of Cherie Amour and a bottle of Mermaid Tears from two years before. She thought the Cherie would still be very good and the Mermaid Tears excellent. Not many California pinots age as well as some of the burgundies, but the vertical tastings she had done at the vineyard had shown Mermaid Tears to still be vibrant after ten years. Cherie, on the other hand, flattened out maybe five years or so beyond the vintage date. Some of her wines in Janice's basement would likely be best used for cooking.

"I'm going to open both of these to see how they are. Some of the older wines down there might not be very good anymore. I can go through the boxes and sort everything for you while I'm here."

"I thought wine was supposed to get better with age." Janice heaped some cannibalized light strands into a box and set it on the floor, keeping the three good ones and a bunch of rubber bats out on the table.

"Yeah, well, that's only partly true. It depends on the wine and on the storage conditions." She rifled through the junk drawer again as she spoke, finally coming up with a pocket knife that included a corkscrew. "Wines are like people . . . some of them age much better than others."

Janice shot her a look as if about to toss off a retort, then said, "Get on with it, then. Pour yourself something and let's go finish hanging these."

"Now?" Suzanne looked at the clock. It was barely after eight, but the early dark made it feel much later. Twilight would just be kissing the vineyard now, long shadows stretching to offer Craig the cover he would need. She checked the charge on her cell phone.

"What, you have something else to do?"

"It's just . . . when I got here you were out cold on the couch. I thought you were done for the night." Suzanne pulled a wine glass out of the cupboard and rinsed off the film of neglect before splashing a little Cherie in the bowl and swirling it as she held it up to the light. The color was bright ruby, nearly pink at the edge, and the legs were still lovely. All the fruit and a hint of spice were still there, it was much as her last taste of it.

"Sorry if I don't have a nice predictable little schedule. Get used to it. That's one of the perks of living alone," Janice said as she sat down to finish her beer and watch Suzanne's tasting ritual.

Suzanne rinsed the glass and poured an ounce or so of the Mermaid Tears. She swirled it on the counter, wanting to get a little more air into it before tasting. The color, as expected, was deeper, burgundy with magenta at the rim, and the taste was layered with fruit and spice, but now there was a note of leather before the long, long finish. The wine was balanced and soft on the tongue, fragrant and even better than her last encounter with the vintage. Her mouth was watering when she put the glass down.

Sheila Scobba Banning **67**

"I know what you mean," Suzanne said to Janice as she poured more wine and gathered the light strands. "There's a lot to be said for not having anyone else around, doing what you want and never having to explain yourself."

Janice made no move to get up as she watched Suzanne savor the wine in her glass as she moved around the room. "Since when do you live alone?"

Suzanne stopped just before the back door, turned to Janice. "Oh. Yeah. I guess I haven't talked to you in awhile."

Janice inhaled deeply and blew out a stream of smoke but didn't respond.

"Will and I have been separated for . . . I don't know, more than six months? But nothing official . . . until he filed for divorce. Now I officially live alone." Suzanne felt oddly relieved to say it out loud.

Janice nodded and stubbed out her cigarette as she rose slowly from the chair. "Seems like 'Why didn't you tell me?' would be in order here, but you stole my line." She squeezed Suzanne's arm as she passed her at the door with an armful of bats. "The ladder's outside."

They worked without conversation but for the occasional direction from Janice to move a light to the right or left. When they finished, Suzanne moved the ladder to the side of the house and plugged the lights into the extension cord. The cockeyed front porch was outlined with twinkling bats, their larger rubber cousins waving from the tree branches over the sidewalk. Tombstones were scattered across the yard with an assortment of cobwebs, spiders, and skeletal parts adorning them. Between the sidewalk and the curb in a nicely shaded plot illuminated by a glaring spotlight was the headstone Janice had made that afternoon.

Suzanne fingered her cell phone in her pocket, pulled it out to check the time. Still too soon, but the scent of wood smoke from someone's fireplace made her picture flames on her vines, and she shivered. She turned to watch Janice standing with her hand on her right hip surveying the yard, then realized she was standing exactly the same way. There hadn't been much that they shared after Suzanne grew up, and seeing the common gesture made her smile. "Are you sure that one under the tree isn't going to scare away the trick-or-treaters? Or their parents?"

Janice shrugged. "Only the wimpy ones who don't deserve candy anyway. It's not like it has dates on it."

"It does look good though . . . you want us to save it? I don't think they'll let us put you that close to the curb, though."

Janice laughed until she hacked uncontrollably. When she could talk again she said, "If you want to toss that out on the water after me, you're more than welcome!"

"What?"

"I want a Viking funeral, like Daddy."

Suzanne tried to get a better look at her sister's face, consciously slowed her own breath so she could hear better.

"Our dad is buried in the cemetery by the highway. I was just there today. Remember?"

"Don't treat me like an idiot! I told you already, death, not dementia." Janice sounded disgusted. "Let's go in; I'm getting cold."

When they got inside, Suzanne turned to lock the door without thinking.

"Stop," Janice said.

Suzanne pulled her hand back, shaking her head at the open door policy, then walked over to the open bottle of Mermaid Tears to refill her glass. The wine had opened up, had a broader range of fragrance and flavor as if a simple melody had become full orchestration. She looked at the clock. It should be dark at the winery, and Craig should be there. She watched Janice take a beer from the refrigerator and open it, then walk toward the door. "Viking funeral?"

Janice stopped. Sighed. "Can we sit in the living room?"

They arranged themselves without thinking, Janice pushed Molly aside to slide into her usual spot on the couch near the ashtray, Suzanne sat as far away as possible without leaving the room, near a window, which she cracked despite the autumn chill.

Janice lit a cigarette and looked at Suzanne. "Do you remember going to the beach when you were really little?"

"Of course. It was our only vacation ever. We went to California, it must have been . . ." Suzanne frowned, "right before our dad died?"

"No." Janice shook her head and drank from her beer, studying the ship on the label as if the story were written there. "It was after he died."

"But I remember . . ." Suzanne closed her eyes to try to bring the memory into focus. "I remember making a sand castle and running away from the waves with the grownups on the blanket high up on a dune. The air tasted salty and smelled," she hesitated, then finished the thought, "not like a hospital."

"Those grownups weren't Mom and Daddy, they were Les and Bette, cousins on Mom's side. I took you to visit them in L.A. after Mom . . . had a little breakdown."

They sat in silence for some time, Janice smoking and drinking while Suzanne tried to process Janice's version and overwrite her own images of that vacation. The clearest pictures were of the ocean and the beach with the sound of pounding surf and laughter. That was when she knew she would be back. She must have filled in her parents like a drugstore postcard. Wish you were here.

"What was Mom like? Before, I mean." Suzanne thought about the distant woman she'd lived with for eighteen years and tried to distill her questions down to the crucial one. "Was she ever happy?"

Janice smiled a little and drank. "Yeah, she was happy. And she had a beautiful voice. She was always a little reserved, though, more shy than anything. Daddy was the outgoing one, always laughing and making wisecracks. They seemed like opposites, but they made a good pair."

The sisters sat with their own memories, Janice's of a time before their father got sick, Suzanne's of her mother's absence during long shifts at the hospital and the silent stares when she was home, not so much vacant as filled with things she could not or would not share with Suzanne.

"Where does the Viking funeral come in?" Suzanne finally asked.

"Daddy used to joke about it, back before he got so sick he couldn't come home. He was really funny." Janice smiled a private smile and then continued. "He said he'd settle for cremation, but Mom wouldn't go for it. Nobody did that much then, and Mom wanted him buried where she would be." Janice shrugged. "So I made a little talisman bag, took a linen hankie that belonged to his mom and filled it with a picture of Daddy, one of his favorite Gahan Wilson cartoons, and a lock of hair I cut off during visitation at the funeral home."

"You cut off his hair while he was in the casket?" Suzanne interrupted.

Janice shrugged again. "Nobody saw me. Anyway, one night after everyone was asleep, I went down to the beach with a newspaper boat, tucked the bag inside it and set it on fire just before a wave came in."

Suzanne shook her head in disbelief.

Janice shook the beer bottle and peered into it, then took two pills out of the bottles on the coffee table and swallowed them with the last mouthful of beer. "Maybe not exactly what he had in mind, but I thought the gesture was worth making."

"Well, unless you saved some of your hair, I think we'll need a different plan."

Janice laughed and wheezed but managed not to build up to the choking phase. "Don't worry, I already told Donnie to cremate me and go visit you. I figured you'd come up with a good place to send me out into the Pacific."

The phone rang with a loud jangling that made Suzanne start. She yanked her phone out of her pocket and stared at it even as the house phone kept ringing. Janice dug around between the couch cushions and under the pillows until she found the phone.

"Hello? No, no, it's fine. Donnie won't get here until after dinner tomorrow. Sure, I'll have him call you."

Suzanne caught the funny look Janice was giving her and looked down to check for missed calls and messages even though she knew there weren't any.

"You expecting another call?"

"Yes."

Janice waited, and when Suzanne didn't say anything more, she asked, "Does this have anything to do with your soon-to-be ex-husband?"

"Sort of. It's complicated." Suzanne hesitated. "I don't want to bother you with my problems."

"Because they pale compared to mine?"

Suzanne nodded and Janice made a face.

"My problems are over. Yours, on the other hand, sound like they're just getting started. If you want to tell me about it, you'd better do it before talking to me requires the services of a medium."

Suzanne considered how much to say, where to begin. "Will wants to make a lot of changes at the winery, changes I may not be able to stop because everything is community property. Today he interfered with the harvest, something I would never have expected." She paused and drained her glass. "I guess I'm just waiting for some good news."

"I never liked him," Janice said.

"What? You did too! You almost had a better time at our wedding than I did."

Janice waved off the comment. "Weddings are always fun. Besides, what was I going to say, 'Sure he's cute and funny and can't keep his hands off you, but do you think he's really in your league?' I'm not exactly the poster child for traditional long-term relationships."

Suzanne caught herself before she could leap to Will's defense. They weren't on the same side anymore.

"Do you have a good lawyer?"

Janice's voice was a melody of sympathy, sorrow, and hope, the kind of notes heard from only those who had known you long and loved you well. Suzanne blinked back tears. "I think so."

"Good." Janice nodded and rose unsteadily to her feet. I have to go to bed now. I hope you get your good news."

Suzanne went back to the kitchen for another half glass of wine, then poured a little more and put her cell phone on the table in front of her. After hours that measured fifteen minutes in real time, the UB40 version of "Red Red Wine" started playing and she nearly knocked the phone off the table trying to answer.

"Oh my god, Suzanne! The fire! I did what you told me, but it spread so fast. It shot up like a torch, flames everywhere."

Suzanne felt time slowing around her, almost as if she were moving underwater. She looked at the clock on the wall and could hear each second ticking like a hammer pounding on metal. She'd always thought that was just a movie effect, then she realized it was her heartbeat sounding, not the second hand. A rim of black started to close in on her peripheral vision, and she turned to the side to lower her head to her lap while she took deep breaths. The rant from Craig continued in the background as she concentrated on not fainting.

"Craig?" It was almost a whisper.

". . . and the heat, it was like a sauna on steroids!"

She sat up slowly, wiped the clammy sweat from her forehead and found her voice. "Craig!"

"What?"

"Are you okay?"

He stopped mid-sentence and said, "Yes."

She could feel the tears on her face, closed her eyes and saw apocalyptic visions of her vineyard in flames. "And Carlos?"

"He's fine." The hysteria in his voice was dialed back a couple notches. "He's right here."

"Miss Suzanne?"

A sob erupted from her at the sound of his voice. "Carlos! How bad is it?"

"The fire in the vineyard, it started in the roses by the first row of the section we picked today. It took two of the vines before we could put it out. It was fortunate that Mr. Craig was here tonight."

"Wait, just two vines? It sounded like . . . I thought . . ."

"Mr. Craig, he is perhaps," Carlos hesitated, then lowered his voice, "a little excited."

Suzanne burst out laughing, which merged with her tears to produce a gurgling mess of emotional stew.

"Miss Suzanne?"

Even over the phone she caught the note of concern for her mental health in the delivery of the question. "I'm okay, Carlos. Go on."

"They used a smudge pot, the vandals. I do not think it was serious."

"Maybe kids? Did it look like a prank, Carlos? Could that be what happened? It is close to Halloween . . ."

"Ah . . . si. Teenagers . . ." There was silence on the other end of the line as Carlos considered Suzanne's question. "It could have been that way."

"You'll need to spend tomorrow cleaning up and checking to make sure there isn't any other damage, yes? And the next day your men can harvest the grapes that are ready." Suzanne reached over to the counter, afraid to stand, and poured more wine in her glass. She thought she would probably regret it in the morning, but right now she had something to celebrate. "You should call Will now so he won't think you called me. And Carlos? Take as much time as you need when you begin picking again."

"Claro, Miss Suzanne. Muchas gracias."

Suzanne could hear the relief in his voice, if not total comprehension. Craig came back on the line after a muffled burst of coughing.

"Are you okay to drive home?" She could afford to smile now, but she wouldn't tease him about his reaction. At least not yet.

"If I never see this place again, it will be too soon!" The drama was still in his voice, but the edge of hysteria was gone. He coughed again, a dry barking sound.

"Did you inhale a lot of smoke?" Suzanne asked.

"I'm fine. Or I will be once I get away from here and have a good stiff drink."

"You saved my vineyard, Craig. I'll make it up to you when I get back."

"When will that be?"

Suzanne looked around the dingy kitchen, took in the full ashtray and leftover Halloween decorations and the permanently unlocked door. "I don't know. I honestly don't know."

Suzanne turned out the lights as she passed through the rooms on her way to bed. She used the outlet behind the dresser to plug in her cell phone charger, changed her clothes, then went to brush her teeth, feeling suddenly exhausted. The sound of Janice snoring stopped as Suzanne walked out of the bathroom. She stood outside the bedroom door, listening, waiting for another sound. She felt like she had the one time she babysat for an infant when she was fourteen. At first she had been so grateful when the baby stopped crying and fell asleep, but then she spent the rest of the night tiptoeing up to the door to make sure the baby was still breathing. She decided that night that babysitting was too stressful. There was a *snork* followed by a long sigh, and Janice's soft snoring began again.

As she lingered in the hallway listening to Janice breathe, the tone announcing a text message went off on her phone. Suzanne covered the short distance and grabbed the phone before the ring finished sounding a second time. It was from Craig. "fyi Carlos looks a tad green . . . maybe flu?"

"Great," she said out loud. Her vineyard manager might just be suffering the after effects of fighting the fire, but he might also be fighting of a virus he didn't want to tell her about. It wouldn't be the first time he had worked sick; he considered that a badge of honor. Suzanne flipped the phone open and closed, debating whether she should call Carlos. She hated not being there to pick and sort and inspect the grapes, but if she couldn't be, Carlos had to be. There was no one else. And he was, after all, a grownup. Finally, she snapped the phone shut, turned out the lights in the shrine to Americana, and slid under the thick covers of the bed. The strange events of the day circled her fading consciousness, filling her dreams with burning ships, smoldering vines, and Styrofoam tombstones carved with the names of everyone she loved.

Chapter 7

Cold Soak:

a pre-fermentation maceration involving aqueous extraction of compounds from the skin/pulp/seeds to increase flavor complexity and intensity of aroma and color

A door banged downstairs and an indecipherable cheer went up.

What little comfort and restoration sleep held for Suzanne that night was cut short by raucous laughter and loud voices. The disorientation of waking abruptly in an unfamiliar bed made her first wonder what party she was sleeping through, then why there were ceramic geese mooning her.

"This is why normal people lock their doors," Suzanne muttered as she rolled over and covered her head with the pillow. No amount of buffering could block out the noise, though, and she rose reluctantly, yawning and stretching. She looked at her phone. It was just after eight, no messages or missed calls. She resisted the urge to call the vineyard so early and instead pulled on a pair of jeans and a sweater so she could go downstairs and get some coffee. She looked in the mirror, running her hands through her hair and wiping the black bits of inadequately cleansed mascara from under her eyes. Suzanne knew it was unreasonable for a guest to resent the presence of other people before breakfast, but she did, anyway. When she opened the bedroom door, Molly waddled in as if she had been waiting there for some time. She squeezed past Suzanne and attempted to jump up on the bed, making it on the second try.

Suzanne considered throwing the cat out, but decided it had greater territorial claim than she did. "All I ask is no hairballs and nothing dead in the bed, okay?"

Molly responded with a tiny meow that sounded more like it came from a kitten on helium than from the slab of fur beached against the pillows. Her little Hitler mustache stretched as she yawned and closed her eyes.

"Hiel kitty." Suzanne left the door ajar for the cat and went downstairs.

The voices grew clearer at the landing, one man and several women. It sounded like they were debating the merits of different sizes of bubble wrap.

"Sleeping Beauty awakes!" Janice announced Suzanne's arrival to the rest of the group with a flourish. "You remember my sister, Suzanne?"

The two older women sitting with Janice at the table did look vaguely familiar in the way that everyone Suzanne saw in town looked a little like someone she went to school with or knew growing up. It was a small town, so almost by definition they had to be related to someone she had known. Many people moved away, but few new people came and stayed. The man standing in the doorway was wearing a FedEx uniform and gulping a cup of coffee.

"Of course we remember her," the one with curly gray hair and wire glasses said. "You were always so smart. My Robby was two years ahead of you in school."

"Sure," Suzanne said, not really sure at all. "Nice to see you again." She got a cup from the cupboard and poured herself some coffee, leaning against the door jamb at the same angle as the delivery man across the room.

"Suzanne Mathews?" The FedEx man asked as he set down his coffee. "That envelope on the table is for you." He turned to Janice. "Thanks for the coffee. I've got two more deliveries to make."

"It's not from the winery," Janice said.

She looked tired today, almost translucent around the eyes, and her hands shook. Suzanne wondered if that was a bad sign or just indication of some imbalance between her meds and her self-meds. Instead of a silk pirate scarf she wore an angora beret in a dark purple shade somewhere between plum and blackberry.

"It's from a law firm," the woman with the shockingly white pageboy said. "Maybe it's from your ex-husband."

Suzanne glared at her sister over the top of her coffee mug, but Janice just shrugged and lit a cigarette. "Twitter's got nothing on you people," Suzanne muttered.

"What?" Robby's mom asked.

"Just wondering what you ladies are up to today," Suzanne said as she lifted the envelope from the table and slid it under her arm without opening nor even looking at it. The two women made no effort to disguise their disappointment.

"Muriel and Patsy have been coming by to help me sort things and box them up for the church. We should be finishing up today."

"Church?" Suzanne looked from Janice to the women and back.

"You know, little building, pointy steeple, open the doors and see all the people?" Janice said.

The ladies cackled, and Suzanne responded, "I understand the concept, I just never expected to hear it used in the same sentence with *you*," which made the two women cackle all the louder as Janice joined in.

"They aren't picky about the source of their charitable contributions, and I'm glad to get rid of everything so Donnie doesn't have to do it," Janice drained her coffee and carried the cup to the sink. "Which reminds me, he'll be here in time for dinner. That call I got last night was from my lawyer. There are still a couple things we need to sign while I'm still considered competent." She snorted at the term, then opened a bottle of beer.

The two women looked down at the table at the mention of the lawyer, then into their coffee cups and out the back door, avoiding eye contact with Janice or Suzanne. Sorting old clothes and packing up knickknacks was the sort of good works they did all the time, but Janice's blunt acknowledgment of her rapidly declining health made the connection to death impossible to avoid.

"Let's go, ladies." Janice shuffled past Suzanne. "We'll be on the porch if you want to help."

Suzanne refilled her cup and took it upstairs. The kitchen table with the audible chatter from the front of the house and the perpetually unlocked back door felt too exposed for opening the FedEx package. When Janice had squeezed past her in the doorway, Suzanne caught a whiff of overripe fruit and fermentation. Part of it was just the metabolism of alcohol, but part of it was something else, something she hadn't smelled since visiting her father's bedside so long ago the images in the memories were like blurred snapshots and could not be trusted. She thought all hospitals had an unpleasant sour tang, but maybe it hadn't been the hospital after all. Maybe that smell was actually the scent of a body consuming itself. Death smelled almost like maceration gone terribly wrong.

Not bothering to close the door behind her, Suzanne sat on the bed and peeled back the cardboard strip on the envelope. Molly didn't even crack an eye at the movement as if she were just another taxidermied detail courtesy of Troop 49. Suzanne read the notice straight through, then went back to read key paragraphs, then read it two more times before she stopped. No amount of rereading was going to infuse the pages with any more sense. It wasn't so much the legalese in which the document was written as it was the major themes. Abandonment of property and dereliction of duty seemed unlikely charges after so few days, but Suzanne didn't see any other interpretation. At least she knew why Will wasn't returning her calls yesterday; he thought the package would have been delivered yesterday afternoon.

Suzanne rubbed her temples to ward off the headache building there. "What the hell am I doing here?"

"I believe I asked you that when you got here." Janice stood in the doorway, her tread so light the creaking floorboards hadn't alerted Suzanne. "I just wanted to let you know that there's a box of things for you to go through, things you might want or might want to see before they go."

"Thanks."

Janice adjusted the fluffy beret. "Bad news?"

"Weird news. But since it's filled with officially-worded threats, I guess it must be bad, just because I have to deal with it." Unlikely as Will's charges were to hold up, Suzanne wanted to get it to her lawyer right away. "Do you have a fax?"

"Nope. Mine broke. There's one at the *ampm* and one at Hy-Vee, but I've been going to Mark's office and using his when I needed to."

"Maybe I should call him." Just saying it made Suzanne feel a little flushed.

"Don't call, just go over. He's uptown, a block off Main Street across from the Dairy Queen. If he's not in, his secretary can do it for you." Janice turned slowly to head back downstairs. "You know, he hasn't had more than a handful of dates since his divorce. None at all this year." Her voice trailed off as she descended the stairs.

Suzanne shook her head and went to take a shower.

The day was brisk, but Suzanne's sweater was warm enough for the walk downtown. The morning air of fall in Iowa was warmer than many nights in the mountains, so even though her packing had consisted of cramming jeans and sweaters and underwear into a bag along with her toiletries, she wasn't completely unprepared. The temperature might have been comparable to California, but the experience of it was completely different. The seasons in Iowa did not change gradually and within a moderate range, they covered a full spectrum marked with dramatic transitions. The chill in the air here did not carry the damp of the fog that would warm as the day wore on; it was a sharper cold that hinted at the hard freeze to come.

Mark's office was in a restored Victorian that looked like a well-dressed woman who had lost her bearings and ended up in the wrong part of town. A parking lot spread to the end of the block on one side, and a plain brick box of a building with appliances in the windows stood on the other side. The Victorian was painted a warm gold with cinnamon trim and white highlights, the attention to detail worthy of San Francisco's postcard row. A framed sign beside the front door read "Jorgenson Assurance." Suzanne searched for a doorbell, then pounded the brass lion's head on the door three times. When she got no response, Suzanne turned and walked down the steps, but she heard the door open behind her before she reached the bottom.

"Suzanne! Come back!"

She turned to see Mark standing in the doorway in running shorts and a t-shirt soaked through in a *V* at the chest. He grabbed the hem to wipe his face, revealing most of his abdomen. She hadn't seen him shirtless in a very long time, and he had filled in and developed just enough chest hair to be sexy. A thin line of dark hair ran from his chest past his navel and disappeared into his shorts, signaling like landing lights on a runway. Suzanne walked back up the stairs quickly so he wouldn't catch her looking.

"Is that how you dress for work?" she teased.

"Yeah. Casual Friday takes on new meaning when you're self-employed in a small town." Mark grinned. "I'd hug you, but I'm all sweaty. I had a longer run than usual today. Fortunately, I live upstairs. A hot shower and I'll be good as new." He stepped back inside and gestured toward the interior. "Welcome to my office."

Suzanne passed by close enough to feel the heat radiating off him. The large room which was probably the parlor in the previous life of the house contained the reception desk, a small conference table with chairs, and two low leather chairs separated by a wooden cube stacked with magazines. It was both welcoming and professional, but she saw no office equipment other than a phone.

"I need to send a fax," she held up the FedEx package by way of explanation. "Janice said you let her use yours, and I was hoping I might be included in that arrangement under the nepotism clause."

"Of course. In here."

Mark opened a set of old pocket doors into a smaller room of indeterminate origin, maybe a pantry or linen closet. It was filled with file cabinets and equipment, including a printer/fax/copy machine. He punched buttons and it made the humming sound of an electrical device waking and coming to attention.

"Here." Mark held out his hand for her fax. When Suzanne didn't move, he turned and looked at her. "Oh, I'm sorry. It's personal." He turned back to the machine and gestured as he explained the operation. "Just put whatever you want to fax, up to eleven pages, here, face up. Punch in the number, and the pages will scan and send as a set." His tone was a little wounded.

"No, it's not that." Suzanne pulled out the notice and handed it to him. "Please?"

Suzanne entered Hannah Jackson's number while he arranged the legal document in the tray. He hit send, and they stood watching the machine in awkward silence, like strangers on an elevator.

"It's my husband. Ex. Well, almost. He's threatening . . ." She burst into tears before she could finish.

Mark responded to her distress without hesitating, pulling her into an embrace and holding her until she'd stopped crying. Suzanne relaxed into him, remaining in his arms beyond the need for comfort.

"Feel free to wipe your nose on the shirt," Mark said, "it's pretty nasty already."

Suzanne burst out laughing at that and took a step back, leaving her hand on his forearm. "You're such a smooth talker." She thought it was strange to be so comfortable with a man she hadn't seen in decades and so at odds with the man she had chosen to share her life. Of course, she had chosen Mark, too, but he had been tied to Iowa, and Suzanne was going away.

The fax machine signaled its completion, and Suzanne reached up to hug him in thanks. The brief contact brought her face to the side of his neck, and she tasted salt as she pulled away. When she licked her lips, everything shifted between them, like in the optical illusion where instead of a vase you suddenly see the lady. What had been playful flirting and attraction became the certain urgency of desire. Mark took the original from the fax and handed it to Suzanne, her fingers grazing his in the exchange. She looked into his eyes, trying to decide what to say, when the door in the outer room opened with a bang.

"Sorry I'm late, Mark. My babysitter had a flat," the secretary announced her arrival. Disappointed and a little relieved, Suzanne took a step back. "Thanks for the use of the fax," she said.

"Anytime." Mark listened to the sounds of his receptionist settling in and smiled ruefully. "I think I'll make that a cold shower."

Instead of returning immediately to Janice's house, Suzanne strolled through the downtown area, a business district which consisted of four blocks of retail along Main Street and additional shops and services for one block perpendicular on either side. Suzanne talked on the phone as she walked, nodding and smiling to the strangers she passed who greeted her just the same.

She had to try the vineyard phone and Carlos's cell before she got him. "Carlos. How are things in the light of day?"

"Very good, Miss Suzanne. The damage was very slight, but the cleanup requires attention. It is very warm today. Tomorrow will be a good day for harvest." He punctuated the assertion with a cough that sounded deeper than Craig's the night before.

Suzanne could hear the smile in his voice before it was consumed by a burst of hacking. "And what about you, Carlos? How are you feeling?"

"I am fine. I will have the men ready to harvest again tomorrow."

She listened behind the words, but couldn't find an opening. "If you are sick—"

Carlos cut her off before she could finish. "No, Miss Suzanne. It is just from the fire. I will not let you down."

In person, she might have been able to finesse the exchange into something he would be willing to talk about. Of course, in person she wouldn't need to. Suzanne sighed.

"I know, Carlos. You are a rock. Is Will there?"

"No. Mr. Will came as soon as it was light, but he left when he saw we would not be picking today."

"Thank you, Carlos. Thank you for everything."

Suzanne wondered whether she should wait to hear from Hanna Jackson before talking to Will, but she decided if she didn't call about the fire right away, that would just give him one more thing to add to the list of her imagined derelictions. Her call went immediately to voicemail, which she found infuriating, unsurprising, and maybe even a little bit fortuitous.

"Will. I just talked with Carlos. The fire sounds like petty vandalism, but I've asked him to keep an extra watch on the vines and close the gate at the end of the driveway at night. Lucky we didn't lose any time since nothing was ready to pick today, anyway." Suzanne smiled as she said the last line, recording both her continued involvement despite the distance and her professional opinion on the harvest strategy for him and his lawyer.

The store fronts she passed were representative of every kind of merchandise you might need, sometimes in odd combinations. Jewelry. High-end clothing. Bargain clothing. Shoes. Books and sporting goods. Antiques and doughnuts. Beauty salon. Beauty salon. Bar. Bar. Bar. Bar. Pet store. Coffee shop. The only chain store in the whole mix was a five and dime at the opposite end of Main Street from the Court House.

The name had grated on Suzanne as a child, offending her natural sense of logic, but when she was a little older, she recognized that "nickel and dime" was not something any shopkeeper was going to advertise.

There were a lot of empty store fronts, at least one on every block on both sides of the street. It reminded her of driving through Silicon Valley after the bottom dropped out of the market. A software company fails in Sunnyvale, California, and three thousand people lose their jobs with only a see-through highrise to mark the death of their aspirations. A fabric store in Winterwood, Iowa, goes deeper and deeper into the red until one family loses everything, leaving space for lease in a stone building from the 1900s where two generations of quilters had met and high school kids got summer jobs. Standing at the center of the fading downtown, Suzanne thought maybe the failure of the tiny family business caused the greater devastation. Small towns had fewer opportunities, little margin for error, and so much interdependence that one failed business could infect the rest, like a glassy winged sharpshooter spreading disease through a vineyard, starving the fruit on the vine.

Suzanne spotted a section up the block that looked fresher, as if someone had started a tiny urban renewal project. One of the stores was a coffee shop done in dark woods and brass and glass block with sculptural pinpoint spots overhead and framed pastel drawings of still life arrangements and nudes on the walls. It looked like it had been teleported directly from Palo Alto. Just as she was about to walk in, Suzanne's phone rang, so she stepped back from the door and moved toward the empty space beside it to take the call from her lawyer.

"Suzanne. I got your message and reviewed the notice from Will's attorney. This is an outlandish set of accusations intended to eat up my time and your money, but we should take it as a shot across the bow. I know this firm, and they are telling us not to fool around or waste time with a low-ball offer. Ridiculous as this accusation sounds, they can bury you in paperwork composed purely of spurious charges, discovery requests, and expert reviews."

"And that's legal?"

Hannah's voice was somewhere between amused and exasperated. "That's how some divorce attorneys make all their money. Now, in this situation, any court would look sympathetically at your need to care for your sister. As long as you have made arrangements for competent people to assume your duties while you are away, they would have a hard time establishing dereliction of duty, unless your absence could be shown to cause loss of income for the corporation or damage to the product."

Suzanne listened to Hannah without speaking, pacing up and down in front of the coffee shop and nodding at her reflection. She stopped at the lawyer's last sentence and stared into the muted tones of her transparent self in the glass.

"Suzanne?"

"We're harvesting right now, and I have never been away from the vineyard for more than a day during harvest. But Carlos, my vineyard manager, is staying onsite. He knows what I expect from the fruit and how long to cold soak each lot, so he can manage." *Unless he gets sick, then I'm totally screwed,* she thought but didn't say. The ghostly woman looking back at her looked a little sick, herself.

Now the silence was on the other end of the line. Finally Hannah said, "If I understand you correctly, your absence from the vineyard at this time is unprecedented. Even though they have a pretty thin argument on the harm to marital assets, the best way to prevent them from pursuing that line is for you to come home."

"What about Will contradicting my instructions and telling the crew to harvest before Brix and physiological ripeness met my standards? Doesn't that sound like an even bigger liability?"

Anger swept aside fear as Suzanne outlined for her lawyer what had happened at the vineyard the day before, leaving out the part about how the fire actually started. She concluded the torrent of complaint to Hannah with the voice message she left on Will's phone. Her reflection was gesturing wildly like a homeless woman arguing with her own demons.

"Okay, I don't entirely understand what your issue with the harvest schedule is, but it sounds like it does matter to you. If both your directions to your manager and the history of your harvest specifications can be documented, this gives us something very strong to work with. I need you to write this up, including as much technical detail as possible, and get it to me as soon as you're done. And Suzanne? I know you can't avoid talking to Will, because he is still your business partner, but I want you to be very careful about what you record or write to him."

Suzanne sighed. "Okay."

"In fact, I would prefer you avoid putting anything in writing unless you can run it by me first," the lawyer added.

Suzanne wrapped up the call still staring at her reflection. Had it really come to that? Sending notes to her husband through a lawyer? "You have to come home," she said to herself. "Yeah, sure, where have I heard that before?"

The laughter hit her as she rounded the corner to Janice's house, a clear signal that Muriel and Patsy were still sorting and loading boxes. They waved to her from the screened porch as she approached, so she walked up the canted front steps instead of walking around to the kitchen door.

"That one over there is yours," Janice said, pointing to a box near the living room door. "The girls are about to load up the rest, but you can take that one up to your room and take your time with it."

Janice's color looked a little better than it had earlier, and Suzanne couldn't see any tremors. Maybe nothing had changed, and every day held a cycle of ups and downs that currently had more ups, but very soon would have more downs until the constantly shifting balance settled down to zero. Suzanne felt a sudden tightening in her throat and turned away to pick up the box as she blinked back tears.

"Thanks," she said.

"Did you get your fax sent?" Janice asked.

"Yes," Suzanne said over her shoulder, "I'll fill you in later."

She carried the heavy box up the stairs and dropped it on the floor at the foot of the bed. The cat had rolled her extremities under herself, transformed from animal to throw pillow. The thump of the box caused no disruption to her nap.

Suzanne took out her phone to call Craig, then put it back. She paced the room, picking up geese and willow hearts and potpourri baskets and putting them back down again until she stopped before the black and white photos beside the dresser. The girl with the startling eyes, the boy with the cat, the teenager and hippie baby. Half the family was already gone, and half of what remained wouldn't make it to Thanksgiving. She looked out the window to the half-bare branches scattering orange and gold confetti as they waved in the breeze and made a choice.

Downstairs the women were stacking boxes into the back of an SUV with four-wheel drive. They all looked up when they heard the porch boards creak.

"Could I use the computer again?"

"Go ahead," Janice said. "Anytime. I'm going to go up for a nap after this, so no rush."

Suzanne walked over to the desk, pulled up the browser, and began searching for flights back to California.

Chapter 8

Fermentation:

the process by which grape sugars (glucose and fructose)
are converted to alcohol through the action of yeast

"Well, I can't really complain about your leaving since I didn't invite you in the first place," Janice said as she started upstairs to lie down.

She had taken Suzanne's announcement of imminent departure as she took everything, not so much complacently as imperturbably. Suzanne wasn't sure if the sting she felt from the jab at the end was intended or was entirely of her own creation. She listened to Janice's footsteps on the stairs and across the ceiling until she heard the creak of the bed springs, then she went to her room to pack.

The cat had moved on to her next designated nap location, so Suzanne had the room to herself. She looked at the suitcase she hadn't even bothered to transfer anything out of, the t-shirt she slept in draped over the foot of the bed, and her toiletry bag on the dresser. Suzanne tucked the tiny bottles of shampoo and moisturizer into the red vinyl pouch, zipped it closed and wedged it between the two stacks of clothes, and zipped the suitcase closed, too. Seeing how few things she had brought with her, she realized that, at least subconsciously, she hadn't been planning to stay long right from the beginning.

Suzanne folded her e-ticket printout and tucked it into her purse beside her wallet. Donnie should be on the road, and she would have time for dinner with him and Janice before her midnight run to the airport for the early morning flight. She wasn't looking forward to seeing him now, knowing that his response would not be quite so even-tempered as his mother's. He had asked her to come and she had gotten on the next flight out, but she had never said she could stay as long as it took. She had never told him she would be with Janice until the end. Of course, she hadn't said she wouldn't be, either. The last time she'd had a phone call telling her to come immediately was when Janice had called after their mother's accident. She had skipped her finals and driven home to help sort everything out. Finals weren't harvest, though, and Janice was still alive.

As if in response to her thoughts, Suzanne heard Janice *snork* followed by the rustling of the covers as she shifted in bed. Now that the decision was made, Suzanne felt restless, wanted to leave immediately, even if it meant sitting in the airport for hours, but she knew she needed to stay at least long enough to see Donnie. She wheeled her bag across the room and put her purse on top, then closed the door softly and got out her phone.

Mark picked up on the second ring. "Suzanne! I was just thinking about you."

She laughed, thinking about their interrupted morning and feeling the same electrical zing as when their hands had touched. "I'll bet you were!"

"I can't wait to see you tomorrow. Maybe I could cook you dinner here instead of going out."

Suzanne pictured an intimate dinner in the Victorian, dining room with wallpaper and wood moldings halfway up and a dark table with claws for legs. Mark would make something simple but delicious, like steak with a salad or a mushroom pasta and she could raid the wine library Janice had unintentionally created in the basement.

"Suzanne?"

Mark's voice brought her back to reality. "Sorry. That's why I called; I have to cancel tomorrow. I'm going back to California in the morning."

"What's wrong? Are you okay?"

Suzanne paused on the verge of giving him the facile brush-off "fine" and took a deep breath. "I don't know. I have to be there for harvest, and the divorce is . . . complicated."

Now the silence was on Mark's end of the line. Finally, he asked, "Are you coming back?"

"Yes." Suzanne surprised herself with her emphatic delivery. "Yes, as soon as we get all the grapes in. Maybe a couple weeks."

"Okay, then it's reschedule, not cancel. We'll make a new plan when you come back."

She wasn't sure what she heard in his voice, some complex blend of warmth and concern and disappointment and longing. It was so layered and nuanced she could almost taste it, even if she couldn't quite name it.

"I'd like that," she said.

Suzanne closed her phone and perched on the edge of the bed. Her wandering gaze fell on the box Janice and her pals had given her from the porch. She slid down onto the plush rug beside the bed and shifted into a half-lotus position as she dragged the box over to her. There was a small album with a worn cloth cover, a lidded shoe box covered with dust, three matching hard plastic cases in yellow, blue, and red, a postcard featuring the ocean at sunset written in a child's hand, and a wine glass inscribed with Will and Suzanne's names and wedding date. She pulled everything out and fanned it across the floor in front of her like a memorabilia rainbow.

The three plastic cases housed the DVDs of the original Star Trek series, one communicator-shaped case per season. The reruns had been ubiquitous for so long, it was hard to believe the show had had such a short run. She was touched that Janice would think of giving them to her instead of giving them away. Kirk, Spock, Scotty, McCoy, Chekov, Uhura, Sulu, they were all as much part of her childhood as any of the kids she went to school with. The ongoing Kirk vs. Spock debate she had with Janice evolved over the years as they chose the perfect man, switched when their tastes changed, and argued each side convincingly. Passion vs. reason. Logic vs. intuition. They had finally agreed that it was an artificial constraint; the best answer involved both. And then they made lewd jokes about it. Suzanne smiled and loaded them back into the box.

The wine glass had been the favor all the guests received at their wedding, not the finest hand-blown crystal, but not a cheap clunky glass, either. Suzanne lifted the glass by the base so the light from the window shone through it. It was coated with a film of oily dust, the sort that accumulates after years of sitting unused on a cabinet shelf. Janice had probably never used it after the wedding; it might be the only one remaining, like an artifact from an earlier civilization. Suzanne remembered a quiet dinner at home with Will on their first anniversary, eating surprisingly good thawed cake and drinking from the wedding glasses. At the end of the meal, Suzanne had spontaneously thrown hers into the fireplace where it shattered against the back wall. Will had been momentarily shocked, then had drained his glass and followed suit with a laugh. Rubbing fingerprint smears into the glass with her thumb, Suzanne wondered if Will's reaction had been less about surprise than horror and maybe disappointment.

The postcard was from her to their mother, sent from the trip with Janice after their father had died. Suzanne frowned and flipped it over and back again. It was odd reading the primitive handwriting of her earlier self from a time she had apparently rewritten in her memory. She had no idea why they hadn't come across that when they went through their mother's possessions after her death. She put it on top of the DVD cases to remember to ask Janice.

Suzanne lifted the lid of the shoebox, uncovering a dense collection of trinkets. She picked up the peacock feather sitting on top and found it was attached to a hair clip. She smiled at the memory of seeing it in her hair in the mirror, but she couldn't attach a year to the image. She decided to save the box of treasure for last. Just as Suzanne opened the small album she heard the kitchen door bang open downstairs followed by Donnie's voice shouting, "Anybody home?" She caught a glimpse of an old black and white photo with a scalloped edge before closing the book and tossing it into the box. She took the stairs in twos and spun into the kitchen with one hand on the door sill for balance.

"Donnie!"

They embraced fiercely, squeezing out the years and miles between them like a mechanical press, then stepped back to take in the changes.

"You have gray hair." He said.

"Yeah, and I need reading glasses, too. Just wait, your turn will come." In the years since his last trip to San Francisco, Donnie had changed little. A bit thicker around the middle, maybe, and a line between his brows that would soon be permanently etched. Suzanne felt the space between them fill with sorrow and regret and all the complications of the unwanted knowledge they now shared.

"Is Mom resting?"

Suzanne nodded. "She seems to sleep in bursts throughout the day. She wanted to have enough energy for your trip to see the lawyer."

Donnie winced and picked up his duffle bag. "Let me put this upstairs and we can talk." He hesitated. "Oh, I forgot you're in the creepy guest room. I think the front bedroom still has a bed under all those boxes."

"I think the boxes are all gone; the church ladies were here today. But you can take the guest room if you want. I have to leave for the airport probably by one, so I can just nap on the couch."

"What?" Donnie turned all the way around to face her. "How can you leave now? What if something happens to Mom?" A strawberry blond with a smattering of freckles and little other pigment, Donnie flushed a dramatic shade bordering on purple when he became emotional. Suzanne had found it amusing as a child to tease him or make him laugh just to see the color he turned. There was no amusement to be found in his scarlet anger now, though, only shame. The letter he branded her with was for abandonment, and she did not need to wear it to feel its sting.

"Something already has happened to her, Donnie. My being here isn't going to change that."

They glared at each other, but before either could continue, they heard the bedsprings upstairs followed by Janice's voice.

"Would you two keep it down? You're loud enough to wake the dead!" Donnie winced.

Suzanne lowered her voice. "Harvest has started and the first grapes are nearly finished with cold soak. I need to be there for the yeast inoculation. I need . . ." She shrugged and turned her palms up. "Donnie, Will filed for divorce and he could destroy everything I've worked for." The last word was choked off as her throat closed and she blinked back tears.

Donnie dropped his bag and stepped toward her, hugging her hard, then searching her eyes. "I'm sorry. I didn't know."

The toilet flushed upstairs, and they both looked at the ceiling.

"Maceration is a little more than two weeks. When the wine is in barrel, I'll have months . . ." Suzanne stopped at his pained expression. "I'll come back after the primary fermentation. I'll come sooner if you call me. But I have to go now."

He nodded, more in acknowledgment than acceptance, then went upstairs to drop off his bag. Suzanne heard him greet Janice, then their voices fell into a conversational rise and fall. She moved into the kitchen to avoid eavesdropping and began putting away the dishes in the drainer beside the sink. When she was nearly finished, Janice and Donnie walked in, the punch line to the story delivered just as they entered the kitchen.

". . . so Muriel says, 'What mice?' completely deadpan. It was the perfect Gaslight! We laughed until we peed."

Suzanne put a stack of plates away, then turned to them and laughed before she could suppress it. Janice had put on an actual pirate bandana, black and covered with tiny skulls and crossbones, knotted above her right ear.

"Go ahead, get it over with," Janice said. "I always wear this one when I have an appointment with Barry just to remind him I know exactly what a shyster he is. Besides, it's time to shift into full Halloween mode."

Suzanne, still laughing, said, "That opening is so easy I'm not even going to bother."

Janice dismissed the remark with a wave as she rifled through the collection of kitchen clutter on the table and the counter behind her until she found a pack of cigarettes.

"I have to take some drugs and then we can go," she said to Donnie before turning back to Suzanne. "What time do you have to leave?"

"Midnight, maybe one; there shouldn't be a long security line so early in the morning."

Janice nodded. "Why don't you thaw something for dinner while we're gone. Pick out whatever you think sounds good from the freezer."

"But not one of those three-bean casseroles. Or anything with tuna and noodles," Donnie added. "I just can't eat any more of that."

Janice whacked him on arm. "Ingrate! Who raised you?"

When she went to the living room to get her meds, Donnie leaned close to Suzanne. "Can't you wait a couple more days?"

His urgency made Suzanne step back. "It's done."

Donnie straightened and rearranged his expression as Janice returned, not making eye-contact with Suzanne. She walked them to the door, then stood on the stoop and watched them drive away. She dreaded the prospect of having her evening filled with Donnie's campaign to make her stay; she felt tired just thinking about it. For one brief flash, Suzanne imagined grabbing her bag and leaving now, driving to the airport, having dinner alone closer to where she wanted to be, skipping the family drama entirely . . . but she rejected the impulse and went to the freezer.

The freezer was packed with baggies and plastic containers and casserole dishes and unidentifiable foil pouches of varying size. Apparently the foreknowledge of death affected people in much the same way grief did. Some people prayed, other people cooked. And the people who knew Janice cooked in volume. Suzanne pulled out half a dozen packages and laid them on the table. All were neatly labeled with a sharpie, so at least she didn't have to open and reseal everything. The set did, indeed, contain both three-bean casserole and tuna and noodles, so Donnie's complaint was probably justified. After two more sorts, she assembled a comfort food selection of meatloaf, mashed potatoes, and chocolate cake from the stockpile of donations. She made a fresh salad to go with the neighbors' contributions, left the cake on the counter, set the oven on low, and put the meatloaf in the microwave to defrost after removing the foil. With dinner in motion, Suzanne went down into the basement to get wine.

The loamy earth scent hit her again halfway down the stairs. The air was cool enough to raise goose bumps on her arms. She had remembered to grab a flashlight from the drawer, and she headed directly for the stacked wine boxes, checking the dates and the winery names. The cellar might get a little too cold in winter to be considered perfect storage, but it was awfully close. Her sister had created an enviable wine library neither knowing nor caring that was the case. Suzanne chose three bottles, a cabernet nearly twenty years old that should be excellent, a pinot fifteen years old that was likely far past its peak and nearly invisible to the tongue, and a bottle of Mermaid Tears from two years before. That vintage had been one of her favorites, and if Janice would not get to taste this year's wine, Suzanne wanted to at least give her a glimpse of the best that she could do.

Janice and Donnie drove up in twilight, and Janice went to turn on the front yard decoration lights before doing anything else. She gave a side-long glance to the dining room table as she passed it. "Are we expecting company?"

"I decided Donnie's close enough." Suzanne had cleared the accumulated junk from the table in the formal dining room and set places there instead of at the kitchen table.

"If we drink three bottles of wine, I don't think you'll be driving to the airport tonight," Donnie said, inspecting Suzanne's choices which were lined up, open, at the end of the table.

"We don't have to drink them all, in fact, they might not all be drinkable," Suzanne said as she pulled the meat loaf and mashed potatoes from the oven and set them on the table. Molly appeared from the living room and leapt onto the dining room table with unexpected grace for anything of that girth. "No!" produced no response beyond a twitch of her little Hitler mustache.

"Good luck with that," Janice said.

Donnie grabbed the cat and put her on the floor.

"You serve, I'll pour," Suzanne said to Donnie.

The older pinot was, indeed, past its prime, but it retained a surprising hint of raspberry and anise. The cab was dark and rich, with all the tannins smoothed into a soft layering of black fruit and cedar and subtle spices and earth on the nose. It was probably better a couple years before, too, but it hadn't lost much, and had come to resemble a bordeaux. The Mermaid Tears was exactly what it should be, red fruit and lavender on the nose, silk across the tongue, and a finish that never seemed to end. She poured three glasses.

"We'll start with this."

When they were all sitting, with Janice dropping bits of meatloaf on the floor for the cat, Suzanne raised her glass. "This is the best wine I've made so far, and I am grateful to be able to share it with you tonight. To family."

"To family!" They echoed.

Donnie raised his eyebrows after drinking. "Wow."

Suzanne smiled. "Glad you like it."

"I can see where you might get used to this," Janice said.

Suzanne clinked her glass against her sister's. "Coming from you, I'll take that as a compliment."

Janice took very small bites and few of them, mostly rearranging the food on her plate into abstract architectural forms as she drank a glass of each of the three wines and then had a second glass of the Mermaid Tears.

"Did you know your mom picked my name?" Suzanne asked Donnie as the three of them relived family legends and revisited old jokes.

He frowned. "I remember that Suzanne song you used to sing all the time. Was that it?"

"Yeah, who knew?"

"I did," Janice said as she poured the last of two different wines into her glass. Suzanne winced but refrained from comment.

"What about my song?" Donnie asked.

"Your song?" Suzanne turned from Donnie to Janice. "Wait," she narrowed her eyes, "I remember! 'Dove my chebby to the lebby but the lebby was dwy!'" She was overcome with laughter, wiping tears away with her napkin.

"Go ahead, make fun of my speech impediment." Donnie was brightly flushed but laughing, too.

"It's not considered an impediment when you're three years old," Janice said. She was smiling at them indulgently, shaking her head as if they had taken leave of their senses. "I almost named you Buddy instead of Don, so count your blessings."

"Your musical taste definitely ran to dense stories with obscure metaphors," Suzanne said.

Janice ran a finger under her scarf, then pulled it off with one hand and scratched her head vigorously with the other. "Well, that one wasn't so much my choice as Donnie's father. It's the song his band was playing when I first saw him."

Suzanne held herself completely still, waiting for more. She noticed Donnie was doing the same. Janice rarely spoke of Donnie's father and had always brushed off questions about him.

"It was that summer we were in California . . . I always had a weakness for redheads. And bass players."

Janice stared across the room as if she were seeing something other than the living room beyond, a tiny smile barely lifting the corners of her mouth. For a moment, Suzanne could see the teenager from the photo in the guest room upstairs. Then as she watched, all Janice's features sagged as if gravity had suddenly increased and she looked very tired.

"I've got to go to bed. Don't get up," she said as she rose unsteadily. She paused behind Suzanne's chair and gave her a quick hug from behind. "Good luck. And safe travels."

Donnie and Suzanne watched Janice go up to bed, then carried the dishes out to the sink.

"That may be the most I've heard her say about your dad ever," Suzanne said.

"I know. Just the last couple weeks she's started making little comments, not like dropping hints but just . . . like she's thinking about him. When she was first diagnosed, she told me a little about him, why they didn't work out . . ." he pressed his lips into a hard line and crossed his arms. "I can't believe you're leaving. I really can't."

His voice was pitched low so his mother wouldn't hear and so laden with emotion it came out more growl than whisper. Even though Suzanne knew the attack would be coming, she wasn't braced for it in the afterglow of the congenial dinner.

"Donnie—"

He cut her off. "Don't give me that placating tone. You might be my aunt, but I am not a child. She's your only sister and she is dying. Right now. How can you walk away from that? And where the hell do you get off making a toast to family? I mean, I'm sorry about your marriage and whatever other crap has been dumped on you, but this is the absolute end of my mother's life. You should want to spend every single minute with her that you can."

Donnie's voice had started to rise, so he stopped himself and took a deep breath. The flush spread from his neck to his forehead and a vein throbbed at his temple. Suzanne was surprised to find that she didn't feel defensive nor even resentful. She just felt tired.

"I can't be two places at once. Giving up my life won't add any more days or weeks to hers," Suzanne said softly. "I'm doing exactly what you are: being here when I can and being prepared to come back on short notice when I'm not."

The color in his cheeks didn't change, but all his features twisted in on themselves like he'd just bitten into a lemon, then he burst into tears and collapsed onto a chair. Suzanne moved to the chair next to his and wrapped her arms around him, holding him tighter as he sobbed into her shoulder. He cried like a child, completely unrestrained. Something about his emotional deluge induced the opposite reaction in Suzanne. Instead of feeling her own throat closing up, she was washed with a sense of calm. Donnie stopped crying after ten minutes, but they sat huddled together for half an hour more, not speaking at all, before Donnie said good-bye and went upstairs to get ready for bed.

Suzanne finished tidying the kitchen, too wound up to try to nap before the drive to the airport. Finally, she went upstairs to get her things. Standing in the hallway, she looked at her few belongings and the box of things Janice had saved for her. Suzanne decided to leave everything behind but the clothes she was wearing and her purse. She hadn't brought that much with her to begin with, and she hoped seeing her suitcase and the box outside his door would serve as a tangible promise of return for Donnie when he woke up in the morning.

The trip to the airport was slightly surreal, the blackness she drove through punctuated by an occasional eerie light in a cluster of trees that signaled a farm. Twice Suzanne passed the twenty-four-hour service cities that spring up at the intersection of two highways, but only a handful of cars and semis passed her the entire trip. The emptiness and quiet of the sleep-deprived drive leant a post-apocalyptic feel to her solitude. What she felt, though, was pre-apocalyptic, as if only she could stop the countdown to Armageddon in the last second, but she didn't know which button to push.

Chapter 9

Inoculation:
winemakers often inoculate their must with known strains
of reliable yeast to activate primary fermentation

Leaving in the dark with Donnie and Janice asleep had felt like sneaking away, and not in the way that might involve assignation and breathless anticipation. The coffee she drank during the drive kept Suzanne alert, but it no doubt contributed to her strange emotional state that had settled into a sort of free-floating anxiety. Unfortunately, labeling it didn't make it go away.

The color block pattern of the Great Plains farmland gave way to the sharp herringbone of the Rocky Mountains as Suzanne stared out the window. She was full of too many thoughts to read or even listen to music, but she had a magazine open on her tray table and her iPod earbuds in place to prevent her neighbor from striking up a conversation. As tired as she was, sleep still eluded her. Suzanne had crossed over into a state of slightly queasy too tired to sleep, but she lowered the shade and closed her eyes, anyway.

"The Captain has turned on the seatbelt sign for our final approach. Please place your seat backs and tray tables in the fully upright and locked position in preparation for landing."

Suzanne started in her seat at the flight attendant's voice, bumping her tray table and knocking her magazine to the floor. She smiled and shook her head at the woman seated on the aisle and composed herself while she collected her belongings. She didn't feel refreshed, but her stomach was calm and her thoughts weren't frenetic and unfocused. The foothills just before San Jose were golden brown filigreed with the dark green of trees. Suzanne took a deep breath and let it out slowly. She could feel her shoulders lower and the tension drain from her muscles. It was good to be home.

She was momentarily confused by the empty overhead bin, then remembered leaving her bag behind and smiled as she exited the plane. The smile faded when she turned the corner out of the security check point. Standing with the cluster of smiling grandparents, searching spouses, and texting students waiting for the flight to arrive was a beautiful blonde she recognized. Laura.

Suzanne stopped when she saw her, thinking it was a coincidence and wondering if she could avoid being seen. Then Laura caught her eye and held up a little sign like the kind limo drivers use that said "Mathews" in thick black letters. She smiled a tentative smile and jiggled the sign in a way that reminded Suzanne of the ad barkers who dance and spin logos on corners. After three people bumped against her, a boulder in the river of people moving toward baggage claim, Suzanne took a deep breath and walked over to Laura.

"Are you looking for me?"

Laura lowered the sign. "I thought you might need a ride to the winery."

"I'll get a cab." Suzanne was terse but polite. She didn't want to make a scene, but she also wanted to scream at Laura's audacity. And part of her wanted to ask how she could ever have been her friend and still be so cruel. "How did you even know I was coming?"

Laura's lower lip trembled, then slid sideways as her teeth seized it from behind. She blinked once and said, "I heard Will talking to Carlos.

I'd like to offer you a ride. I'd like for you to ride with me." She paused and added, "I'm really sorry about your sister."

"Let's go outside." Suzanne gestured toward the automatic doors, desperate for some fresh air. She felt ambushed and suspicious, but a note of comfort and gratitude was creeping in. Just to have someone who knew her acknowledge the other part of her life in that moment was a relief, even if Laura couldn't be trusted. Suzanne mentally berated herself for not having called Craig to pick her up, even if she had already asked more of him than any friend should be expected to deliver.

The walkway was noisy, filled with traffic sounds and police whistles and shouts. The lane near the curb filled and emptied and filled again as people were picked up, but the outer lane zipped by, angling for the best position to head for 880 or 101. Desperate smokers clustered around the ashtrays placed at legal intervals away from the exits. Suzanne looked everywhere but at Laura.

"If you don't want to go with me . . ." Laura broke off and started again. "I need to apologize."

Suzanne *snorked* involuntarily, then covered her mouth. "Oh, ya think?" Whether it was the sleep deprivation or the rampant stress of the week, or just the absurdity of the situation, Suzanne felt a wave of hysteria sweeping over her. "What could you possibly have to apologize for? Calling me names? Sleeping with my husband?"

Laura looked as if she had been struck, but she stood her ground. "For being a bad friend. For not being there for you when you needed me most."

The surprising comment cut off Suzanne's giggles. Laura looked like she was about to cry. When she noticed the smokers were looking on with more interest than she preferred, Suzanne said, "I'll ride with you on one condition."

"What?"

"We leave right now before this starts to look like a preview for the Lifetime Channel."

Laura laughed and wiped her eyes discreetly as she pointed. "I'm parked over here. Do you need to get your bag?"

"I've just got this."

They walked in awkward silence, Suzanne both weary and wary of Laura's motives. She did need a ride, though, and she didn't think she was in any actual physical danger. She would have to be vigilant about what she said, though, just as if her conversation were being recorded for Will. And if Laura were less vigilant about her own comments, there might be something useful to be gained.

"Do you want to stop for coffee?" Laura asked as she pulled out of the short-term parking.

As she was about to say no, Suzanne realized that coffee sounded really good just then. "Could we just do a drive-through?" She wanted to get to the vineyard as fast as she could, and the prospect of facing Laura across a table was harder to imagine than riding beside her in a car.

Laura pulled up to a corner espresso stand near the freeway entrance and ordered a latte for herself before turning to Suzanne who added a large black coffee and a blueberry scone to the order. They ate and drank without conversation as Laura negotiated the route that would take them to the freeway. Laura blew across the hole in the coffee lid, and it whistled a little like playing an empty bottle. Suzanne felt a smile that didn't quite reach her lips.

The first time Suzanne saw Laura cool her coffee that way they had been at the Mountain Winery waiting to see Diana Krall. The temperature shift in the summer could be quite dramatic after sunset, and they got coffee to take into the amphitheater with them. Will had gone in to their seats with a bottle of wine divided into two big plastic cups and three small plastic cups for drinking. The stage was still being reset from the opening act, so Suzanne and Laura stood looking out over the lights of the valley for a few minutes before going in.

"This is my favorite view of the Valley," Suzanne said, "all the lights like stars on the ground, the constellations named Mountain View and San Jose instead of Orion and Pleiades, but a glimpse of heaven just the same."

"It reminds me of Christmas," Laura said, "the lights even look like they twinkle." She blew across her coffee cup lid and a low note sounded like a distant fog horn.

"Are you cooling that coffee or playing it?" Suzanne asked.

Laura laughed. "Five years of flute lessons as a child totally messed up the way I blow."

Suzanne choked on her coffee. "That has so many nested lewd connotations I can't even make a joke. It would just be too easy."

They were still laughing when they took their seats, Will and Laura on either side of Suzanne.

Suzanne looked over at Laura driving the car and realized she didn't care that Will and Laura were having sex, didn't care even that they were essentially living together. What really hurt was not that Will had chosen Laura, but that it felt like Laura had chosen Will over her. He was the one she shared intimate moments and salacious jokes with now, and Suzanne hadn't had coffee with her in a very long time. The silence continued, each woman with her own thoughts, until they had merged into the southbound morning traffic on 101.

"So," Laura began, then cleared her throat.

Suzanne waited.

"Will came home from the Computer History event so upset he wouldn't even talk about what happened; I had to drag it out of him. Finally he told me how you yelled at him in public and threw him out." Laura hesitated, then continued. "It was only later that the details came out, that you did tell him to leave, but maybe it wasn't exactly public humiliation . . ." She looked over at Suzanne to gauge her reaction then continued. "He was in so much pain and I was angry at you for causing it and . . . I know that doesn't excuse the message I left. I'm sorry."

Suzanne looked out at the Coyote Creek Golf Course flashing past and sifted through her feelings before replying.

"You should be." She felt Laura bristle beside her. "But thank you for telling me." She thought about the CHM event, a night that now seemed months in the past. "I probably shouldn't do event appearances with Will right now." *Or ever again*, she thought to herself.

"When he told me about your sister," Laura paused as if searching for and rejecting words, "I wanted to call you . . ."

"Call me what?" Suzanne cut in automatically as if in jest, but her tone had an edge that made Laura glance sideways at her.

Laura sighed and drove in silence until they reached the exit that would take them up into the mountains.

"I love him. I'm in love with him."

"I was, too," Suzanne said.

"How long has the past tense been accurate?" Laura looked at Suzanne as she asked the question.

Suzanne met her eyes, then looked away without answering. She watched the oaks flow past the car, giving way to open fields and the distinctive *T* pattern of staked grape vines.

"I didn't sleep with him before you separated," Laura continued. "I didn't choose him over you. I'm not that girl," her voice broke and she waited for control before going on. "Our friendship is worth fighting for."

Suzanne scrolled through her memories of dinners and movies and hikes and book discussions and all the bits of shared history that accumulate to cement a relationship. Laura might be right about their friendship, but Suzanne didn't see how she could ignore what Will was trying to do. She felt a flash of paranoia, wondering if this were an intentional fishing expedition, then became completely disgusted. Second-guessing the motives of everyone she talked to and screening everything she said so it couldn't be used against her was no way to live.

"I don't know if I can add another fight to my to-do list." Suzanne rested her hand on the center console, not touching Laura's arm but still an intimate gesture. "Maybe to you it seems like Will's plan is just a small change or maybe it even seems exciting, but to me it feels like a knife held to my throat."

She watched the color rise in Laura's cheeks as they reached the long driveway to the vineyard. "You can let me out here," she said. "I'd like to walk up to see how everything looks."

Laura stopped the car and nodded. "Okay."

Suzanne picked up her purse and the trash from her breakfast and slid out of the car, pausing with one hand on the door. "I'm not saying the damage is beyond repair, just that it might be awhile." She searched for something else to say, but nothing came. "Thanks for the ride."

Laura said, "You're welcome," and backed out of the drive without making eye contact again.

After dropping her purse at the house and changing into work clothes, Suzanne walked out to meet the men in the section they were harvesting. The day was perfect, sunny and warm with not a hint of early winter rain clouds. Carlos turned as she approached.

"Miss Suzanne!" A grin spread across his face, and he looked ready to hug her before he thought better of it.

He was flushed and beads of perspiration dotted his forehead, but it looked like exertion not illness. Suzanne decided not to ask him just yet if he was feeling okay. "It's good to see you, Carlos. How are we doing?"

"The sections we are picking today are at twenty-four and twenty-four point five. It is possible that the final vines will reach twenty-five if we have two more days like today."

They smiled at each other as if they shared a secret, and Suzanne nodded. "Good." She bent to lift a whole cluster out of the large basket the men were filling from the vines on either side. "The stems look good."

She pulled off a grape and chewed it slowly, seeds and all. "The first containers should be finished with cold soak. I'll inoculate half of them today and let the other half begin fermentation with wild yeast."

Carlos turned to the vines to lift the next cluster off. "It is good to have you back," he said without looking up.

Suzanne smiled. "It's even better to be here. I need to go look at the fire damage and then I'll be back to help."

The section had been fully picked, and Suzanne could see the blackened ends of the two rows even from a distance. The end posts were charred, and three vines were singed, though they looked like they might be fine. Two rose bushes were completely gone, the Forever Yours consumed by the flames of a different passion. Suzanne picked up a twig, but it crumbled to ashes in her hand.

"I've been waiting for you."

Suzanne gasped and spun around, her heart pounding. "To sneak up on me?"

Will tilted his palms upward in a gesture of surrender. "Sorry. No, I didn't intend to startle you. I just knew you would come here as soon as you got in."

Suzanne forced herself to uncross her arms and put her hands in her pockets. "Why are you here?"

"I work here, remember?" Will either didn't notice his arms were crossed or didn't care.

Suzanne took a deep breath, let it out slowly, repeated the action two more times. "I mean, why were you waiting for me? If you have something to say, say it to my lawyer. As you can see, I haven't 'abandoned my responsibilities,' so you can let go of that little pipe dream."

Will's mouth tensed. "That was the lawyer's idea. That's what he gets paid to do."

"Really? Why not just hire a hit man? It's probably cheaper and faster."

Will winced. "Laura already gave me shit about it; you don't need to join the party."

Suzanne waited without speaking; a tiny piece of her glad to know Laura had taken her side even before they spoke.

"I wanted to tell you that you can go back. You can trust me to finish the harvest."

"You have got to be kidding me." Suzanne shook her head. "What do I look like, new kid? You've already contradicted my instructions to Carlos once, why should I believe you won't do it again?" She toed the raked dirt in the burned spot, burying another blackened twig in the process.

"I suppose you blame me for the fire, too." Will sounded indignant.

"No," Suzanne said, "I don't. It's just a moot point because I'm *here* and I'm staying."

"I thought Janice was dying." Will looked both perplexed and irritated, as if he were expecting a completely different response to his offer.

"Not today she isn't. In a couple weeks I can have all the wine in barrels. If I need to go back sooner, I will." Suzanne bit off her response, angry that she had said as much as she had.

"We can get through the fermentation without you," Will said.

Suzanne searched his face, trying to read his intent. Was it a genuine, generous offer, or was it a trap to bolster his position? "How many days will you cold soak? How much whole cluster will you use and how much will you de-stem? How many times a day will you punch down the cap and how long will you let the primary fermentation go before you press to barrel?"

Will flapped his hand as if at a mosquito. "Doesn't Carlos know all that?"

"He does know the general timeline, and he knows when to ask me for a decision," she narrowed her eyes, "but he would have to be in full control of the process without interference." She stopped herself. "It doesn't matter. I'm not going anywhere."

"Fine." Will shrugged. "Have it your way." He turned abruptly and Suzanne heard him mutter "You always do" as he walked away.

She could feel a dull throbbing headache coming on, which wasn't surprising considering what her last two hours had covered. Or maybe it was her last two days. Or two weeks. She rubbed her eyes then massaged the back of her neck with her thumbs. There was too much noise, too many things to think about, but she knew how to make them all go away. Suzanne touched the singed vine beside her then went to join the crew picking grapes.

"So, bitch, how long were you going to wait before calling me?"

Suzanne smiled at the voice without opening her eyes, still half asleep with the phone to her ear. "I love you, too, Craig."

"What's wrong? Why do you sound so groggy? Have you been drugged? Should I call the police?"

"No. Craig. Stop. I was just sleeping. It's okay." She stretched and sat up. "Stop being such a drama queen."

"Excuse me? I'm the drama queen? Who's the pyromaniac here?" Craig broke off mid-rant. "Okay, technically that would be me, but I mean, who put the whole *Firestarter* scenario in motion?"

Suzanne looked around the room, tried to gauge the time, the day, the date. She was on her living room couch and it was dark, so that was a start. "Craig? What time is it? And what day?"

"Oh. My. God! You have been drugged. I'm coming over there right now!"

"No! No. Well, you can if you want to, but seriously, I just can't see a clock. I fell asleep on the couch." Suzanne heaved a big sigh. "Craig, you may be the best person I know. You may be the only true friend I have. Would it be too much to ask for you to cut me some slack?"

There was silence on the line, and then Craig said, "Is this some Jedi mind-control thing that works on everyone, or is it just me? These are not the droids you're looking for?"

Suzanne burst out laughing. "Seriously, though. When is this?"

Craig heaved a sigh to launch a thousand ships. "Saturday night? California?"

"Is California a time?" Suzanne asked.

"Compared to Iowa? Yeah," Craig answered.

"Nice." Suzanne stood and stretched and wandered into the kitchen to forage in the refrigerator. "I'm sorry I didn't call you as soon as I got back, but I'm in the middle of a divorce, not a Hitchcock movie. Though things have been weird. Laura picked me up at the airport so she could apologize and then Will showed up at the vineyard."

"Get out! What happened?"

Suzanne finished chewing the piece of Roquefort she had popped into her mouth. "She drove me home and went away unhappy; he told me I could go be with Janice while he made the wine and went away irritated when I declined."

"Are you beginning to think it was something you said?" Craig asked.

"I'm certain. I just don't care right now." Suzanne pulled a baguette out of the freezer and put it in the oven to warm. "Will was waiting for me by the burned spot." Suzanne listened to the silence as she pulled prosciutto, grapes, and a half-full bottle of sauvignon blanc out of the refrigerator. "Craig?"

"Do you think . . ."

"He suspects? No. And the damage doesn't look that bad. It's possible I could lose one or two clones on the end, but it was worth it. This could be the vintage of a century, and we bought the time to get the fruit where it needed to be. You bought the time."

Craig sighed. "Should I let you take me to dinner tomorrow?"

"I'll be working all day, but I guess I have to eat sometime," Suzanne said. "Or how about Monday? I need to see my attorney and we can have dinner after. Should I ask where I'm taking you?"

"No, just bring your best plastic"

Suzanne shook her head as they ended the call, amused by Craig, as always, but reminded of how much she had asked him to do for her.

He was as much her family as Donnie and Janice, maybe even more for having been chosen.

She pulled the bread out of the oven with a mitt and sliced it in half, then tore off a section and layered it with prosciutto. She pulled the rubber stopper out of the wine and poured a glass, then bit into the open-faced sandwich with a crunch. The warm saltiness that filled her mouth made her flash on the brief encounter with Mark's neck the day before. If she hadn't come back, she'd be at dinner with him right now. She licked the salt from her lips. Or maybe dinner would be over by now. Suzanne took a sip of wine and let the chill spread over her tongue, stone fruit and floral notes filling her mouth before she swallowed. She mentally added Mark to the list of reasons to go back to Iowa as soon as she could, a list that hadn't existed before.

Chapter 10

Punch Down:
breaking up and pushing down the skin cap during fermentation
to keep it moist and ensure the desired extraction

Sunday passed in a satisfying blur of picking and sorting and tasting. Suzanne worked alongside the crew, pulling jack stems by hand from the newly harvested blocks before transferring the fruit to open containers for cold soak in the same sequence as the fruit already off the vine. She plucked and ate one or two grapes from each basket that came in, the Brix measurement gave the sugar content but nothing about the flavor profile. She grew more excited with each of the berries she tasted. There was still work to be done, but she had never grown any better fruit than this. She relished the annual transition from viticulturist to winemaker even more this year.

The containers from the first blocks picked had begun their primary fermentation, and the CO_2 produced in the process lifted the fruit solids to form a cap that needed to be punched down three or four times per day to keep it moist and in contact with the juice, adding color and flavor. All the color for the wine would come from the skins, and the tannins necessary for structure would come from the stems left on the whole clusters. The inclusion of more whole clusters increased the vanilla and clove notes, which would be balanced with the bright red and dark berry flavors of the crushed grapes. This was one of Suzanne's favorite parts of the transformation of grape to wine, not just the balancing act needed to extract the best flavors, but the tactile involvement with a chemical process. Punch down reminded her of kneading bread, though it was a much gentler process. When she had worked at wineries that produced bigger reds, zinfandels and cabernets, they would punch the cap down manually with a flat metal disc attached to a long poll, like a potato masher on steroids. Pushing down the solids on dozens of containers every six hours for two weeks was a better workout than any gym could offer. With fragile pinots, though, Suzanne always used a broad mesh screen and a very slow press. Somehow the gentler process was even more physically demanding.

Suzanne shivered in the cool air as the last light was swallowed by the mountains. She untied the sweater from around her waist and pulled it on as she waited for Carlos beside the barrel room. This was the same aquamarine cotton pullover she had worn home on the plane, now stretched and dirt-smeared from nearly two days in the field. Suzanne always got compliments when she wore the sweater; its soft blue-green color brought out nuance in the hue of her eyes that made people look twice. She had been wearing it when she walked to Mark's office, too, a memory that warmed her even more than the garment. The chill that day and now might be nearly the same, but her time in Iowa felt like the kind of dream that seems perfectly clear when you first wake up but makes no sense at all when you try to explain it to someone else, an Escher setting full of strange fears, unexpected sex, and people you barely know. Just like a dream, even if she couldn't explain it, she felt it every time she closed her eyes.

"Miss Suzanne? Todo bien?"

She opened her eyes and smiled. "Si, Carlos. Todo bien, gracias. I was just . . . thinking."

"Maybe you work too hard today."

Suzanne laughed. "No, I don't think that's it. Harvest may be exhausting, but I never get tired of it."

Carlos frowned for an instant and then grinned, flashing dimples a model would kill for. The smile turned into a wet cough ending with a wince. It was not the relentless smoker's hack of her sister, but it was definitely more than a little tickle in his throat.

"Are you okay, Carlos? Have you been to the doctor?" Suzanne had avoided asking him directly even as she watched him during the day. Craig had been right about his color, but he had been working at the same pace as always, not hesitating, not resting more than anyone else.

He stuffed his bandana back into his shirt pocket. "There has been something at school. Kids bring home everything." He shrugged and smiled again, but with more teeth than dimples.

Suzanne squinted at him, the natural light was gone and the floodlights above the fermentation vats washed out everything. She resisted the urge to put the back of her hand on his forehead and cheek.

She nodded, finally, and asked, "Where are we?"

"The final blocks, the two that are always last to ripen, will be ready tomorrow."

"Really? All of them?" Suzanne could hear the six-year-old at Christmas sound in her voice and didn't bother to restrain it.

"Si," Carlos said. "There could be a few vines with one more day, but not enough to count."

They turned to face the vineyard together, as if on cue, though they could see little beyond the border of illumination that circled the building. Suzanne and Carlos stood in silence for a long time, then Carlos suffered another bout of coughing. Before Suzanne could say anything, he spoke into his bandana.

"How is your sister?"

Suzanne stopped mid-breath, respecting the line he had drawn between them. "She is still . . . dying. Soon."

Carlos glanced over at her and then away, looked at the moon rising over the mountains. "Lo siento," he said quietly. "Lo siento mucho."

They stood watching the gibbous moon until it broke free of the

Santa Cruz ridge, then nodded their farewells with no more words to be said.

Soaking in a hot-tub-temperature bath frothed with bubbles, Suzanne unleashed all the jumbled thoughts and conflicting inclinations she had compartmentalized while she focused on work. Eyes closed, head back, she let the free-associations circle and twist until they began to sort into coherent patterns. The winery. The harvest. Her marriage. Her family. The first three contained most of what mattered to her, and they were inextricably linked. Her family hadn't taken up very much space in her thoughts since she had driven west after burying her mother, but now Janice and Donnie needed her, and she surprised herself by wanting to be there for them.

Suzanne didn't know what to think about Will. He had seemed almost reasonable when they talked yesterday, but he had behaved so unreasonably while she was away. Her suspicions about his motives only made her feel worse, though, because if she couldn't trust him now, maybe she never should have. Who was the idiot in that scenario?

Back when the second release of Mermaid Tears had started winning medals and generating buzz, Will and Suzanne had gone out to celebrate the vindication that the first showing hadn't been a lucky fluke. Over several hours they savored multiple courses each paired with wine, followed by desserts served with port and sauternes. Exquisite bites lubricated with generous amounts of alcohol filled them with a warm contentment that was mirrored by the golden halo of the candlelight. In that moment, Will had taken her hand in both of his and looked into her eyes.

"I have never known any woman, any*one* like you. You're so," he groped for the right word, "you're so . . . certain. No, not just that . . .

you're passionate." He squeezed her hand and smiled. "In many ways. Sometimes I still wonder why you picked me."

Surprised and touched by the declaration, Suzanne said, "I thought you picked me." Will shook his head. "That's not how it works for you. You're the one who makes things happen. Other people are just along for the ride." He leaned forward and kissed the back of her hand. "Thank you for taking me with you."

Suzanne hadn't thought about that evening in a long time, but the details were still vivid. She knew Will had meant what he said that night. Maybe he just got tired of the ride. She ran more hot water. How could she disentangle their lives? Will didn't make the wine, but she would be lying if she said he hadn't helped make it possible. She needed to come up with an offer that would keep him from forcing the sale of part or all of her winery, but what did he want?

Before she could begin to analyze the problem, her thoughts were interrupted by the phone ringing in the other room. She waited until the machine picked up, then held her breath and strained to hear the message. It was Donnie. She climbed out of the tub and wrapped herself in a towel, rushing to grab the phone before he finished.

"Donnie! I'm here; sorry, I was in the bath. How are you doing?"

He sighed. "I was out of line trying to guilt you into staying. I'm still pissed, though."

Suzanne leaned against the wall, hugging the towel to her. "And where are you right now, Donnie?"

"I'm back at my house."

Suzanne snorted.

"I know; I get it," Donnie said. "It's just . . . I don't think I can do this myself, I really don't."

"You don't have to. Janice has people looking out for her, checking in on her. She's got everything arranged the way she wants it, even if neither one of us is staying with her." Suzanne wasn't sure whether she was working harder to convince Donnie or herself.

"You're probably right." He paused, then added, "What about you? How are you doing?"

"The last of the grapes will be picked tomorrow, and I have a meeting with my lawyer to discuss what I want and what I can live with if I can't have what I want. I'm . . . optimistic."

After exchanging farewells with Donnie, Suzanne found her bath was cold. She opened the drain and pulled on some sweats, then logged on to her e-mail account and typed:

Janice—you've become such a layabout, I don't know when to call without interrupting your beauty sleep. Know that I'm thinking about you, though, even when you don't hear from me.

She yawned and stretched, fatigue filling her veins like a sedative. Suzanne knew her life was still teetering on the brink of chaos, knew that a spectacular harvest meant nothing in the language of community property and offered no miraculous out for her sister, but it had been a solid good day. Strategy for dealing with Will could wait until morning.

October in California can see the first spitting rain of the season, but it nearly always includes a week or two of Indian summer. Suzanne checked the temperature on the fermenting vats and punched down the caps, then met Carlos where his crew was picking in shirt sleeves with sweat plumes already spreading down from their necks. The fog had not come in the night before and the day was warming fast, a vibrant blue and gold day like something out of Rodger's and Hammerstein. Maybe it wasn't a bright canary yellow, but it did infuse her with a soaring joy. She left instructions with Carlos, then had a quick shower before heading north to meet with her lawyer and have dinner with Craig.

Suzanne felt invigorated as she locked the car and strode into the office of Hannah Jackson, her thoughts neatly outlined. If Will wanted more recognition for his contribution, maybe it was as simple as giving him a new title and larger responsibilities. Let him decide what he wanted to be called. Let him put Suzanne Mathews on a few wine glasses and picnic baskets. As long as whatever he chose was good quality, and she would insist on that stipulation, maybe branding wasn't such a big deal. They could continue to own the business jointly, but as business partners rather than romantic ones. He could keep the condo on California Avenue, and she would have to come up with the difference between the assessed value of the house and the condo, somehow. She didn't really like having him retain part ownership of the land, but compared to the Solomon solution property laws could demand, working with him was something she could live with.

The attorney rose to shake Suzanne's hand as she entered. Hannah Jackson was once again perfectly put together in a crisp linen suit and plain gold jewelry whose simplicity was synonymous with expensive. Suzanne smiled, more at her own thoughts than at Hannah or her firm handshake. It wasn't that Suzanne didn't look good, it was just that she didn't remember looking that creaseless and spotless ever.

Hannah Jackson spoke as she gestured for Suzanne to sit. "I've gone over the charges from your husband's attorney and the background details you sent along with the outline of your responsibilities and specific skills. I had a counterclaim filed this morning to have the claim of abandonment and dereliction of duty dismissed. As I indicated, that was more likely intended to burn funds and keep you off balance. However, their proposal arrived this morning. I haven't reviewed the full document, but we need to discuss your options."

Suzanne summarized her thoughts on Will and an equitable division of assets. The lawyer held up her hand before Suzanne could continue with details.

"Your husband's offer is quite generous financially, and it makes concessions beyond a strict community property division of tangible assets." She paused and gave Suzanne a piercing look before continuing. "It does, however, include a stipulation that if you cannot agree on a final settlement that includes expansion of the business with outside investors, he will insist that you either buy him out or that all jointly-held property be liquidated. His attorney has stated unequivocally that those points will not be negotiated."

Suzanne was momentarily stunned. "What? He can do that?"

The lawyer brushed her hair behind her ear and leaned back in her chair with the same smooth gesture. "He can't dictate the settlement terms, and he cannot countermand court orders, but I believe what he is doing is telling you where his line is drawn in the sand."

"So if we offer a counter proposal that keeps the winery jointly held . . ."

"That offer will be refused." Hannah Jackson templed her forefingers and offered the barest of smiles. "But while they are correct that the court would likely order either a buyout or sale of assets, they would not be able to control the timeline, and we would require an outside valuation to prevent them from artificially elevating the buyout cost for leverage."

Suzanne felt a little queasy.

"You should discuss the business implications with Jeff." She pulled a paper out of the file on the desk. "I can send him a copy and request that Will's attorney cc him on all future correspondence, if you authorize it." She slid the page over to Suzanne and offered a pen. "My job is to represent your interests, though, and that encompasses more than just the bottom line."

"Exactly!" Suzanne punctuated her statements with her hands. "Thank you. It's not that I'm against making money. I'm not even opposed to branding, necessarily, but the history of winemaking in California is littered with commercial zombies risen from the carcasses of family wineries. And anyone who's been in Silicon Valley for longer than a couple days knows that you don't invite a VC to the table if you intend to keep your seat at the head."

Hannah waited for her to finish talking, then slid the signed release into the folder. "The priorities you've given me are to maintain control of Suzanne Mathews Winery and to have the divorce process move as quickly as possible."

Suzanne winced involuntarily at "divorce".

"Right now those two are in conflict."

"Keeping the winery is the most important thing," Suzanne said without hesitation.

The lawyer nodded. "We could offer mediation. While it is unlikely to bridge the gap between your position and Will's, it could give us some idea of where his resolve is weaker or what he might be willing to concede."

"Would his attorney agree to mediation?"

"Probably—for the very same reason we're interested."

"So mediation is actually a tool for tricking your opponent into revealing something you can use against them?"

Hanna Jackson raised one eyebrow and smiled. "Well, that may be an excessively cynical analysis, but in this case, that's the idea."

Suzanne sighed. "Okay. Set it up."

Suzanne had heard the phrase "mad enough to spit" many times, but she hadn't really felt it until now. If Will were here, spitting at him might be the least of what she would do. She ground her teeth all the way to the restaurant, even the prospect of time with Craig had no power to soothe her. She had been ready to make concessions, wanted to settle things without more friction, but she had clearly underestimated the scope of what Will wanted. Or maybe she didn't even remotely understand.

The drive was a blur of irrelevant color and meaningless buildings. Suzanne pulled into the parking space at the restaurant fast, and the car rocked back from the concrete stopper. She strode through the front door and up to the table where Craig sat waiting, barely acknowledging the host on the way by. Her purse dropped onto the chair beside her with a harsh jangling of keys. Craig looked up, startled, and signaled the waiter.

"I think she needs a drink." He turned back to Suzanne as the waiter approached. "Stop glaring at me."

Suzanne closed her eyes and held her breath for a moment, then said, "I'm not glaring at you . . ." she offered a weak smile. "I'm glaring with you?"

Craig grimaced and waved her off. "Oh, no, you are *not* going to get away with that. This is supposed to be my pampering payback dinner, and you storm in here with a bad attitude like . . ."

Their eyes met and he stopped talking as a boy with gel-spiked hair and many hours of gym time arrived.

"Would you like something to drink, Ma'am?"

Suzanne nodded. "Yes. Yes, I would. Single malt, between eighteen and twenty-five years old, rocks, water on the side. And make it a double."

The waiter opened his mouth as if to ask questions, then scribbled on his pad and walked away.

Craig raised an eyebrow at her. "I haven't seen you drink scotch in a long time. You might as well tell me what's up so we can get it over with."

"Will drew a line in the sand. Accept his growth model with additional partners or sell everything and divide the cash."

"There must be other options."

"Oh, sure," Suzanne said. "I could buy him out—at full market value of the land, the buildings, and the projected earnings of the winery." She snorted.

The waiter arrived and put the scotch down in front of her. "It's Laphroaig," he said, then added hesitantly, "most people ask for scotch by brand or look at the menu."

"I'm not most people." Suzanne caught his anxiety and smiled. "Sorry, it wasn't supposed to be a test. I was sure you'd have a couple scotches that would work, and it was faster than reading the menu or asking you to list them. This is great, thanks."

The waiter paused for a moment, waiting for her to taste the drink, then hurried back to the bar.

"Please don't frighten the cute waitboys," Craig said. He looked at her over the rim of his martini and smirked. "Not most people, indeed."

Suzanne choked on a mouthful of Laphroaig. "I'd complain about your timing, but at least you didn't make me spit it out."

Craig lifted his glass. "I always knew you swallowed."

They both laughed as Suzanne touched her glass to his. "The restorative power of a good double entendre may be even better than a double scotch."

"Well, thank god the evening has been rescued," Craig said. "Forget about Will, I want to hear about the farm boy." When Suzanne didn't respond immediately, he added, "The old boyfriend in Iowa?"

"Oh, right, it was 'farm' that threw me off," Suzanne said. "His name is Mark, and he's living in our hometown and became friends with Janice because his mom was in the same support group."

Craig's demeanor shifted. He looked from the tablecloth to Suzanne to the salt and pepper as he asked, "How is your sister doing?"

"Great. For someone who's almost dead."

Craig looked at her, startled.

"I'm serious," Suzanne said. "She's irreverent and sharp and exactly the same as she's ever been, except she's so thin I'm sure I could carry her, and she tires to the point of exhaustion several times a day."

"Is she in denial?"

"No, her attitude is more like, she has spent her whole life doing what she wanted and speaking her mind, why would she stop now?"

Craig drained his glass and signaled the waiter for another. "Is she scared?"

Suzanne swirled the ice in her glass, watching the patterns shift before taking another sip. "That I don't know."

When Craig's drink arrived, the waiter asked if they were ready to order.

"Yes," Craig said. "We'll do the Chef's Tasting with the wine pairings."

The waiter looked from Craig to Suzanne as if he had misread the cues about whose party it was. Suzanne smiled and nodded to the waiter. "Whatever he wants. It looks like it's going to be a long night."

"Oh, it is," Craig said. "You'd better get started. Now tell me about this Mark guy. I want all the juicy details."

Suzanne drove home thinking about how some people can change the emotional tone of everything around them. Craig had a playfulness that was infectious and a sense of joy that was irrepressible. She was lucky to have Craig as a friend, and she had told him that at dinner. Laughing with Craig had siphoned off her intense anger, but the residue left a bitter taste.

The gate to the long gravel drive was open. She had told Carlos she would close it when she got home, as was their policy since the vandalism. Suzanne drove in, then stopped the car and got out to pull the long wood and barbed-wire gate shut behind the car. There was moonlight enough to see the bare vines stretching into the dark, arm-in-arm like friends holding each other up as they staggered home after a night on the town. She shivered in the chill and inhaled deeply. Even without the fog coming in, she could feel the ocean. Suzanne slid into the car and continued up to the house, surprised to see a car out in front. It was Will's.

Suzanne turned off the engine and sat in the dark, the ticking of the cooling metal sounding to her like a time bomb. Her first instinct was to go out to the shed and check the fermenting grapes, but if Will's car was here, then so was he. Hannah Jackson didn't want her to talk to Will directly, but it was too late to call for advice, and it wasn't as if she had invited him. She took a deep breath and let it out slowly. The warm glow and soft edges created by the meal and the wine and the company were gone. She clenched her teeth as she got out of the car and went inside.

"Suzanny!" Will rose from the couch as she walked in and dumped her keys into the mermaid dish by the door. She tensed and he must have seen it.

"Sorry. Suzanne. The door was unlocked, so . . . I hope I didn't surprise you."

A dozen snarky responses leapt instantly to mind, but Suzanne bit her tongue. "Why are you here, Will? It's late and I'm tired." She dropped her purse on the kitchen counter on her way to get a bottle of water. She could feel Will turn to follow her movements, though he waited for her in the living room.

"I just wanted to talk. I wanted to say . . ." his voice trailed off in search of a conclusion.

Suzanne leaned against the door frame and drained half a bottle of Pellegrino. "Wanted to say what?"

Will ran both hands through his hair. "I don't think it has to—we have to—I think we can do this without getting really nasty." He blew out his breath as if it had been long held. "I think we should forget the lawyers and do this ourselves."

Suzanne finished the little bottle and put it on the counter behind her without breaking eye contact with Will. "Okay, let's see . . . what's the shortest distance between a family winery and 'bring in outside investors or die'? Isn't that what you said?"

Will stepped away from the couch. "No, that isn't what I said. That's why we should talk. I made a mistake."

Had Will shown up earlier in the day, or on a night that didn't include both scotch and wine, or even if he had been waiting outside instead of in the living room, Suzanne might have let that go, but he had burned all his benefit of the doubt with his greeting. She crossed the room so fast that Will stepped back toward the door. "A mistake? A mistake?! Like sleeping with my friend? Or stealing my name? Or accusing me—*me*—of dereliction of duty? Or are you talking about blackmailing me into letting you water down my winery?"

Will flushed a splotchy color Suzanne didn't recall seeing before. "Your winery? *Your* winery? That's the real issue, isn't it? Nobody but you can do anything. Well you're wrong. Without me, Cherie Amor and Mermaid Tears would be just another couple of anonymous pinots. I introduced them to the world; I got them the recognition they deserved."

Suzanne looked at him and knew she could not have this conversation now. "Get out."

"No! I'm not leaving until we finish this!"

"Fine, then I'll go." Suzanne started toward the door, but Will got there first.

"You aren't going anywhere," he said.

Suzanne narrowed her eyes. "Get out of my way."

When Will didn't move, she tried to shoulder past him and he grabbed her.

"Let me go right now, or I'm calling the police!"

Will let go of her but leaned against the door with his arms crossed. With a look equal parts disgust and smugness he said, "Fine. Call them. This is my house, too."

Suzanne grabbed the knob and blocked Will with her hip, but he shoved her back from the door. She stumbled, her eyes landing on the fireplace. She crossed the room in three strides, grabbing the poker and wielding it like a baseball bat. She braced herself, heart pounding. "I said get out! And don't come in here again without calling. Ever!"

Will glared at her, then his eyes widened and the color drained from his face. "I'm sorry." He held up his hands in surrender, then opened the door without turning away from Suzanne. "I wasn't going to . . . I'm sorry. I'm going."

Suzanne carried the poker to the door and flipped the deadbolt behind him. She listened to the idling engine as Will opened the gate, finally relaxing her grip on the poker when the tires squealed then faded to silence.

Chapter 11

Maceration:
the process whereby tannins, coloring agents, and flavor compounds
are leached from the skin, seeds, and stems of the grape into the must

Suzanne moved from one open-topped tank to the next checking the temperature, punching down the cap, then forgetting which direction she was going or skipping the punch down and having to retrace her steps. The confrontation with Will had left her agitated and unable to sleep, so she had started her rounds as soon as the sky was light enough to read the thermometers. The last few blocks picked were still in cold soak, but the rest of the fruit was bubbling along nicely in the neighborhood of eighty-two degrees. Yawning and stretching toward the cloudless sky, Suzanne had one more reason to be grateful harvest was finished. The marine layer hadn't come in, still held at bay by a high pressure system that showed no signs of moving on. There was quite likely a very hot week ahead.

A tiny lizard materialized out of the camouflage of the rocks at her feet and darted under the tank. Catching a reptile doing pushups usually made Suzanne smile, but today even the morning air and brightening horizon were insufficient to lift her spirits. Never had Suzanne imagined herself in a situation where she felt physically threatened by someone she knew. Worse yet, never would she have imagined considering violence herself. But there she was last night, face to face with her husband—her *husband* for god's sake—and she had been brandishing a weapon anticipating a physical assault.

Suzanne sighed and resumed her inspection of the fermentation vats. The familiar motions of routine tasks helped quiet her tumbling thoughts. She recognized now that she had always been a little superior about domestic violence, knew it crossed socioeconomic, ethnic, and gender lines, paid lip service to the "it can happen to anyone" line, but knew for a fact *she* would never allow that kind of situation to develop under any circumstances. Not that she would classify the incident with Will as domestic violence, but it seemed like the beginning of a skid that could change the definition of never.

The sound of gravel crunching in the driveway made Suzanne stop and look up. She was relieved to see Carlos arriving in his pickup truck, an older model that was immaculate, even during the rainy season. He climbed out of the truck and walked toward her, pausing to bark into a crumpled bandana. His coughing had a phlegmy sound Suzanne couldn't ignore.

"Carlos! You should be home in bed."

"Buenos dias, Miss Suzanne."

"Buenos dias, Carlos," Suzanne said impatiently. "I'm serious. You are having the men clean up the rows today, yes? Once you get them started, I want you to go home."

The vineyard manager shook his head. "No, Miss Suzanne. I can stay."

"Carlos," Suzanne put her hand on his forearm, "I will be here. You should rest." When he did not respond she added, "Por favor. I don't need you right now. I do need you to be well."

Carlos looked up at that, looked into her eyes and nodded. "Claro."

Suzanne smiled. "Muchas gracias, Carlos. I'll finish this and do the midday punch down, too."

"Ricardo can help you," he said as he turned to walk away. "I will tell him."

She watched him until he entered the shed to prep for the crew, then finished the punch down with a willful sense of focus. When the last gauge was checked, Suzanne went back to the house to call her lawyer and try to sleep.

Hours later, dripping sweat from working in the noon sun, Suzanne decided she had time for a quick shower before the phone appointment with Hannah Jackson. Her sense of time had been thrown off by staying up all night, as if several days had passed during her dreamless nap. After the midday punch down, Ricardo had helped her set up the cooling rings on the fermenting vats. Everything was still under eighty-five degrees, but even one more day of the heat wave would drive the internal temperature too high and start burning off the flavor. Suzanne decided to bring everything down by five degrees. With so much whole cluster fruit in the mix, she wasn't really worried about fermentation getting stuck, but she didn't want to risk letting the temperature get so high the wild yeast started dying. Peeling off her damp clothes and standing under a spray of hot water, Suzanne still felt disoriented. The Indian summer heat contrasted so dramatically with the Iowa cool of the week before that she might have taken a time machine instead of a commercial flight.

As the water pounded her aching shoulders and ran down her back, Suzanne found herself humming. When she realized what it was, she sang, ". . . There are heroes in the seaweed, there are children in the morning, they are leaning out for love and they will lean that way forever, while Suzanne holds the mirror." She switched back to humming, turned off the water and dried off. She hadn't sung that song in years, hadn't thought about it in even longer. The vivid images and strange metaphors felt familiar in her mouth but didn't sound the same. She wiped a clear circle into the steam on the mirror and saw in her own eyes the same shade of sorrow that had defined her mother. Maybe all songs, all stories change their meaning over time because you see the words with eyes that have seen so much more. If Janice had chosen some other poem, would Suzanne be a different person?

She dressed quickly and dialed Hannah Jackson's number, pacing as she waited.

"I know you told me not to talk to Will, but he was waiting for me when I got home last night."

Suzanne told the story three times, first all the way through without interruption, then slowly while the lawyer took notes, then in minute detail as Hannah questioned her on specific points.

"Well," the lawyer said, "this may impede the prospect of mediation, but it does alter the balance of power. We can file a restraining order first thing in the morning and you will not have to worry about Will setting foot on the property nor contacting you until the divorce is final and possibly longer, if that's what you want."

Suzanne stopped pacing and looked out over the vineyard. "A restraining order?"

"Yes."

"But he didn't really do anything . . ."

"Did he keep you from leaving the house?"

"Well, yes, but . . ."

"That's false imprisonment," Hannah Jackson said.

Suzanne frowned. "Seriously?"

"Yes. And he . . . 'grabbed your arms' and also 'pushed you away from the door'?"

Suzanne could tell the lawyer was reading from her notes. "What about the fireplace poker?"

"Based on your description, that was a defensive move which demonstrates your genuine fear of attack."

"But . . ." Suzanne wasn't sure how to respond. The lawyer's version of her argument with Will didn't sound quite right, yet nothing in it had been really inaccurate. It just sounded so much worse the way Hannah slanted it.

"Suzanne. I can hear your reluctance, but this is how the game is played. And it *is* a game, but not some little Candy Land bit of diversion—this is Risk, and you just scored a really good roll. It's time to start massing your armies."

Suzanne resumed her pacing as she thought, noticed the fireplace poker was askew and stopped to adjust it.

"Okay. What happens next?"

"We will file the incident form on your behalf and a temporary restraining order will be granted pending a court hearing, usually fourteen days from the date the temporary order is granted. The respondent must also be served, which my office will do immediately after the automatic approval by the court. You will need to appear in court at the time of the hearing, and the specifics of the permanent restraining order will be negotiated then."

"Permanent?" Suzanne felt vaguely queasy and sat down on the couch.

"That's just a term. It could be three months, six months, one year . . . or you could fail to appear and the order would be rescinded."

"So we're using it as leverage, a negotiating tool, but I won't necessarily have to testify and no police report needs to be filed?"

"That's right."

Suzanne could see the advantages of following this path, even if she didn't feel completely comfortable.

"And Suzanne?" Hannah Jackson said, "The respondent in a restraining order often files a counter claim. Don't be surprised if Will's attorney serves you after this goes through. It's what I would advise if he were my client."

The rest of the week passed almost as if life were normal. Carlos had stayed home, reluctantly, at the advice of his doctor, and Suzanne did his work along with her own. Ricardo had helped her erect a canopy above the open-top fermenters to provide additional temperature control along with the cooling rings, but he was no substitute for Carlos. Suzanne worried that Carlos was sicker than he wanted her to believe, but she wasn't

Suzanne blew a piece of hair off her face and squeezed her eyes shut. She couldn't decide if she was sorry she hadn't seen this message sooner or was really grateful. When Hannah Jackson had asked what her goal was, it had been pretty simple to boil down. Keep control of her winery *whatever it takes.* That was easier to say when she had no idea how far she might need to go, the kinds of choices and actions that one little word "whatever" might encompass. She had set something in motion that was definitely an escalation, but was it justified? Her ambition, her dreams for her wines, had never been in such direct conflict with her relationships before, and the cognitive dissonance it produced surprised her. She considered not responding, then typed "Thanks," and sent it.

The message from Donnie was a terse note telling her he was driving down to the house again for the weekend and would send her an update. She glanced at the clock on her computer. He would be there by now but probably wouldn't write or call until the next day. There were three messages from Janice, the first two a morbid joke and one of those chain mails with a scathing note added, because Janice hated those more than any spam. The last message was a reply to Suzanne's.

You can call me anytime. Just don't expect me to answer. If you leave a message, then I still get to hear your voice. In fact, leave me a song. When you were little, you used to sing all the time. I don't remember the last time I heard you sing.

Suzanne scrolled up and then back down again, checking to be sure there wasn't any more to it and that it was really for her. Janice wanted her to sing into her machine? Suzanne wasn't sure if the request was a sign of decline or another bit of memory that her sister had held onto for her long after she had let it go. She thought about the photograph in the guest room that showed Janice holding her as a baby. Clouded images of Janice teaching her songs, singing for the nurses, were all she could summon, but it was more than she had before. Suzanne wondered if much of anyone's early childhood existed only in the minds of others. She decided maybe a song wasn't that much to ask.

She saved Mark's message for last as a reward for getting through everything else. It was from earlier that day.

> *If you drove to the airport now and got on a plane, our date would only be 1 week late . . . :-)*
> *Janice was more tired than usual at dinner Wednesday, and we had to cut it short. She didn't eat much, but she insisted I get a bottle of wine from the basement to take with us, then reprimanded the manager for not offering any of your wines. The fatigue hasn't taken any of the vinegar out of her, that's for sure. I think the pain might be worse, but she doesn't talk about it.*
> *Tell me how your harvest is going . . . and your divorce. If you want. Hurry back.*

Suzanne reached out to touch the words on the screen with her finger tips. His concern for Janice came through, but without the panic or fear or guilt that she and Donnie couldn't entirely repress. He was a surprising gift in the midst of crisis. She smiled and hit reply.

"Why don't you come here?" she began.

Between Saturday's rounds of punch down, Suzanne patrolled the barrel room with a wine thief, checking the progress of last year's vintage. Sliding the angled glass tube into the top of a barrel, she would siphon off a couple ounces to taste. She nodded to herself as she spat out a mouthful. Another four months, maybe six, and this wine could be bottled. It was good, but this year's was going to blow it away. The more she thought about it, the more she thought she should increase the percentage of new French oak she was using. She needed to track down the extra barrels right now, though, if she wanted to make that happen.

The cool of the barrel room was a welcome respite from the heat. Forecasters predicted a return to normal seasonal temperatures at the beginning of the week, but it was hard to remember what normal was supposed to be. Walking through the rows of barrels stacked three high, footsteps echoing on the cold concrete slab, breathing the fragrance of oak and stone and a touch of mustiness, Suzanne felt completely at peace. This was like a library, it was her cathedral, and Suzanne felt her thoughts quiet as she followed a labyrinthian path. She had no power over life and death, and love was messy and complicated—like everything that involved other people. But she could make wine. This she could do, and as for everything else, she would just have to make the best decisions she could with the information she had.

That relaxed calm carried her through the day, even as the late afternoon turned muggy in a peculiar Midwestern summer way. When the phone rang, she was so reluctant to break the serene isolation, she waited for the machine to pick up. It was Craig.

"You haven't set foot off that farm for days now! If you don't get out soon, someone's going to find you holed up in your bedroom with six-inch fingernails surrounded by empty ice cream cartons and mason jars full of—"

"Enough!" Suzanne cut him off, laughing. "I think there are quite a few steps between staying home for a few days and channeling Howard Hughes, but thanks for that lovely graphic image."

"You're welcome. C'mon. Don't be a hermit. Let's have dinner and you can update me on your sordid soap opera of a life."

Suzanne was about to protest, but decided the description wasn't that far off.

"Why don't you come over and have dinner here?"

"Out," Craig said. "*Out*, means in a restaurant, somewhere not your little cave. Among other things."

"Okay, I give up." Suzanne shook her head, as much at herself as at Craig's persistence. "How about the diner next to the cigar bar in town?"

"How about margaritas and camarones at Fiesta?" he countered.

"Maybe something a little closer?" Suzanne really meant she wasn't quite up for the gregarious social scene at the Mexican restaurant where everyone was family.

Craig sighed. "How about Los Gatos?"

"James Randall it is. I'll call."

The tiny house that looked like Grandma's Victorian cottage housed a twenty-four-seat dining room that managed to be both charming and hip. The menu changed with the seasons and what was available at the market, but it was predominantly small plates with a few large entrees. The wine list was eclectic and included many small production and local wines.

Craig was waiting when Suzanne arrived.

"Don't think I didn't notice that you picked the one place that would still feel like you were at home." He lifted his wine glass. "They even have Cherie."

The waiter brought water as soon as she was seated. "Welcome back, Miss Mathews. Would you like a moment to look at the wine list?"

"I'm thinking something floral, aromatic, summery. Maybe a verdejo? Or a rose! Do you have a rose?"

"We have a sparkling rose by the half bottle."

"Perfect. Bring a glass for him, too."

"Do we have something to celebrate?" Craig asked.

Suzanne reached over and picked up Craig's wine glass. She held it up to the light, swirled it just enough to release the bouquet, breathed deeply and took a tiny sip before handing it back to him.

"Maybe when we don't have anything to celebrate is the time we need to most."

Craig's tone shifted from playful to serious. "You're pretty philosophical tonight."

Suzanne looked at her friend, grateful he had insisted on seeing her. "I decided today that figuring out how my life became such a mess is not as important as figuring out how to clean it up. And cleaning up the mess may not be as important as getting through it."

The waiter arrived with the sparkling wine, deftly removing the cork with a twist of the bottle and a small pop. Suzanne tasted it and nodded, and the waiter filled their glasses. They toasted each other and drank, as a man who had been standing by the host station approached the table.

"Are you Suzanne Mathews of the Suzanne Mathews Winery?"

"I am." Suzanne smiled.

"Ooh, paparazzi," Craig said.

"I love your wines," he said, "and I have this for you."

The man deftly inserted an envelope into Suzanne's open hand and walked out of the restaurant.

Craig's eyebrows shot up as Suzanne opened it. "What is it?"

"It's a restraining order," Suzanne said. "I've just been served."

She picked up her champagne glass, toasted Craig and drained it.

Chapter 12

Must:

freshly pressed juice containing the skin, seeds, and stems,
the solid portion is known as pommace; the first step in winemaking

It was earthquake weather. Suzanne knew there was no connection between shifting tectonic plates and the muggy Midwestern density of the air, but every occurrence of this combination of heat and humidity, infrequent but regular, was widely referred to as earthquake weather. What it really felt like to Suzanne was tornado weather, but that possibility was too rare to register in the Californian lexicon. Trepidation linked to changes in barometric pressure was surely hardwired into the primitive brain, but recognizing the foolishness of attaching that anxiety to the nearest available natural disaster didn't prevent Suzanne from doing it.

Sweat trickled down Suzanne's cleavage, no doubt matched by damp crescents beneath her breasts and under her arms. She considered stripping off her shorts and tank to sit naked, pretending to be in a sauna at some spa, but she was too hot to make more effort than turning the page of the newspaper. She pulled out the local section first, half expecting to see "Mountain Vintner Served More Than Dinner" or find her name on the police blotter, but she knew neither of those made any sense. Still, she felt like a criminal. She had to stay one hundred feet away from the condo in Palo Alto, one hundred feet away from Will anywhere. She couldn't contact him except through his lawyer, no calls and no e-mails. If she violated those requirements, she could be arrested. Arrested for making a phone call. Just remembering the phrase "fear of personal bodily harm" made her cringe and blush. Had Will felt that way, too, when he was served?

Suzanne pulled her hair up into a ponytail and held it with one hand, looking over to the barn and the fermentation containers then scanning the hills beyond. She picked out the black smudge where the fire had burned the roses and moved into the grapes before Carlos and Craig put it out. She closed her eyes. That had either been brilliant or one of the dumbest things she had ever done. She smiled halfway. Maybe it was both. That act may have saved the vintage, but if she couldn't save her winery, would it matter? She sighed. Yes. It *did* matter. Whatever the future brought, she wouldn't lower her standards, and she would not let this vintage suffer from distraction. If this turned out to be her final production under the Suzanne Mathews label, let it be the one to define her career.

The Sunday morning newspaper ritual could not hold her attention. Her eyes kept sliding off the edge of the page instead of dropping down to the next sentence. It was too early to call Janice with a song, because she didn't want to do it while Donnie might still be there. Singing into the answering machine seemed a little odd, but it was doable. The possibility of her sister and nephew standing and listening to it while she sang, though, made her feel self-conscious in a way that was a throwback to childhood. She still needed to choose a song. She had rejected the obvious choice of "her" song, but when she tried to remember what Janice liked forty years ago, all she could come up with were melancholy songs filled with loss and yearning. She had to wonder if those tunes reflected Janice's inclination or her own. "Sounds of Silence" hit too close to home, and even the earliest song Suzanne could remember her mother singing to her, "You Are My Sunshine," had a disturbing desperation to the lyrics in odd counterpoint to the upbeat tempo.

Suzanne's thoughts chained through a series of songs and years and people, ending with the last time she saw Mark before she transferred to Davis. They had gone to a concert in Ames, not a big touring show, but a dive bar with a local band that covered pop songs and oldies with a veneer of blues. It hadn't felt like the end of anything, more like the beginning. It hadn't felt like goodbye. When the singer launched into "Big Yellow Taxi," Mark had drained his glass and kissed her hard and asked if she was ready to go. The way he looked into her eyes made her forget to breathe, and she stood without finishing her drink. They didn't even make it into the car, let alone back to campus. Pressed hard against the car, lips, tongues, hands, she had unbuckled his belt as they kissed, then dragged his pants down with her as she knelt to take him in her mouth. Before he could finish he had stopped her, pulled her up and lifted her against the car with her skirt bunching at her waist as she wrapped her legs around him. The climax had been fast and loud. Suzanne felt her face warm at the memory of the dimly-lit but very public parking lot and was grateful there had been no YouTube when she was young.

Slipping into a greater recline on the chaise, Suzanne dropped her feet to the ground on either side and draped her arms off the chair. Eyes closed, head back, she took a long slow breath. The heat was moist but not stifling, and the air still held the dry-leaf, moist-soil, fermenting-grape notes she had come to associate with fall. She slid her right hand up under her tank top and grazed first one nipple then the other with her fingernails. Lifting her heels to shift pressure to the balls of her bare feet, she raised her hips just enough to move the hand down inside her shorts. She pressed up against the hand pressing down, slipped one finger inside and moaned. Suzanne heard the crunch of gravel on the driveway, but she was too close to stop or to care. She arched her back and tensed her thigh muscles, pressed her left hand down on top of the right and finished, the chaise creaking in rhythm with her.

At the sound of a car door slamming, she yanked her hand out and wiped it on her shorts, then grabbed the paper and tried to get her breathing under control. Teri was planning to come discuss the schedule of pourings and events through the end of the year, an undertaking which was going to be greatly complicated by the mutual restraining orders. She had been head down, keeping a low profile and avoiding taking sides, so Suzanne had seen little of her since the Computer History Museum event. She probably shared some of the same worries the field crew had. Suzanne listened to the footsteps coming around the house and dropped the newspaper, smiling at Teri's early arrival.

It wasn't Teri. It was Trevor Constantine.

She wasn't going to stand, a conscious display of both disrespect and dismissal, but when he took off his sunglasses and ran his eyes over her like he was contemplating an all-you-can-eat buffet, she changed her mind.

"Mr. Constantine. What brings you here? Besides your pretentious car, I mean."

"Whoa, why so hostile?" He held up his hands in a defensive gesture. "You can't even see my car from here. And it's Trevor."

"You're right, that was unfair." Suzanne walked forward past him until she could see the front of the house. A sleek red sports car sparkled in the sun, so close to the ground it looked like something had stepped on it. "My mistake. Your compensatory phallic symbol." She smiled. "Trevor."

Constantine laughed and shook his head. "I see what Will meant about you."

Suzanne bristled.

"But to paraphrase your line at the museum event, sometimes a car is just a car." He winked. "Inadequacy is not a problem for me."

Rolling her eyes, Suzanne crossed her arms over his default visual target. "I'm sorry, Trevor, but I'm very busy. If you'd like a tour, you can call Teri, our promotions manager, to arrange a private visit."

"I do want a tour, but that can wait. I came to make you a proposition." He leered. "A business proposition."

"Not interested," Suzanne said.

"Don't be so hasty." Constantine spun slowly in place, looking out across the vineyard as if measuring the boundaries. "Divorce can be very expensive."

"And how would you know?"

"I can know that without making the mistake of getting married. Genius should be serviced, not bound. If you'd figured that out sooner, you wouldn't be in this position."

Suzanne had been about to throw him off the property, but she was curious to know what he was up to. "And what position is that?"

"Will has big plans, and he could make you a lot of money. For that to work, though, you have to play along. He doesn't really care what you do, though. Whether he's got part interest in Suzanne Mathews Winery or a big chunk of real estate, he's ready to move on. This winery is just a stepping stone, not a passion. If you dig in your heels on the investors, he's ready to sell this place and start over."

Constantine's words struck like a blow to the solar plexus. Not that she trusted him, but he had been involved with Will on his deal from the beginning. She had been sure that whatever else Will wanted, he wanted more control of the winery. *This* winery.

"But I can help you." Constantine watched her closely, the frat boy facade gone, and nothing in his eyes but the predatory glint that made his reputation. "I could buy him out. It would still be a two-person corporate partnership, with me replacing Will." He spread his arms wide, palms up. "It's a sweet deal. I put up the cash, and you keep doing what you do best."

Suzanne narrowed her eyes, but that did not improve her perception of Constantine. "Why do I detect a whiff of brimstone?"

A micro-expression that might have been confusion but could have been annoyance flitted across his face before he burst out laughing. "Good one! But this is not a Faustian bargain." He made an *X* over his chest with a forefinger. "Promise. This is the deal that buys back your soul from divorce hell."

sure how much of the concern was for him and how much was purely selfish. She sent a basket of fruit and cheese as a get-well wish and fervently hoped he would be back Monday, as he had promised.

The temporary restraining order had been granted ex-parte, as Hannah Jackson had predicted, and Will had been served. Suzanne felt some relief knowing Will would not spring out of the barrel room or turn up on her doorstep, even if she'd had moral qualms initially. Perhaps forced separation really was what they needed right now. At least she could focus. The first grapes picked were nearly ready to press, and in two weeks all the wine should be in barrel. She could be in Iowa in time for Halloween with Janice. The thought made her smile followed by a strange ache she didn't want to explore.

Suzanne closed the driveway gate behind the crew at the end of the day and settled into the couch with her laptop and a glass of wine. Clearing her inbox offered both the comfort of a quiet evening at home and the sense of accomplishment that comes from crossing a dull task off the to-do list. It had also become a necessity. Each time she had looked at her computer over the last couple days, she had found excuses to do other things, but any longer and the backlog would be unmanageable.

First she weeded out the marketing updates and newsletters that weren't quite spam but didn't need to be read, then responded to messages related to the winery, most of which had been screened by the promotions manager. After an hour of scanning, responding and deleting, she was left with personal mail from Laura, Donnie, Janice, and Mark. She stretched, walked to the kitchen to refill her wine glass, and started with Laura's. The message was from Tuesday night with no subject line.

Will wants you to know that he feels bad about how things went last night, and he's sorry. (His lawyer told him not to contact you.)
I want you to know that I told Will this is the only time I will be the intermediary.
I'm still hoping we can all be friends.

Suzanne felt simultaneously repulsed and buoyed, as if the doctor had just informed her that her severed hand could be saved, but only by covering her fingers with leeches. "I'm not sure what to say, Mr. . . . Trevor. What do you get out of the deal?"

His face lifted back into his hail fellow personna, a mildly disturbing transformation. "Me? Why, I get prestige and bragging rights and hopefully some return on my investment. Not to mention all the wine I can drink." He winked.

Suzanne smiled back at him. "There must be something more."

"Well, I might like to amp up the marketing a tad, just to make sure I *am* getting some return, but no other investors, and nothing we wouldn't have completely spelled out in writing before you had to commit. That's a much better deal than any marriage can offer."

He put his sunglasses back on and pulled out a business card as he moved closer to Suzanne. Remembering his last handshake, Suzanne gave a quick grasp to his right hand before accepting the card from his left. He smiled but said nothing. Suzanne didn't bother re-crossing her arms.

"I'll think about your offer," she said.

"That's all any man ever asks." Constantine tipped an imaginary hat in her direction and crunched across the gravel back to his car.

The configuration of the vehicle required an entry that was borderline obscene, a contortion performed smoothly as Suzanne watched. He started the car, backed up, and drove away all without ever looking back in her direction.

"I'm sorry if I'm speaking out of line here, but you guys are *not* making my job any easier. This all seems so unnecessary." Teri was half joking, half serious as she scolded Suzanne without looking up from her laptop. They had been working on the schedule for half an hour, sitting at the table on the back patio in a shady spot with a breeze. She typed a staccato beat then asked, "Okay, what about the winemaker dinner in December? You have to be there, but the contact is Will's friend. We wouldn't be in there otherwise."

"December is a long way off," Suzanne said. "I can't think that far ahead right now. Let's just look at what we've got through the end of October. And into early November."

Suzanne watched her assistant as she searched and typed, wondering just how much Teri had observed and overheard, especially in the last year. Teri was good with people, but her real affinity was for organization, spreadsheets and details. When she was engrossed with her work, it was easy to forget she was in the same room with you. Employees in a small business are like kids, they hear and understand much more than anyone knows.

"Just the wine shop tasting, the sommelier meet and greet, and the station identification for the local news, then." Teri ran her hand through the short side of her hair, the magenta highlights fluttering against their dark background. "The wine shop is you—that's next week—the sommelier is Will, and the blurb filming can go either way."

"Let Will do it," Suzanne said. "No, wait." She thought about Will in front of a news camera. Maybe they were just shooting a promo spot, but they were a news crew. Will in front of a camera talking about the expansion plans. Will in front of a camera talking about the restraining order. "We should have them do the shoot here, with the vineyard as the background. I'm sure that's what they had in mind. For a few weeks, anyway, that means they'll have to talk to me."

Teri typed silently and chewed on the inside of her cheek.

"What?" Suzanne asked.

"How long will the . . . restraining orders be . . ." Teri gave up looking for the end of the sentence and looked at Suzanne.

Suzanne picked up her glass of iced tea and drank. She had hit it off with Teri from the beginning, and their relationship was congenial and familiar. But in that moment, Suzanne recognized that that was the extent of their connection. Teri was more colleague than confidante, and she was not someone with whom Suzanne would or could share her innermost thoughts. Few people fell into that group, which used to include Will and Laura and now may have narrowed down to Craig. And maybe Mark.

"I know it seems strange, but the restraining orders are mostly a legal strategy. Will and I disagree on the best future for the winery, and that disagreement is complicated by the divorce. Right now it's hard for us to work together, but it's possible we can work something out before we have to appear before a judge on the restraining orders." Suzanne spoke evenly, careful not to raise her voice or Teri's curiosity. "It could be no more than a couple weeks."

Teri started to type, then stopped abruptly. "Am I going to have to take sides?"

Before Suzanne could respond, Teri continued.

"Because if this is going to get ugly, I'm out of here. When my brother got divorced, my sister-in-law wanted me to say she should get full custody of the kids. I couldn't believe it. She was my best friend, but he's my brother. I tried to talk to them, but it was like they both went crazy. I was actually subpoenaed to testify." Her voice broke. "It was horrible."

"I'm sorry you had to go through that, Teri." Suzanne considered pointing out that even if she quit, it wouldn't protect her from having to testify, but that clearly wouldn't help. "I don't know what's going to happen, but I want to keep things as uncomplicated as possible."

Teri shot her a look without commenting, and Suzanne held up her hand like a crossing guard.

"I know, I know. A restraining order doesn't sound like keeping it simple." Suzanne felt Will's fingers dig into her arms, felt her own grip on the poker, but pushed the memory away. That explanation was not for Teri. "But I just want to protect my winery, not hurt Will." She smiled. "If you think I'm starting to get crazy, you tell me, and I promise to listen. Okay?"

Teri pursed her lips and frowned, but Suzanne could see the corners of her mouth twitching beneath the faux severe expression. "Okay." She closed her laptop and picked up her glass to take to the kitchen on her way out. "I'm meeting with Will in the morning. I'll let you know if there are any changes to the schedule after that."

"Thanks."

Suzanne walked Teri to the door, then continued out to the fermentation vats to check the temperatures and punch down the caps one more time. Some of the vats were moving faster than usual, but nothing to worry about. She would probably start free run midweek, then press the caps on the first two vats and have wine in barrel by the end of the week, with the rest coming over the course of the following week. Suzanne smiled just imagining this wine in barrels, soaking up a hint of toasted oak to complement the red berry and spice from the fruit, developing the silky finish she was certain it would have. She inhaled deeply, a suggestion of violets coming after the pungent fermentation fog. This one was going to need longer in the barrel before bottling, longer in the bottle before release, too.

The smile faded. How was that going to play out with the divorce? Would Will get half the inventory? Could half this historic vintage be mishandled and wasted? Not that fruit this perfect could be easily ruined, but the difference between a good wine and an epic once-in-a-lifetime wine didn't happen only on the vine. The touch of the winemaker was crucial, and this wine, these grapes, were hers. Suzanne finished the punch down and walked back to the house. The sun was sliding toward the mountains, and the lengthening shadows brought the temperature out of earthquake weather and into Mediterranean balmy.

Suzanne poured herself a glass of wine, picked up the phone and slumped down on the couch. What if she took Constantine's offer? Could it really be that simple? One deal with the right devil and no more worries about what might happen next? She closed her eyes and leaned her head back. It was too good to be true. She knew it was, but it was nice to think even for a minute that maybe she could hold everything together essentially unchanged. Or maybe she needed to be like Will, prepared to walk away and start over. Suzanne sat that way for a long time. Eventually, she opened her eyes, stretched and sat up straight. She took a sip of the crisp bright white in her glass, then dialed Janice's number, waited for the machine to pick up, and began to sing.

"Bows and flows of angel hair and ice cream castles in the air . . ."

Chapter 13

Free Run:
the juice that runs off the vat without any pressing

Monday did not so much dawn as brighten slowly, like an incandescent bulb on a dimmer switch. The marine layer had come back in a cool gray veil. Suzanne wasn't convinced the Indian summer heat wave had broken, but she was sure it would stay below one hundred degrees. She took her coffee with her to punch down the tanks, eager to get to work.

The first grapes harvested were nearly finished with primary fermentation, and she could have the free run wine in the settling tank by the end of the day and ready for barrel Wednesday morning. Each of the small open-topped fermenters was developing its own character, the one hundred percent whole cluster different than the thirty percent, the wild yeast vats not quite like those inoculated. Suzanne would keep them all separate in the barrel, too, just as she kept the grapes from each parcel separate. Only after the wine spent more than a year in French oak would she select and blend to create her signature wine. The anticipation of those tastings and the final bottling from this particular fruit made Suzanne grin.

Trying to imagine her life in fifteen or twenty months made the smile evaporate. It was hard enough to picture next week at this point; next year seemed an impossibly long time away. The rhythm of the vineyard and the timeline of the wine was such that each vintage overlapped the next, a cycle spiraling forward through time. As these grapes were ripening, last year's barrels were being tasted and topped off. Somewhere between pruning the vines and bud-break last year's wine would be bottled and half the barrels would be sold and replaced with new French oak when next year's were ready for crush. Right about then Suzanne would be barrel tasting the vintage fermenting right now to check its progress, even though it would still be young and tightly wound, it would be the first glimpse—and first test—of what she expected to be greatness.

She pushed down the cap on the final fermentation vat and retrieved her coffee cup. The path for this fruit from here to the bottle was so obstructed she could barely make it out. She needed to clear away the distractions, to protect not just the land, but this vintage. That thought was followed immediately by a decision to call Trevor Constantine. Suzanne was surprised by the sudden resolve and the sour taste that accompanied it, but she couldn't afford to eliminate any option without at least exploring it.

"Desperate times, desperate measures," she muttered to herself as she walked back to the house. Gravel crunching and the rumbling of an engine that had to belong to Carlos's truck made her veer off toward the driveway and speed up until she was practically skipping out to meet him. When she saw his arm waving, Suzanne slowed and waited while he parked. The man who slid out of the cab was so altered from the one she had sent home only a week before that she was momentarily speechless.

"Hola, Miss Suzanne."

Carlos was naturally thin, but now his clothes hung in folds gathered in the middle by a shiny new belt. Suzanne thought it leant a vaguely monk-like quality to his attire. His smile was genuine, but his cheeks had a strange blue-gray tinge instead of the warm caramel color they usually held and his eyes looked smudged with purple.

"Carlos, what . . . I mean . . . como estas?"

"Bien. Bien, gracias."

Suzanne shook her head. "You can't be bien. Carlos, what's going on?"

He met her eyes and said, "It is pneumonia, but I have had three days of antibiotics. Already I am much better."

Suzanne scanned his face. "What did your doctor say about working?"

Carlos coughed, then shrugged and looked past her to the fermentation vats. "He said to rest. Not overdo. I will have Ricardo and Hector do the heavy work."

As ridiculously grateful as Suzanne was to have Carlos back at work, she was certain it was a bad idea. Carlos must have seen the doubt on her face.

He held up a hand. "I will not work long. And I will rest." His assurances had a dignified finality.

"Okay." Suzanne relented, as much for her own interests as for his unspoken need to be there. Carlos shared her connection to the vineyard in a way no one else did. He probably felt he had already missed too much work, had failed to fulfill his responsibilities. She would just have to watch to be sure he really wasn't pushing his limits.

The sound of another vehicle turning into the drive made them both look.

"Ricardo was a big help last week, but he's not you," Suzanne said. She smiled as Carlos took a sudden interest in the toes of his cowboy boots. "I've finished this morning's punch down."

"Gracias, Miss Suzanne."

Carlos smiled, put on his hat, and walked slowly to the barrel room.

After showering and getting more coffee, Suzanne took her laptop out to the patio. Donnie hadn't called the night before, so he must have sent an e-mail update on Janice. She scrolled through her new mail until she found his.

Things are about the same. Mom started sleeping on the couch. She said it's to see the Halloween decorations, but I think the stairs are too much work now.

*Her attitude is the same—bad! (haha) Saturday we drank some of
your wine and made up tasting notes, "not fully open but still imper-
tinent, refined with a hint of slut, etc." We thought the descriptions fit
you even better than the wine. (kidding!) Mom talked about my dad
again. Yours, too.*

I'm in meetings all day, but call later when you can.

Suzanne smiled at Donnie's jokes and thought about Janice's move
to the living room. She was already spending most of her time there,
so it could have just been convenience that motivated the change, but
she shared her nephew's concern that it was a sign of something else.
Suzanne was used to measuring weeks and even days, but with wine each
timeline led to another phase, a new beginning. That was not the nature
of Janice's counting of weeks. She didn't feel like she was in denial, but
accepting the finality was elusive. While she had spent a week juggling
her domestic problems and finishing harvest, she had missed an eighth
or a fifth or maybe even more of what remained of her sister's life. She
had already been absent from a big chunk of the life that had come
before, but there had always been more time. Until there wasn't.

She leaned back and looked out across the mountains. Suzanne envied
Donnie the stories Janice was telling about the past. Their past. She
hadn't realized how hungry she was for the information until she'd had
a little taste of it during her time in Iowa. The Viking funeral, the story
of her naming and Donnie's, even the revelation that the family vacation
she remembered didn't include her parents. She had spent her whole
life looking forward, believed the future to be not only more important
than the past but often only tangentially related to it. Now she had to
wonder if that attitude had been the self-preservation of a child whose
past was crumbling beneath her feet. Had she subconsciously focused
on the future because she couldn't afford to tether herself to the rapidly
vanishing past?

Suzanne blew her bangs out of her eyes and adjusted her ponytail.

The question felt uncomfortably true, as if it were something obvious that everyone else had always known. Not that she hadn't had a few psychology classes, not that she didn't read *Science* magazine, but she had considered the research on early childhood development, things like birth order and spacing and breast versus bottle to be somewhat dubious, geared for public entertainment and not as rigorous as chemistry when it came to sample size and replicability. But for all the risk in extrapolating larger assumptions from anecdotal evidence, when it was your own anecdote, it was hard to deny the viability. Who might she have been if her father hadn't died before she even knew him, if she hadn't spent all of her childhood trying to make her mother smile?

She shook her head. Who she was now was what she had to work with, and the rest was pointless navel-gazing. She scrolled down until she saw a message from Mark dated the day before.

Suzanne,
I talked Janice out of a bottle of Mermaid Tears from a couple years ago and opened it Saturday night. Not the same as having you here, but at least it was something touched by you. I think I'll do that every Saturday until you show up for our date. :)
Janice was upbeat and lively when I saw her last, but short bursts of energy are often followed by a decline. I'm not trying to scare you, but I want you to be prepared.
I hope your life there is sorting itself out.
Mark

"Your life there" as opposed to "your life here"? Suzanne wondered what he meant, since as far as she was concerned her life was where she was and required no modifier. There was no arguing that she had a lot of sorting out to do, but the line left her feeling unsettled.

Before she had finished working her way through all the e-mail, Teri called.

"There's a problem with the news promo," Teri said after greeting Suzanne. "Will agrees you should do it, but he wants to have final approval of the cut."

Suzanne frowned. He must be having some of the same concerns she'd had about what might be said or done when the other wasn't there. It was bad enough to feel so paranoid, herself, but to have someone else feeling paranoid about what *she* might do was even worse.

"Tell him we'll both review the spots and we won't let them run anything we don't agree on. How does that sound?"

"That should work. I've got a request for another pouring in two weeks, but they haven't confirmed, so don't worry about it yet."

"Did Will say . . ." Suzanne stopped herself from asking if Will had said anything about the divorce or about her before she dragged Teri into the mess she had promised to avoid. "Did Will say he was available for that one if it happens?" She heard Teri let out her breath.

"I told him we'd talk about it if and when they confirm."

Suzanne smiled so it would be heard in her voice. "Thanks, Teri."

There are many kinds of uncertainty, and Suzanne was very comfortable with quite a few. But too many facets of her life were not only out of her control, but seemed to be barely within her sphere of influence. Suzanne put the phone back in its base and walked to the front door. She picked Constantine's card out of the mermaid dish where she had tossed it and called his office to set up an appointment. When his secretary told her Mr. Constantine had given instructions to make time available for Suzanne any time she requested it, she chose the following morning. Wondering what big deal she was squeezing off his calendar and why she merited such priority, she wasn't sure whether she should be flattered, or very, very afraid.

By the time she took the Sandhill exit off 280 the next day, Suzanne was pretty sure the correct response was fear. Between rounds of punch down and checking on Carlos, she had made a few phone calls and done as much "off the record" research as she could without raising too many questions. The last thing she wanted was for the Silicon Valley rumor mill to get wind of her meeting with Trevor Constantine. Actually, the last thing she wanted was to have Will hear about it, so she had chosen her contacts carefully and had given as her reason the fact that Will had been in discussion with Constantine and she was just doing due diligence.

The parking lot was full of Jaguars, Porches, and there was even a Tesla. Suzanne wondered if there was a separate lot in the back for Japanese cars, but decided to park between two white BMWs and see if any alarms sounded. She had considered coming directly from the morning punch down wearing jeans and surrounded by the aroma of fermenting grapes, but she decided that was juvenile. Instead she wore a black skirt that ended just above the knee, a black and white hound-stooth jacket, and a silk blouse the color of blood. When she'd put up her hair and added pearl earrings and lipstick to match the blouse before leaving the house, she thought she looked good enough to give her per-fectly-turned-out divorce lawyer a run for her money.

Suzanne reviewed her goal as she walked into the building, repeating it like a mantra. She was there to listen, not to talk. The information she had gathered was an odd mix of solid business feedback and corporate gossip. Constantine had started his first company while he was still in school and sold it before he was twenty-five. He started another com-pany which he sold at enormous personal profit three years later. His separation from a venture capital firm after a brief stint was so loudly trumpeted as "by mutual agreement" that everyone knew it was acri-monious, and he started investing on his own. Constantine dabbled in real estate, opened a restaurant, then started an investment fund and personal wealth management company. His fingerprints were all over the Bay Area in unexpected places. He was hard to read, harder to anticipate, and had a knack for identifying vulnerability. One thing everyone agreed on, though, was that if he was on your side, your side always won. There had been two or maybe three sexual harassment suits over the years and one civil suit following a car accident, all of which vanished quietly with no further public comment from the plaintiffs.

The receptionist showed her into a bright room full of chrome and leather furniture and told Suzanne to help herself to coffee, water, or juice. Suzanne had been expecting something dark and club-like with wing-back chairs and scotch, so the room was a surprise. Constantine wasn't there yet, so she didn't sit, either, instead admiring the view of the Foothills from the expanse of glass on two sides of the room. She turned when the door opened and saw Constantine lift his gaze from the chair where she was supposed to be and scan to where she stood. He gave a low whistle, and Suzanne felt her jaw clench. She forced herself to smile and consciously relaxed her shoulders as she walked over and extended her hand.

"Trevor. Thank you for meeting with me so quickly."

"Well if I had known you were going to go all out, I would have suggested dinner instead of the office." He winked and gestured to the set of chairs with a low table between. "Maybe we'll save that for the celebration."

Suzanne just smiled and waited.

Constantine put a leather portfolio on the table then leaned way back in his chair, lacing his fingers together behind his head and propping one ankle up on the other knee.

"Everything you need to know is in that binder. You can take it home, show it to your lawyer, crunch the numbers until they beg for mercy, but here's the upshot. You will make a cash offer to buy out Will's share of all tangible and intangible property and all future rights. I will provide that cash and become your full partner in Suzanne Mathews Winery. I will share equally in all profits from wine sales but will have no input on the vines, the wines, or your life. In exchange, you will agree to a minimum number of sponsorship opportunities each year, be they tangible or intangible. You will have the right to refuse any of them, but you must approve some of them by the terms of the contract. Profits on all SMW non-wine products and promotions will be split seventy/thirty with the larger portion going to me."

Suzanne raised her eyebrows but didn't respond.

"The details have some room for negotiation, but don't sit on your hands. Will has two more investors interested in backing his business plan. He wants to have everything in place to make an offer to buy *you* out before anything goes before a judge. Not that he expects you to accept any offer he makes, but the more unreasonable he can make you look, the better it looks for him when you do go to court."

"Why are you telling me all this?" Suzanne walked across the room to get a bottle of water and sat back down, keeping her weight balanced on the edge of the cushion. "Aren't you skirting your own confidentiality agreements?"

Constantine lifted one brow. "Skirts are easy to get around if you know what you're doing."

Suzanne rolled her eyes before she could quash the impulse and Constantine laughed.

"Okay, okay," he said, "not my best effort."

"Why do you want half-interest in a winery?"

"Why did Meg Whitman run for Governor?" Constantine shrugged.

"That doesn't really answer my question. Why should I even read this?" Suzanne gestured to the portfolio.

Constantine sat up straight and leaned toward her, elbows resting on his knees. "My friends in Napa and the Russian River say the same thing they're saying all up and down the Santa Cruz Mountains. Martin Ranch, Burrell School, Windy Oaks, even the proprietress at Suzanne Mathews couldn't resist commenting to a few people that this year all the stars aligned for their pinot noir grapes. The rainfall, the temperature, everything came together to produce what will be at least the vintage of a decade and maybe the vintage of the century."

Suzanne felt all the saliva in her mouth dry up.

"There is just no way for you to come out of your divorce with all of that perfect wine, because half of it belongs to your husband. You would have to sacrifice a significant percentage of your share of other assets in exchange for that kind of control, and I think you would give up a lot to keep your baby. Now, Will may not know that right now, but he will as soon as I buy into his little venture."

Suzanne was unable to break his gaze, mesmerized like the next meal for a python.

Constantine offered a smug tight-lipped smile. "Either way I get part of your winery. I just like having fewer partners." He picked up the folio and held it out to Suzanne as he stood. "Don't take too long. I'm meeting with Will next Monday, and I might get tired of waiting."

She rose and found the voice to say, "I'll be in touch."

"I know," Constantine said, already turning toward the door.

Suzanne hoped he hadn't seen her hand shaking as she reached for the binder.

Chapter 14

Press:

the application of pressure to extract the last juice from the pommace

"I'm being blackmailed!"

Suzanne slammed the leather folio Constantine had given her onto her business attorney's desk, then crossed her arms and paced back and forth while he opened it, put on his glasses and started to read.

She had driven away from her meeting in a daze, speeding down 280 on autopilot until the shock and fear that had paralyzed her thought processes were overridden by a searing rage. She had taken the next exit and gone directly to Jeff's office, determined to wait as long as it took for the next five minutes he could give her.

"He knew exactly where to hit me, tell me he understands the value of this vintage like we have a bond and then flip that knowledge around to rub my nose in it. I am such an idiot!" Suzanne threw her hands in the air. "Even knowing his M.O., I didn't look for my own weaknesses." She made a sour face. "Make that 'opportunities' Constantine could exploit."

Jeff looked up and said in his soothing baritone. "Suzanne? Would you like to sit down?"

"No! I would not like to sit down! I'd like to take my pruning shears and feed Constantine his cojones for breakfast! I'd like to get a rocket launcher and take out Constantine's whole building! I'd like not to have to defend a business I started with my own hands. Literally! I'd like to be putting free run wine into the settling tank and pressing the must and transferring the settled wine to barrels. I'd like . . ." Suzanne met Jeff's eyes as her tirade wound down. She took a ragged breath and sat. "I don't even like opera . . . when did my life become one?"

The lawyer flashed a smile and went back to skimming the document. "This partnership agreement does not appear to be as outrageous as the conversation you described, though I'll have to study it in more detail." He paused and reread a section. "It does specifically assign control of the wine growing and wine making process to you. There is also a provision for establishing full ownership for you of the house, proper, and the land on which it stands."

Suzanne frowned. "Really? That seems awfully . . . reasonable."

Jeff nodded. "I know. We'll have to be careful not to miss the finer points of sponsorship and collateral materials provisions. Trevor Constantine is not known for his gift-giving, so somewhere in there he is being paid back with interest. And Suzanne?" Jeff lowered his head to look at her over his reading glasses. "I want you to refrain from using words like 'blackmail' with anyone but me."

Suzanne nodded, feeling as if she were being reprimanded. She knew he was only protecting her, though, knew he was right about the pervasiveness of Constantine's reach. She did not want to give him any ammunition, or at least not any more than he already had. "Thanks, Jeff. And I'm sorry for barging in and screwing up your schedule." Suzanne stood. "I owe you a bottle of wine."

The attorney rose and shook her hand. "You were right to come immediately. If you wait a few minutes, we can have copies of this made right now. I'll get a copy to Hannah so she can factor it into your divorce negotiations, and I recommend you read yours thoroughly as soon as you can. If anything stands out that we should know about, e-mail both of us."

"What about his insinuation that I have to decide before Monday or it will be too late?"

Jeff frowned. "He may attach any deadline he'd like to, of course, but your decision should be based on the merits of the offer."

Though it was already afternoon when she returned to the vineyard, and she was feeling queasy from stress and hunger, Suzanne headed directly for the barrel room. She passed three empty fermenters on the way and a fourth beside them that had only the must left in a sludge at the bottom waiting to be pressed. Carlos was leaning against the settling tank, but she could not tell if he was lost in thought or in need of support. He straightened and turned toward her as she approached.

"Hola, Carlos. Where are we?"

Carlos removed his hat and wiped his brow with his sleeve. Punch down's telltale spots darkened his cuff like splattered blood. "Yesterday's wine has settled and is in barrel. Ricardo will finish today's press. I am on my way home, unless there is anything else you need, Miss Suzanne."

"No, gracias, Carlos. I want you to rest when you can. This wine . . ." she trailed off as the words lodged in her throat. The morning, the week, the month washed over her, the undertow of despair dragging at her knees. Suzanne struggled to maintain her composure.

"Si, senora." Carlos clasped her wrist lightly but firmly, anchoring her to the moment. "This wine . . . esta es tu obra maestra."

Suzanne burst into tears and smiled at the same time. Carlos dropped his eyes and released her wrist. He inspected the creases in his hat before settling it on his head.

"Hasta manana, Miss Suzanne."

"Hasta manana, Carlos."

Suzanne watched him walk slowly to his truck and climb in, part of her wanting to run after him and ask him to stay. She knew he would push too hard if he stayed, though, and she was grateful he was following her earlier request to guard his health.

She reached up and pulled the clip out of her hair, shaking the updo loose with her fingers so vigorously the motion almost shifted from massage to torture. She put the clip in her pocket and walked into the barrel room, pulling the door closed behind her.

The oak barrels filling the warehouse reminded her just a little of the building where the Ark of the Covenant was buried at the end of *Raiders of the Lost Ark*. This room wasn't so cavernous that you could ever really lose anything in it, but the sense of endless possibility and concealed treasure was still there. Fans whirred softly in the ceiling high above, the only sound in the cool dimly-lit space except her own breathing as she walked back to see the new barrels. The room once again worked its magic for Suzanne, the soaring beams and the monumental racks that always made her want to whisper. She closed her eyes and wrapped her arms around her waist as she inhaled deeply. The fragrance was related to wine, but not like the bouquet of a glass of pinot noir, more like a rich balsamic vinegar.

The damp soil fragrance with slight must reminded her of Janice's basement, the storm cellar become wine cellar through Suzanne's relentless sharing of her latest releases. Knowing that her resume as a vintner was sitting there barely touched gave her a sense of exhilaration laced with disappointment. Some of the wines could no longer be found anywhere else, so tasting them again would be like reliving a lovely moment long-forgotten. It was gratifying to see her collected body of work stacked in one place almost like a tribute, but the real tribute would have been drinking the wines, even if nothing was ever said about them. Perhaps that was expecting too much, as if her transformation of her sister's basement had been less the act of a fairy godmother than a perpetual five-year-old. Look what I made!

That thought transported her to the basement, filled not with boxes of wine as she'd last seen it, but with boxes of books and off-season clothes and family "heirlooms" no one was willing to throw out. It was one of her favorite spots for hide-and-seek, even though it seemed so obvious. No one else liked to go down there because it was too dark and full of spider webs. She knew they were only daddy longlegs, though, so it wasn't really scary. She would squeeze behind a box, wrap her arms around her legs, bury her face in her knees and become invisible.

Suzanne did exactly that the day of her father's funeral, though no one was seeking when she hid. That scene came back to her, the overlapping voices, the food everywhere in great vats of segregated smells, the unrecognizable leg maze, the way her mom cried at all the wrong times and wouldn't look at her. Suzanne had stayed in the cellar until Janice found her much later.

"Miss Suzanne?"

Ricardo's hesitant voice called softly from the doorway.

Suzanne took another deep breath and opened her eyes.

"Si. I'm here." Suzanne reached out to run her fingers over the barrel next to her, before going to meet him.

"One of the tanks, I think it might be stuck." His brow was furrowed in an almost comical contrast to his age, but if fermentation had stopped prematurely in one of the vats, that would be good cause for worry. She took off her jacket and pulled an old work shirt off the hook by the door, buttoning it over her red silk blouse as she walked.

"Let's go take a look."

Night on the mountain was quiet in a way that made Suzanne feel like the last person on earth. No lights were visible outside but the stars, which did not stop Suzanne from staring out the window at nothing. She had been reading and rereading Constantine's contract for hours, first with coffee, then with a glass of wine, then armed with nothing but growing fatigue. Each section of the document sent her thoughts off on a circuitous route from wine to Will to Janice and back to harvest, and she couldn't focus long enough to find the trap she was sure was in there somewhere. She considered going to bed, but she knew she wouldn't sleep.

Suzanne stood and stretched and walked over to the phone.

"Remember that line from Amadeus about too many notes?" she asked. "Well, I've got too many words. Or too many thoughts."

There was a groan at the other end of the line.

"Do you know what time it is?" Craig said. "If I pretend this is a wrong number, will you leave me alone?"

She checked the clock. It was after midnight.

"Sorry, I didn't think. Besides, aren't you a night owl?"

"I just finished a big project . . . too tired to celebrate." He finished with an elaborate yawn.

"Go back to sleep. I can talk to you tomorrow."

"Great," Craig said. "An insomniac and a tease. You might as well tell me what's going on, I'm awake now."

"My head is crammed so full of problems that I can't focus on anything, and everything is a crisis. It's like being in a room filled with babbling voices and trying to hear one person on the other side." Suzanne walked as she talked, moving aimlessly from one room to the next.

"Um, are any of these voices telling you to hurt people?"

Suzanne snorted. "Not actual voices, you idiot, but thanks for asking. It's the voice outside my head that wants to hurt people, but my lawyer already warned me about that." She dropped heavily onto the couch and stretched out. "I'm going over this partnership proposal from Constantine, picturing working with him, and doing that, I have to think about Will's plan and the divorce settlement. Thinking about the divorce makes me freak out about losing the winery and that makes me panic about finishing this year's harvest by myself if Carlos doesn't keep getting better. Thinking about the timeline for crush makes me think about the deadline to respond to Constantine. Thinking about the deadline makes me think about . . . Janice."

Craig was silent.

"Janice has started sleeping on the couch because she can't handle the stairs anymore." Suzanne said. "I think . . ." She couldn't finish the sentence.

"Do you want to go?" Craig asked.

"I can't."

"Well, what *can* you do?"

"That's the problem. I *can* do a lot of things, but I can't do them all." Suzanne stood up and started pacing.

"That's always true," Craig said, "but I don't think I've ever heard you sound so . . . I don't know, confused? Indecisive?"

She stopped in front of the framed poster of the Mermaid Tears label and stared into her own eyes. "You're right. Because I never have been. Even when I moved to California, left what little family I have behind, left Mark, I didn't have to struggle with the choice. It was easy. I knew what I wanted most."

"What do you want now?" Craig asked.

"Maybe the question isn't about what I want anymore." Suzanne ran her forefinger over the sparkling tear on the mermaid's cheek. "Maybe the question is what can I have?"

Suzanne spent all of Wednesday outside. She did the punch downs and helped Carlos and Ricardo with the free run and press of the vats that had finished primary fermentation. Ricardo had been mistaken about one of the containers being stuck, and everything was progressing smoothly. She made only one comment when Carlos was unsteady and did not mention his frequent pauses to catch his breath, but she tried to finish her own tasks faster so she could help with his. Mostly they worked in comfortable silence, side by side, finishing each other's motions the way a married couple might finish each other's sentences. Suzanne was pleased to find Carlos explaining things to Ricardo and introducing him to aspects of the process that he had previously done himself.

When the work with the wine was done, Suzanne walked the property, up and down the vineyard rows, to the highest elevation and back down again. She looked down at the house and the open-topped fermenters from the ridge; she looked up at the undulating rows from the long drive. She did not open her computer or make any calls. She left Constantine's offer on the dining room table untouched. The decision to shut out everything but the wine came after her conversation with Craig. Chaos may be unavoidable, but indecision was a choice. If she could focus on one thing, even for a day, if she could just do her job, she could have a reprieve from trying to untangle the Gordian knot of her life.

Somewhere Will was spinning his own winery dreams with Laura by his side, somewhere lawyers were toiling away by the billable minute at her expense, somewhere Constantine was floating sparkly things hoping for a bite, somewhere Donnie was working and worrying and avoiding his grief, and somewhere right now, Mark and Janice should be having their weekly dinner. Should be, unless Janice's inability to negotiate the stairs anymore also meant she wasn't leaving the house. Suzanne knew Alexander's solution to the Gordian knot problem, and she was the one holding the sword.

Chapter 15

Malolactic Fermentation:
the conversion by bacteria of malic acid into CO2
and lactic acid, used to reduce the acid in red wine
by organic rather than chemical means (secondary fermentation)

Suzanne had always been able to sleep on planes, but a redeye to New York is not the same as a redeye to Minneapolis. Between the takeoff safety mime show and the long prep for landing, the available nap time is cut down to maybe two hours under the best of circumstances. Throw in the turbulence of a late-October thunderstorm dropping snow on the Rockies and hail on the plains, and rest isn't really an option. She watched the light show ten thousand feet down and miles to the south. Her moment of clarity, the certainty that she wanted to be with Janice, had come that morning. She could not speed up her divorce or the primary fermentation, but she could be with her sister in the last days of her life.

The woman next to her was gripping both arm rests so hard the veins in her hands bulged, and from the way her lips were moving, Suzanne was pretty sure she was praying. The woman's husband on the aisle was snoring lightly, thanks to the two tiny bottles of scotch he drank as soon as the plane took off. Suzanne moved her airsick bag to the front of the seat-back pocket as a talisman against nausea and put her iPod on shuffle. When the plane finally touched down, the passengers burst into spontaneous cheers. Had the seatbelt light not still been on, Suzanne was sure the pilot would have gotten a standing ovation.

The river of disoriented travelers streamed past empty gates and down the escalator to baggage claim. Little tributaries branched off at the restrooms, and the few travelers with only carry-on bags washed up on the curb outside, Suzanne among them. She squinted at every pair of approaching headlights as if she might recognize Donnie's car from the beams. When a car finally did stop in front of her, the passenger window slid down and the voice inside said, "You look like hell!" Suzanne threw her bag in the back and got in beside Donnie.

"We can't all look as good as you."

"True," he said, "but you could at least look human."

Suzanne backhanded his shoulder. "You're such a jerk. It was a rough flight. If I doze off on the way down, you'll know why."

"Go ahead and sleep. We can talk later."

"That's okay," Suzanne said, "I want to hear the stories. But can we get some coffee?"

Donnie made a quick pass through a roadside coffee stand before merging onto the Interstate. Suzanne blew over her cup and watched Donnie's face in the strobe-like flashes of the passing traffic. When they had left the city limits, he began.

"You know the part about going to California after your dad died and Gram had a breakdown, right? Mom didn't say much about Gram, because even though she was eighteen, nobody told her anything." He looked sideways at Suzanne. "You know how it is. Anyway, she took you to California to stay with Gram's cousins. You stayed for almost a month. After the first few days, Mom started going out every night on her own, mostly just to walk on the beach."

Suzanne recalled Janice's description of going out after everyone was asleep to burn the symbols of their father in a paper boat. Maybe that was the beginning of the late night outings.

"One night she heard music and crashed this house party where my dad's band was playing. He was singing "American Pie" when she walked in. She said it was like in a movie where a light glows around one person and everything else blurs to background."

"Wait, Janice said that?"

"Well, not exactly . . ." Donnie admitted. "What she actually said was that the place was so packed she couldn't see anything until she squeezed through on one side and the only unobstructed view was of an electric guitar, a tie-dyed shirt, and my dad's hands."

Suzanne laughed. "That's more like it. Then what?"

"She met him after the set, and they made a date for the next night. She saw him every day until you went back home, and they made plans for Mom to move out there."

"Really?" Suzanne frowned, trying to imagine Janice living in California. "What happened?"

"When Mom found out she was pregnant, Tom—that was his name—wanted her to go back right away."

"Why didn't she?"

Donnie looked at Suzanne. "She said Gram couldn't be left alone yet, and she needed to take care of you."

Suzanne knew Janice had lived with them and taken care of her when she was little, but it had never occurred to her that it had been any kind of sacrifice. She had assumed just the opposite, that Janice had stayed at home because it was easier than raising a baby alone. Even if that were true, Janice had chosen taking care of them over the possibility of a life in California with Donnie's father. As she imagined how different Janice's life might have been, and how drastically her own might have been altered, she realized Donnie was still talking.

"He offered to help pay for an abortion, but it wasn't like she could get one anywhere around here back then. And she didn't want to leave." Donnie glanced at Suzanne and back at the road. "So Tom came to Iowa for a couple months after I was born, picking up gigs whenever he could, most a two or three hour drive away. It just wasn't going to work for long. He sent money when he could, she sent pictures when she knew where he was. Eventually . . ." Donnie shrugged.

Suzanne shook her head. All the years she had spent feeling invisible, trying to get her mother to really see her, holding on to a moment of direct eye contact like a life preserver, and it turns out it was Janice who saved her. "I used to think . . . maybe it would have been easier . . . if Mom had died, too, because she didn't seem to want to be here, anyway. I had no idea how close that came to happening." Suzanne wiped her eyes and looked over at Donnie. "I have never said that out loud."

Donnie nodded. "Gram did spend most of her time at the hospital, working or volunteering when her shift was over." He took his hand off the steering wheel for a moment to touch Suzanne's hand. "But I probably had different expectations than you did."

Suzanne snorted. "Yeah. That's the problem with expectations . . . no matter what you want from someone, they can't give you what they don't have."

"I'm sure Gram loved you." Donnie jumped in so fast he flushed, which made Suzanne smile.

"I know she loved me . . . in the way she could," Suzanne said. "But I learned to rely on myself. I never doubted that was a good thing; I just didn't know Janice made it possible."

Staring out the window as the fields flashed past, Suzanne kept thinking they should be stopped to a crawl in commute traffic, but this wasn't the Bay Area. The motion of the car and the warm air from the vents were irresistible in combination, and she nodded off just as dawn broke.

"Suzanne?" Donnie's voice woke her what felt like minutes after she'd fallen asleep. "I'm going to drive straight home and go out for groceries later, unless you need to pick something up right away."

Suzanne yawned and stretched. She did not feel rested, but had probably gotten a longer nap in the car than on the plane. "No, I'm okay."

"Good. I asked Patsy to wait until we got there. Mom's friends have been staying in shifts when she lets them." He sighed. "She didn't like the hospice worker because she didn't know who Joni Mitchell was and never knew any of the *Jeopardy* questions when they watched on TV." He shot Suzanne a meaningful look. "She yelled out wrong answers."

They were still laughing as they pulled into the driveway. The front yard cemetery was now covered in cobwebs and ravens perched on several of the headstones. Suzanne had to walk up to one to be sure it wasn't real, because it was life-sized and covered with feathers. She couldn't bring herself to look at the grave under the big tree by the street.

"It looks like the Halloween fairies have been here. I thought we were finished decorating when I left."

"I know. I put up a few more things, then Patsy and Muriel came by with extra cobwebs and Mark set up the fog machine so we wouldn't have to get dry ice." Donnie surveyed the yard. "We don't know where the birds came from. Or the flowers. People have been leaving them at night. First there was one raven, a few days later another. I think they're . . ." Donnie choked up and couldn't speak.

Suzanne reached out and took his hand. "Tributes?"

He nodded and wiped his eyes. She followed his gaze to the grave by the street, the one with Janice's name, and saw the flowers for the first time. Small potted violets, larger pots with mums, individual stems in vases or just laid on the false mound like a blanket. She took a deep ragged breath and squeezed Donnie's hand as they turned to walk inside.

Patsy was sitting at the kitchen table drinking coffee and doing the crossword in the morning paper. "Hey, Donnie. Suzanne. How was your trip?"

"Bumpy," Suzanne said.

Patsy gathered up her belongings and stood. "Janice is sleeping now, but it was a restless night. I think . . ." she broke off mid sentence. "Well, you have a good weekend now." She patted Suzanne on the arm and hugged Donnie on the way out.

They watched her go, neither able to muster more than a muttered "thanks" for the time she spent with Janice.

"There's something to be said for having your parents die when you're young—or at least die quickly," Suzanne said after Patsy's engine started.

Donnie smacked her in the arm.

"I'm just saying . . ." she gave him an exaggerated wounded look, arms outstretched and palms up. "How could we possibly thank someone else for sitting death watch, doing hospice duty—for our family? For *us*? What can we give or do or say to Patsy and Muriel and all the others that would even remotely make this up to them?"

"Okay," Donnie said. "I get that. Just . . . I don't know . . . don't be smug about parental death."

They both half-smiled and scanned the kitchen. Donnie handed his bag to Suzanne with a smirk. "You carry the bags upstairs and I'll make the Hy-Vee run while Mom's sleeping."

"You're on," Suzanne said. "But please buy some salad and fruit? And real coffee, please?"

"Snob."

"I have standards. It's not the same thing."

Suzanne followed his exit with her eyes, then carried both bags upstairs as quietly as possible. Her box from Janice was in the guest room along with the carry-on she left behind. She took Donnie's bag to Janice's room before walking in. Molly wasn't sleeping on the bed, but there was a hair-filled impression by the pillows where she had clearly spent much time. Suzanne walked over to the wall of photos and looked at each in turn, pausing at the one of Janice holding her as a child, before walking back downstairs.

Suzanne crept up to the couch, careful not to wake Janice. Molly was curled up at the end leaning against Janice's feet. She cracked one eye as Suzanne approached but did not react otherwise. In repose her sister was smooth and still, somewhere between marble and a sarcophagus with silvery spikes covering her head, her hair almost long enough now to be a hip punk cut. She seemed so at peace that Suzanne had to smile. And then she realized Janice's chest wasn't moving, nothing was moving! She vaulted the couch, causing Molly to bolt with a speed remarkable for a cat of her girth. Suzanne lifted Janice's neck with one hand while she pushed back on her forehead with the other. No, wait. Chest compressions-only was the new model. Suzanne placed her left hand on top of the right and clenched her fingers together, centering her locked outstretched arms over her sister's sternum. Before she could do the first compression, Janice gasped and sat bolt upright like something out of a horror film.

"What in the hell do you think you're doing?"

Suzanne jumped back and flapped her arms in the air, trying to maintain her balance as she fell over the coffee table.

"I thought . . ."

"You thought wrong. I'm breathing, okay?" Janice lay back down. "A little apnea, maybe, but even if I *had* stopped breathing, what part of DNR do you not understand?"

Janice's voice wasn't really loud enough to qualify as shouting, but it delivered the same impact. She glared at Suzanne with an intensity that animated her face, her eyes bright with emotion.

Suzanne's hands were still shaking from the adrenaline rush of finding her sister dead and trying to bring her back. She opened her mouth and closed it and huffed and finally shouted, "I thought the *N* was silent!" She could feel her heart racing and she focused on her breathing to control it. "It was instinct, not insolence."

Janice snorted and lay back down.

"What do you want me to say?" Suzanne stepped toward her. "Sorry I tried to save your life? Or sorry I can't really save your life and nobody else can, either?"

They glared at each other for a moment then Suzanne burst into tears, dropped to her knees, and buried her face in her sister's chest.

Suzanne felt Janice's fingers run down the back of her head.

"If I have to change this nightgown, I'm going to be really pissed."

Suzanne *snorked* and laughed and sat back on her heels, wiping her face and looking around for a tissue. She found a box behind the bottles of pills and piles of magazines on the coffee table and blew her nose.

"You really are the proverbial bad penny, aren't you? Are you going to tell me that your harvest is all done and your marriage is fixed and that's why you're back?"

Janice's voice was soft and trailed off at the end as if she had used up all her air. There was little left of her, she had melted down to a small frame that, even draped in flannel, bore an uncomfortable resemblance to some of the plastic occupants of the front graveyard. Suzanne was sure she could lift Janice and carry her in her arms like a child.

"If I thought I could say it with a straight face, I probably would, but I'm not that good a liar." Suzanne rose and went to sit in the chair by the window. The furniture still smelled of decades of stale smoke, but without the constantly refreshed haze that used to hang in the room, the air was tolerable without having the window open. "Half of this year's wine is in the barrel. All but the whole cluster should finish over the next week or so. My marriage can't be fixed because it isn't broken—it just doesn't exist anymore."

"Ah." Janice sat up to sip from a glass of water with a straw in it.

"If I waited to come back until my life was in order . . ."

"There wouldn't be any of mine left?" Janice finished for her.

Suzanne winced. "I was going to say, 'I'd never be back,' but yours works, too." She dropped her bantering tone. "Donnie said you only get up to go to the bathroom now. And you quit smoking."

Janice sighed. "That boy still has a big mouth. I'm surprised he left off drinking. And eating."

"What about them?" Suzanne tried not to sound alarmed.

"I don't do much of those, either. I don't need to make many trips to the bathroom."

Suzanne scanned the bottles on the table. "What about the pain?"

Janice shrugged. "It's kind of like high humidity or freezing cold.

After a couple weeks you readjust your definition of normal." She closed her eyes and opened them again with the slow-motion blink of a reptile. "I have this liquid morphine now," she gestured toward a small bottle with squeeze-bulb dropper. "It makes me sleepy," she fixed Suzanne with a look, "and apparently a bit too chatty sometimes, but it works better than anything else." She closed her eyes and sank back into the couch. "Speaking of sleepy . . . ." She lifted her hand in a vague gesture of dismissal. Suzanne rose and walked to the kitchen.

The clutter was gone, the ashtrays were empty and spotless. She leaned back out into the dining room and saw that the cleaning fairies appeared to have been there, too. The change was so dramatic Suzanne was surprised it hadn't registered the first time she walked through. There was definitely more missing than just clutter, some pictures from the walls, maybe a small table and a couple lamps, but she wasn't sure exactly what. She sat down at the kitchen table to wait for Donnie, then popped back up and opened the basement door. When she yanked the string on the light over the stairs, she could see that the neatly stacked boxes of wine were still there. Suzanne turned off the light, closed the door, and sat back down at the table. She let her eyes drift around the room from empty space to empty space, then picked up the bronze ashtray in the center of the table and held it like a mirror. The funhouse distortion wasn't flattering, but she did have more color than she was ever going to get naturally.

She dropped the ashtray and stood to make coffee. All her movements felt jerky and disconnected, as if her muscles were receiving mixed signals or some of the signals were being censored. She tried to make as little noise as possible getting out the filter, filling the reservoir, but when she knocked a spoon off the counter and could still hear Janice snoring softly in the living room despite the clanging bounce, she relaxed the effort.

Suzanne drank half a cup of coffee then dumped it in the sink. She didn't really need more coffee, didn't quite know what she needed. The house felt stripped of its personality, Janice's personality, not quite as if it were being staged, but close enough. Janice's goal of getting rid of as much as she could so Donnie wouldn't have to deal with it had obviously been met. It would be much easier for him to sell what he didn't want and put the house on the market. Suzanne was surprised by the sudden sting in her eyes at that thought. She hadn't been in her childhood home more than three or four times since she moved away, but the thought that she would never be able to go there again gave her emotional vertigo.

At the sound of popping gravel, Suzanne walked outside to help Donnie with the groceries. He turned from the back seat to hand her a bag.

"You look even worse than when I left."

Suzanne accepted the bag. "It's been a rough morning."

Donnie checked his watch. "I was only gone twenty minutes."

Suzanne shrugged and walked into the house with Donnie close behind. They set the bags on the table and began searching for the proper placement of each item as if working a jigsaw puzzle together.

"I tried to do CPR," Suzanne finally said.

Donnie was shaking his head before she got to the end of the story. "You're lucky she can't get up very fast or you'd be dead. She is so obsessed about not being taken to the hospital, she has a copy of the DNR under her pillow and another one nailed to the inside porch door like Martin Luther King."

Suzanne paused in front of the cupboard with a can of peaches in her hand. "What?" She frowned, trying to make sense of the image, then broke into a grin. "You mean Martin Luther?"

"Whatever!"

She started giggling. "I bet your mom won't let *you* play *Jeopardy* with her, either."

He threw a loaf of bread at her which she dodged and caught as it rebounded off the refrigerator. She squeezed it back into shape before putting it in the dented metal bread box.

"Anyway," Donnie continued as he folded his empty bag, "Mom is very serious about dying at home." He stuffed the bag between the refrigerator and the wall, then turned back to Suzanne. His blush telegraphed his statement. "I almost did it once, too. She threatened to change her will and made me get the phone so she could call her lawyer."

Suzanne handed Donnie her empty bag and watched him fold it and stash it with the other one as she leaned against the counter. "I can understand not wanting to die in a hospital, wanting to have control over *something* . . . but I guess I don't get how you could ever stop fighting and just give up."

"I don't think it's giving up so much as it's, well . . . letting go," Donnie said.

"Same thing."

"Not exactly. It's like the final stage of grieving. Acceptance." Donnie smiled. "Last week Mark called it 'embracing the inevitable.'"

"I don't know," Suzanne shook her head and frowned. "It seems like . . . if you know you don't have much time, every day, every hour, is more precious."

"It is precious, but for Mom it's not about how long she lives, it's about *how* she lives." Donnie scratched his head furiously with both hands, leaving tufts and whorls in the wake of his fingers. "And how she dies."

Suzanne smiled at the familiar gesture of discomfort.

"Do you remember how your dad died at all?" Donnie asked.

The medicinal scent of rubbing alcohol and overripe fruit washed over her as if she had stepped back into the hospital room with its buzzing, whirring insect swarm sound. She felt her nose wrinkle involuntarily. "Not really. I mostly have impressions, not memories."

"Well, Mom said he looked like he'd been abducted by the Borg. He was full of tubes with machines keeping his organs functioning, but he wasn't really there anymore."

Although she didn't remember it, Suzanne could picture it like in *The Next Generation*, a body no longer completely human connected by wires and lines to fluids and pumps and artificial support. Finally she nodded.

"Janice would kill herself before she would let that happen."

Donnie gave her a meaningful look and held it. "Yes. Yes, she would."

Suzanne blew out her breath in a long slow exhale. She understood him perfectly; Janice had been—was—prepared to prevent anyone from taking her to the hospital.

"She's pretty weak now . . . did she ask you . . . ?" Suzanne left the question hanging.

Donnie held up a hand and waved her off. "I can't talk about it. I just can't."

They stood on opposite sides of the kitchen staring at the floor.

"I need to check in at work," Donnie said suddenly.

"Yeah, me too."

Suzanne went outside to get a better signal on her phone while Donnie used the house phone upstairs. After punch down and press with Carlos and Ricardo the day before, she had written detailed notes and posted them on the fermenters. She decided to increase the percentage of new French oak barrels and to use one hundred percent new oak for the whole cluster wild yeast. Something in the scent even this early cried out for more vanilla and a little toast. Carlos had gone to check immediately to ensure they had the barrels they needed or to acquire what they lacked. When she reached him, he reported that he had the barrels they needed and all was well with the wine.

"Y tu, tambien?"

"Si, Miss Suzanne. Todo bien."

His voice sounded strong even though it was still raspy, and Suzanne feared her time with Janice had lowered her standard of what healthy sounded like. Her parting words were, "Gracias por ayudar, Carlos. Cuidado."

Suzanne ate a banana and a slice of cheese before going upstairs to nap. She felt heavy and slow and weirdly battered, as if she had spent hours doing something physically challenging. She dropped onto the bed and covered her eyes with one arm. Picking grapes, punching down the must during fermentation, walking the rows, pruning the vines, even packing and stacking cases of wine, all of them were easier than talking about her sister dying.

When she opened her eyes again, the room was dark. Suzanne sat up, cold and disoriented, not sure what hour or even day it was. She heard voices downstairs and checked the time on her phone. It was five o'clock. She had to look twice to see the p.m. She turned on the lamp by the bed and pulled out the sweater at the top of her bag. The conversation below was soft, but she could make out Donnie's voice and Janice's. As she passed the stairs on her way to the bathroom, she heard Mark's voice, too. She went back to the room to put on make-up and brush her hair before going downstairs, grinning like an idiot at her reflection. Suzanne looked past her own image in the mirror, then turned around to inspect the room. All the porcelain figures were gone, the geese with bows, the lace doilies all the little faux country knickknacks. The furniture remained along with the three photographs on the wall and Suzanne's luggage and box from Janice.

"Well, well, sleeping beauty awakes," Janice said as Suzanne stepped off the bottom stair.

"I'm not sure about the beauty part, but she does look a lot better than she did this morning," Donnie added. He was sitting on the couch beside Janice with the cat on his lap.

Suzanne held out her hands. "I'm right here, you know."

"Welcome back." Mark rose from his chair and crossed the room in two strides, taking Suzanne in his arms and holding her a little longer than required for a simple greeting. He smelled of musk and eucalyptus, and she turned her face into the back of his neck involuntarily.

"Get a room!" Janice said. She chuckled at her own joke, and the laugh became an uncontrollable hacking that shook her small frame. She doubled over, red-faced and gasping. Everyone else froze, waiting. Even Molly looked up from Donnie's lap. Janice finally inhaled a deep ragged breath and slumped sideways against the arm of the couch with one hand on her chest. With her regular breathing, the room was reanimated.

"Mom, have some water." Donnie grabbed the glass off the coffee table and held it out, dislodging the cat and dumping her to the floor.

Mark and Suzanne separated and went to the back and side of the couch, Suzanne sliding a pillow behind Janice's head while Mark adjusted her blanket.

Janice lifted the hand from her chest and waved them away. "Get the hell off me." She opened her mouth to say more, but stopped as if the effort were too much.

Suzanne and Donnie sat down, but Mark remained standing. "I have to go now." He took Janice's hand and squeezed it, gesturing at a pair of ceramic jars on the table. "Don't forget to use the oils."

"Yeah, yeah," Janice said. "Lavender and chamomile."

Mark turned to Suzanne. "I believe you owe me a dinner. How about I pick you up tomorrow at six?"

She smiled. "I'll be ready."

Janice shifted on the couch, scooting to the edge and bracing herself. "Wait. We'll walk you out."

"We will?" Donnie and Suzanne said at the same time.

"Don't look at me like that. I want to see the yard." She stood slowly, waving a bit as if in a breeze, and accepted the arm Mark held out to steady herself.

Suzanne started to object reflexively but stopped. She looked from Mark to Donnie and back again. Whatever Janice wanted, they ought to be able to make happen. Going outside really wasn't that much to ask.

"Maybe we should carry you," Donnie said.

Janice glared at him. "Or not."

"Wait. The computer chair," Suzanne said. She went to the dining room and wheeled the chair up beside Janice. "Sit."

"What's next? Rollover? Play dead?"

"Well it sure won't be 'speak'," Suzanne said as Mark guided Janice into the chair and wrapped her in a blanket.

Donnie pushed the chair while Mark and Suzanne walked on either side ready to catch Janice or stabilize the chair. "Front or back, do you think?" The question was directed at Mark and Suzanne, but Janice answered.

"Back."

Negotiating the back stairs nearly resulted in spilling Janice onto the ground when Suzanne missed the edge of a step. She scraped her ankle but managed to right the chair and not fall down. Before they began rolling her down the drive toward the front yard, Donnie checked Janice's balance and adjusted the seat back.

"There are some new things since you were outside last, Mom," he said. "It's become sort of a neighborhood effort."

Janice leaned back in the chair with her hands in her lap. "As long as they didn't screw it up."

Donnie exchanged a look with Suzanne and shrugged.

"We can take down anything you don't like," Mark said.

"Wait." Janice held up a hand.

They all stopped.

"The fog machine."

Donnie snapped his fingers. "Sorry. Be right back."

Suzanne shivered and crossed her arms. "Are you warm enough?" she asked Janice.

"I'm fine."

Donnie came bounding around the corner from the front of the house. "Ready."

They walked all the way to the end of the driveway before turning the chair back toward the house. Tendrils of smoke snaked between the

Sheila Scobba Banning **183**

tombstones and began to form a blanket across the ground so the skeletons nearest the porch looked like they were rising out of the fog. The bat lights outlining all the windows and door offered a kitschy counterpoint to the eerie cemetery. A dozen sets of tiny red eyes blinked off and on in the windows, under the porch, and in the nearly bare branches of the tree.

Suzanne jumped when a rat scurried from one tombstone to another in the middle of the yard. When she saw it go back again, she realized it was on a track, part of the decorations. She examined the whole yard more closely, marveling at the overcrowded but ingenious conglomeration. There were two more rats scuttling through the leaves, one from under the porch and back, the other along the roof. A pair of unblinking amber lights moved out from under the porch and continued toward them across the yard. Molly's tale appeared above the thickening fog bank as she walked over and rubbed against Janice's leg.

The ground spots highlighted the giant spiders in the cobwebs and cast long shadows from the ravens and skeletons. A boney finger stretched across the graves, pointing toward the street. The grave with Janice's tombstone was so brightly-lit it looked like an alien abduction scene. The potted plants clustered around the grave were lurid colors in the spotlight. The cut flowers had wilted into a pile of mulch with three red roses on top.

Janice began shaking so hard the chair creaked. She bent forward to cover her face, and Suzanne put a hand on her back. Donnie knelt beside the chair and touched her knee. Suzanne felt Mark move closer, then Donnie said, "Mom?"

Janice sat up and put her hands on Donnie's face. "Perfect!" she said. His expression changed from concern to amusement.

What Suzanne had taken for tears had been silent laughter. She smiled at Donnie, but when she looked at Janice's name and "any day now" carved into the Styrofoam marker, she had to look away.

Chapter 16

Legs:
the ring of clear liquid in a wine glass which, when the wine is swirled,
produces a sheet of continuous droplets; tears of wine

"What *is* this?" Suzanne spit a mouthful of what felt like paste with grit and tasted about the same back onto her fork.

Donnie and Janice both laughed until Janice's laughter evolved into a coughing jag. The familiarity of the effect rendered it no less scary, but Suzanne remained in her seat, watching and waiting. Donnie wiped his eyes, still chuckling, though he shifted to the edge of his chair, tensed to jump up.

"We call it Minnie's Mystery Casserole. We've had three different ones now, one she called tuna, one she called goulash, and this one is supposed to be ham," Donnie said.

Janice caught her breath and pushed the plate away. "I'd make fun of you now, but I'm not going to eat it, either. How about ice cream?"

Donnie got up from the kitchen table to fill his mother's request and returned with a larger bowl than Suzanne expected based on Janice's description of her appetite. Suzanne scraped her own plate into the garbage and got an apple and piece of cheese out of the refrigerator.

"You want anything?" she asked Donnie.

He was liberally dousing his plate of casserole with salt, pepper, and ketchup. "No, thanks. I'm good."

Suzanne shook her head and sat back down, pouring more wine for both of them. Janice had a beer open, but she hadn't done more than taste it. Suzanne and Donnie had exchanged a look when Janice wanted to sit in the kitchen for dinner. It would likely be a short meal. Suzanne watched Janice eat three big bites of ice cream with great enthusiasm, then put her spoon down and lean back. She was still sitting in the rolling desk chair, which she had decided was not only convenient, but fun. From the way Janice was beginning to list to the left, however, Suzanne wondered if it was time to wheel her back to the couch.

"I was hoping maybe tomorrow you could tell me about some of the things in the box of stuff you saved for me. I didn't have a chance to ask about them before I left," Suzanne said.

"You mean before you skipped town," Donnie interrupted.

Suzanne didn't rise to the bait. "It doesn't have to be tomorrow. Whenever you feel up to it."

Janice nodded. "Yeah. That would be fun."

She closed her eyes and didn't open them for so long, Suzanne thought she had dozed off. Janice's skin was translucent in a way that made it look like she was wearing blue-gray eye shadow. Her face tensed suddenly, everything squeezed together and she gripped the edge of the table. Donnie caught Suzanne's eye and gestured with his head toward the living room as he stood.

"I'll take you back for your meds now, okay, Mom?" He didn't wait for an answer before wheeling Janice away from the table.

Suzanne swirled the wine in her glass, a five-year-old Mermaid Tears that was more earthy than most of her wines, like eating berries and plums in a damp forest. She watched the legs rise on the inside of the glass then break and run back down as tears when she stopped spinning the stem. Janice was worse than Suzanne had expected, even factoring in the denial. She resented the rapid decline even as she was grateful Janice was still alive, a dissonant combination that left her emotionally unsettled. She listened to the murmur of voices in the living room.

Maybe the stage of grieving that followed denial and acceptance was greed. *I want as much time as I can possibly have, and I want it all now.* She took her wine and went upstairs to read Will's proposal, nodding to Donnie as she passed through the living room.

"I assume the *Star Trek* collection needs no explanation?" Janice asked.

She was propped up on the couch in a reclining position watching as Suzanne unloaded the box of mementos. Hours had passed, breakfast and lunch, before Janice had been ready to talk. Donnie had said that her energy seemed to peak at one and five—a.m. or p.m.—and Suzanne had watched and waited until she was ready.

"True, but where did you get the communicator boxes?"

Janice smiled. "EBay. That's the real reason I bought the set. I already had all three seasons recorded, but I couldn't resist the cases."

Suzanne opened one of the cases and flipped through the disks inside. "I stopped watching the reruns years ago, but I can still remember every episode."

"Maybe because you watched them every night for ten years?"

"Ha, ha." The postcard in Suzanne's childish hand had slipped down to the bottom of the box. Suzanne pulled it out. "Why didn't we come across this when we went through Mom's stuff after she died?" She handed the card to Janice who held it very close to her face and looked over the top of her glasses.

"It wasn't in Mom's stuff," Janice said flipping the card over to look at the picture, then back again. "It was in mine. No post mark, see?" She handed the beach scene back to Suzanne.

"You never mailed it?"

Janice shrugged. "Mom wasn't getting mail. I wasn't going to tell you that, so I just stuck it in the book I was reading and forgot about it. When I found it later, it reminded me of Donnie's dad, so I held onto it." The corners of her mouth twitched.

Suzanne looked at the perfect California beach sunset captured on the postcard. She didn't remember choosing this card for her mother, but it did not surprise her. How many sunsets had she watched from how many beaches since that first trip to the ocean? Dozens, even hundreds, maybe, but she still felt the same sense of wonder and stillness and awe when she watched the fiery orange disk slide beneath the horizon behind a pounding surf. Suzanne brushed her thumb across the picture, and she could smell the sea breeze and taste the brine on her lips. A longing seized her like a hand squeezing her heart, and she closed her eyes against welling tears.

"Are you okay?" Janice asked.

Suzanne took a deep breath. "I think that's my line." She put down the postcard and picked up the wine glass from her wedding. "This might be the last one of these in existence." She turned the glass in the light from the window, reading the inscription before putting it down. "I'm glad you saved it."

Janice shifted her weight on the couch, pushing up a little to lean more against the back than the arm. "Have you unloaded that deadweight yet?"

Suzanne offered a half-smile, but didn't laugh. "I'm not sure he's the one being unloaded, but yeah, I'm working on it."

They sat together in silence for a long time, until Suzanne spoke again.

"Will's plans to expand the business aren't as bad as I had assumed." She hesitated. "I didn't even read them before."

"But is it what you want?"

"No. But it isn't completely unthinkable," Suzanne said. "And things have gotten . . . complicated. Maybe it isn't always about what I want."

"Since when?" Janice's voice had an edge Suzanne hadn't heard since the last visit. "What you want is the only thing that mattered pretty much since the day you were born."

"What do you mean?"

"You were spoiled."

"Spoiled?" Suzanne heard her voice rise and didn't bother lowering it. "I started working when I was fifteen and walked beans before that. I cooked my own meals, practically raised myself—how is that spoiled?"

"It wasn't what you did, it was your attitude. Like you were born with expectations other people didn't have." Janice paused and took a deep breath. "Not that that's a bad thing. But it made you dissatisfied, always looking to what was ahead." Janice picked up a ceramic jar and rubbed a little lavender oil from it onto the base of her throat and across her forehead. "Sometimes you missed the things right in front of you."

Suzanne caught the reference to Mark and blushed. "What, there's no place like home? I didn't miss as much as you think. I just made different choices than you."

"How's that working out for you?"

Suzanne pressed her lips together even as she felt her hands clench in her lap. She turned and reached into the box, wondering what it said about her that she wanted to slap a dying woman. She opened the box of trinkets with the peacock feather hair clip on top. "Maybe we should do this later."

"I've got about ten more minutes," Janice said. "Let's not waste it."

Ten more minutes of functional energy. Ten more minutes on the doomsday clock of her life. Suzanne took a deep breath and let it out. She pulled out the peacock feather. "I remember this. Sort of."

Janice leaned back into the couch and smiled. "You should. You wore it every day for months. "Tommy brought that for you when he came to stay with us."

"Tommy?" Suzanne frowned. "Donnie's father?"

Janice nodded. "There's a picture of the two of you in the little album."

Suzanne put down the box and opened the photo collection. There weren't very many, small versions of the black and white pictures on the wall in her room, probably the originals, a faded color Polaroid of

Suzanne and Janice at the beach, a stiff-looking pose of Suzanne and her mother at high school graduation, and a photo of the young Suzanne with the peacock feather in her hair sitting on the lap of a man who looked like Donnie with long curly hair.

"That's . . . weird."

Janice chuckled. "Yeah, the resemblance is pretty amazing. Imagine how I felt about ten years ago."

"Maybe Donnie should have this." Suzanne found it hard to stop staring at the strange photo.

"I gave him others. You can make him a copy if you want." Janice's voice began to trail off and her face pinched around the edges.

Suzanne looked at the rocks and shells and sparkly bits in the trinket box and decided they could wait. "Why didn't you go back to California. Later, I mean."

Janice reached for the bottle of morphine on the table and squeezed a drop onto her tongue. "I couldn't wait to get away . . . until I did. That summer you would watch the tide come in like it was the best movie ever made . . . Hours . . . I knew right then you were already gone. I was surprised you stuck around as long as you did." Her eyes closed and the tension drained from her face as her movements slowed down. "Turned out, that wasn't . . . me . . . I only needed . . . books . . . or . . ." she lifted a hand as if it were very heavy and dropped it to her chest.

Suzanne packed everything back into the box. "No place like home," she whispered. She picked up the box then put it back down on the chair by the window, thinking there was more to talk about and might be another opportunity. She checked her phone and walked outside, listening to the number at the winery ring until the machine picked up. The same thing happened with Carlos's cell phone. Frowning, she shuffled up and down the driveway beside the front yard cemetery, kicking the fallen leaves as she went. It was crisp but nice, a temperature that made Suzanne smell roasted apples and cinnamon even when they weren't there.

There were a lot of perfectly reasonable explanations for no one getting the winery phone, and there were even a few for Carlos not picking up his cell phone, but there weren't many that covered both for most of a day. Suzanne dialed again.

"Are you still here or are you gone?" Craig answered the phone without a greeting.

"Gone," Suzanne said. "I left yesterday."

Craig hesitated. "How are things there?"

"Good . . . but really bad, if you know what I mean. Coming back was definitely the right decision. But Craig? I need a favor."

"Oh, no! I am not getting sucked into another crazy scheme! This is not 1-800-arsonist! You know I love you, but I don't think my heart could take another one of your 'favors'—I mean, are you trying to kill me?"

Suzanne waited for the tirade to wind down, then said, "I was just going to ask you to go pick up something at the house and mail it to my dying sister, but if that's too much to ask . . . ."

"Oh, my god! You are just shameless. You know that, right?" Craig heaved a dramatic sigh. "Fine. What is it? And I'm still excluding arson. And murder. And anything else that involves handcuffs that aren't lined with velvet."

"I think I can guarantee all those things." Suzanne watched the FedEx truck approach the house and come to a stop in front. "Seriously, I do want you to go to the house, but I just need you to check in. I can't reach Carlos at any number." She could hear the FedEx man whistling as he checked his clipboard then walked into the back of the truck.

"Isn't this a little early to panic?" Craig asked.

The FedEx man walked out of the truck and up the drive carrying a long box.

"I'm not panicking. If I were panicking, I would have called the police."

"And you know the police, and I, sir, am not the police?"

Suzanne smiled. The Fed Ex man thought it was meant for him and waved. "Something like that. I just . . . need to know." The FedEx man waited patiently for her to finish.

"Okay. I should be able to drive down there this afternoon," Craig said. "Is he staying at the house?"

"I think so. This may be nothing, but it's out of character for Carlos. And Craig?" Suzanne said. "Thanks. I owe you again."

"And you know I'm keeping score."

Suzanne ended the call and gave her attention to the FedEx man. "Janice is sleeping, but I can sign for that."

"Oh, it's not for her, Miss Mathews. It's another one for you. You get a lot of deliveries for somebody that doesn't even live here. You must be awfully popular." He grinned and held the electronic signature device out to her.

Suzanne accepted the oblong box from him, frowning as she walked back into the house. She put it down on the kitchen table and examined the return label. It was a florist she didn't recognize in Chicago. "Chicago?" she muttered as she searched the junk drawer for scissors and opened the box. The perfume was overwhelming; rose, lily, and gardenia. The box was filled with long-stemmed red roses and white lilies with gardenia blossoms scattered across the top. She smiled. Mark always had been one for the big romantic gesture, but this seemed over the top. A gold envelope in crisp velum lay on top of the flowers. The perfume concentrated in the box was almost nauseating in its intensity, and Suzanne felt a little lightheaded as she opened the envelope, imagining the gardenias and rose petals scattered across a bed, their fragrance released as they were crushed . . . the daydream dissolved abruptly when she read the card.

Trevor Constantine.

Suzanne looked over her shoulder involuntarily, as if he might be grinning smugly at her from the back porch.

"What smells like a French whorehouse?" Donnie said as he walked into the kitchen. When Suzanne didn't respond, he added, "Those from Mark?"

"I wish." Suzanne slid the card back into the envelope slowly as if it might explode if she didn't do it just right. She started to put it back on the flowers, then stopped. "And how would you know what a French whorehouse smells like? You sound just like your mom."

Donnie looked stricken. "God forbid! But seriously, what's the story?"

Suzanne shoved the card into her back pocket. "When I figure that out, I'll let you know." Seeing Donnie's perplexed frown, she added, "The flowers aren't a declaration of love, they're a demonstration of power. From the guy who wants to be my business partner."

Donnie looked from Suzanne to the flowers and back again. "I'm not sure whether that's a good thing or a bad thing."

Suzanne picked up a gardenia and examined it. "You and me, both."

"What really galls me is that it's such a heavy-handed peeing on all the trees sort of gesture." Suzanne made no effort to stifle her rising voice, but when she paused mid-rant to take a sip of wine, she caught Mark's expression of barely repressed laughter and glanced at the nearby tables. She smiled and shrugged an apology at the couple beside them, then took a deep breath and picked up the gold envelope from the table. "This is not good wishes, it's a threat."

Mark didn't say anything but watched her intently as she talked. His focused stillness made her stop, too, and for a moment she just looked into his eyes. Suzanne felt comfortable with Mark, but it went beyond the familiarity of an old friend and lover. There was something more that she couldn't quite name, a certainty he didn't have before. It wasn't confidence so much as it was presence, as if he were exactly where he wanted to be all the time. Suzanne smoothed the skirt of her dress with the hand in her lap. She could feel the ridge of the garter and the lace at the top of her stockings through the silk. Suzanne had packed this dress, the bluish gray of a stormy sky, because it drew compliments from strangers every time she wore it. She had rifled through her lingerie drawer for something that would look good without the dress. Just in case.

Suzanne shook the envelope at him. "You know what?" She grinned and took the envelope in both hands. "I don't negotiate with terrorists." She tore the card into four pieces and dumped them on the table, then lifted her glass and touched it to Mark's. "Let's talk about something else. Like you, maybe?"

Mark toasted with her and shook his head. "My life doesn't have quite the level of drama yours does."

Suzanne thought about the last few weeks. "You have no idea. And that's a good thing." She paused and leaned back as the waitress appeared with soup and salad. "This is good." The soup had been described as homemade, but the complex flavor surprised her.

"There are a few people in the world besides Thomas Keller who know how to cook," Mark said.

"If Thomas Keller were my standard for every meal, I'd starve. Or live in poverty," Suzanne said between spoonfuls of soup. "And what do you know from Thomas Keller, anyway?"

Mark smiled. "This may still look like the middle of nowhere, but the internet goes everywhere. And so do planes. I took my daughter to New York when she graduated from Carleton. We had dinner at Per Se."

"Lucky girl." Suzanne pushed her empty bowl aside and leaned forward. "Could I . . . ask what happened to your marriage?"

Mark looked past Suzanne as if searching for the answer on the wall behind her, then met her eyes again and shrugged. "Probably something like what happened to yours. Or maybe nothing like it. I think the tipping point was when Julie left home for college. Karen wanted to travel, go on cruises, do things. I didn't want to leave Mom alone for long stretches. She started going away on her own, and eventually . . ." His voice trailed off.

"I'm sorry you had to go through that."

"I'm sorry you have to."

Suzanne raised her glass to Mark. "Maybe your life doesn't have drama, but you have your own business and a grown daughter somewhere. You took care of your dying mother and now my sister. Those things all sound pretty significant to me." She thought about Mark rearranging his life to move back near his mother, knowing it was something she could never have done. Would never do. "Daunting, even."

Mark poured more wine in Suzanne's glass, then in his own. "When I first started going to grief therapy, I was overwhelmed. Death is so big and we are so powerless . . . but I learned that when you can't change the big things, the little things matter even more." He reached out and covered her hand with his. "Maybe nobody can change the world, but everybody can change one life."

Before Suzanne could respond, UB40 started singing "Red Red Wine" from her purse. She pulled her hand away and reached for the phone. It was Craig. "I'm sorry, I have to take this. Start without me." She squeezed Mark's hand and walked outside as she answered the phone.

"Do you want the good news first or the bad news?" Craig asked.

Suzanne paced in front of the restaurant, holding down the front of her dress with her free hand as the wind caught her hem. "Start with where Carlos is."

"The hospital."

Suzanne stopped pacing. "What? Why? The pneumonia? He said he had drugs and was getting better."

"It took me awhile to piece this together, and I can't swear it's accurate. Ricardo's English cuts in and out when he's worked up and my Spanish sucks under the best of circumstances, but here's what I got: Carlos collapsed and his wife took him to the doctor. He has pneumonia or bronchitis, or maybe both, and his oxygen was so low they admitted him immediately. He called Ricardo—this is where it gets more confusing—and I think threatened to fire him if he told you. Or something like that."

Suzanne sat down on the bench by the entrance and covered her face. "And the wine?"

"Well, that's the good news! Sort of." Craig's voice became harder to hear, as if he had walked into a tunnel and started whispering. "Ricardo and Hector were pressing wine out of one of the big plastic things when I got here. He seemed really happy when he showed me the barrel they just filled, but he was still pretty nervous."

Suzanne waited for more, shivering at the sudden gust of wind. She should have grabbed her wrap on the way out. "Craig?"

"Sorry." His voice was back to normal. I needed to walk away from the barrel room. Suzanne? I saw a sleeping bag and backpack up against the outside of the building. I think Ricardo is sleeping next to the fermenters."

Suzanne ran her hand through her hair, and the wind blew her skirt up high enough that she saw the tops of her stockings. She clamped the dress back down, grateful for the lack of traffic. Carlos was protecting her, wanting to spare her trouble while she was with her dying sister. Ricardo wasn't ready, and he was scared. And she was . . . weirdly calm.

"Okay."

"Okay? That's it? Okay?" Craig's outrage made Suzanne burst out laughing.

"Sorry. I mean thanks. And yes, it is bizarre, and I will take care of it." Suzanne brushed the hair off her face in a quick gesture that didn't leave her hemline time to fly up again. "Should I give Ricardo a key at least?"

"No. He wouldn't use it anyway." Suzanne heard the door open and turned toward it. Mark popped his head out and she held up her index finger to tell him she was almost done. His eyebrows rose when her unattended dress fluttered, but she caught it and smiled. "How about this. Before you go, tell Ricardo that when you talk to me next, you will tell me what a good job he's doing."

"And that will get you what, exactly?" Craig asked.

"It might not get me anything, but it might let him get some sleep tonight. Tomorrow I'll have a plan."

Suzanne sat down before Mark had a chance to get up and dropped her phone into her purse. "Sorry."

Mark gestured toward his half-eaten pork chop. "I've been busy."

The prime rib she had ordered was perfectly cooked, red through the center with a thin rim of brown. She took a bite and chewed, salt and paprika and hints of garlic.

"Is everything okay?" Mark asked.

"Not exactly," Suzanne said. She took another bite, then pushed her plate away and picked up her wine glass. She picked up the pieces of the card from Constantine and stuffed them into her purse. "But desperate times, desperate measures." She shivered, still chilled from being outside, and reached for the pashmina on the back of her chair.

"What were you thinking, sitting out in the wind for so long?"

"I was thinking I wished I had worn underwear."

Mark opened his mouth then closed it again without saying anything. Suzanne looked at him and smiled.

"I'm not very hungry," she said. "Maybe we can take this with us?"

Mark held up his hand and said, "Check!"

The drive back to his house was a matter of minutes, one definite advantage of a small town. Suzanne barely had time to undo the top two buttons of his shirt before the car stopped. She ran her tongue across the bottom of his earlobe one more time before releasing it from her teeth. "Hurry," she said into the side of his neck. They couldn't stop touching each other as Mark fumbled with the keys, and they practically fell through the door. Once inside, Suzanne was in his arms, up against him, arms around his neck. Their kissing was urgent but not rushed; Mark's hands ran down her back and up again, then he grazed her nipple as his right hand moved to lift her skirt. He brushed his fingers across the top of her stocking and continued up her thigh.

"You weren't kidding about the underwear."

Her response was something between a laugh and a whimper as he slid his fingers inside her. She managed to unbuckle his belt, but her hands were shaking so hard she couldn't get the pants unfastened. Mark laughed.

"Wait; wait," he said and took over the task with practiced hands.

Suzanne reached back to unzip her dress. She stepped out of it, then lowered Mark's pants and boxers carefully over his erection and down to the ground.

"I think we've both waited long enough."

Chapter 17

Sediment:
the solid material which collects at the bottom of a wine bottle, the lees

Suzanne awoke from a dream of the ocean tasting salt. She licked her lips and stretched and opened her eyes. Mark shifted beside her and reflexively tightened the arm draped over her. The room grew bright then dark again, shifting patterns of light and shadow that meant big clouds moving fast. She stared up at the ceiling watching scenes from the night before like a movie. After the first time just inside the door, they had moved upstairs to the bedroom. There had been a lot of talking and playful exploration until Mark was ready again, and then there wasn't much they didn't do. Except sleep. Suzanne glanced over at the chair beside the bed with Mark's shirt draped over it. She was pretty sure she had been draped over that chair in about the same position at one point, but the memory was more tactile than visual.

Mark's breathing shifted as he rolled over onto his side and pulled her to him. "Good morning."

Suzanne nestled into him, smiling, and said, "Is that for me, or is that just your usual Sunday morning wake-up call?"

He laughed. "A little of both."

"I'll wait," Suzanne said as he slid out from under the comforter and walked into the bathroom. When he returned, she rose to her knees, arms outstretched, to pull him onto the bed. She ran the tip of her tongue across the hollow of his throat then down the center of his chest to his navel. He tried to pull her up into an embrace, but she caught his hands with hers and lifted her head.

"I want to taste you again before I go."

Mark freed one of his hands and stroked her hair. "Your appetite is more . . . enthusiastic than most."

Suzanne released his other hand so she could continue to touch him while she talked. "Maybe other people don't have my palate." She began a new trail down from his navel, making side excursions up and down his thighs with her lips and tongue while her fingertips worked independently.

Mark started to reply just as Suzanne took him slowly into her mouth, and then neither could speak until they were finished.

"Um . . ," Mark began when he found his voice again. "I was about to say something about your palate, but I can't remember what anymore."

Suzanne giggled. "Well, then, my work here is done." She snuggled beside him and closed her eyes. After some immeasurable time passed she said, "I really do have to go."

"Can't you stay for breakfast?"

"I thought I just did."

They both laughed and Mark said, "But that wasn't pancakes and eggs."

"No . . ," Suzanne frowned, thinking, "more like scallop mousse."

Mark looked something between amused and disgusted. "I've never had scallop mousse, and now I sincerely hope I never do."

Suzanne kissed him once more before climbing out of bed. "Trust me; it's very good."

"I'll stop by later to check on Janice," Mark said.

"I'll be there. I have a lot of work to do." Suzanne finished dressing and gestured for Mark not to get up. When he ignored her, she leaned into him as he opened his arms.

"Are you leaving?"

Suzanne frowned. "Well, yeah, I just told you . . ." she caught something in his eyes, "oh, you mean going back. Really leaving."

He brushed a hair off her cheek and shook his head. "Sorry. That sounded kind of needy, didn't it?"

"It's okay," Suzanne said. "I'm glad you want me to stay." She pressed her palm to his chest and could feel his heartbeat. "I'm staying as long as Janice is alive. Anything I can't take care of from here, I'm going to have to deal with when I get back." She kissed him good-bye. "Don't worry. I have a plan."

Donnie waggled his eyebrows at her when she walked into the kitchen. He was working on his laptop and drinking coffee.

"I'd ask if you got up early to go to church, but since that's the same dress you wore to dinner last night, I'm guessing no."

Suzanne backhanded his shoulder without replying on her way past. She took a cup from the cupboard and poured some coffee.

"How's Janice today?"

Donnie rubbed his eyes and scratched his head. "The same. A little quieter. Horrible. I don't know . . . what can I say? She's been sleeping even more. I think she's upped the morphine."

Suzanne sat down, resting a hand on his forearm and leaning in. "Has she been up?"

"Not since yesterday. No food or water, either." He closed his laptop.

The silence stretched to long minutes. Suzanne felt the shift in the atmosphere of the house the way she felt bud break coming on. Subtle changes in the light and wind, minor variations in the tone of conversation, subliminal indicators that a passage had been made.

"I need to make some calls." Suzanne saw the panic in Donnie's eyes and added, "I'm not leaving, okay?"

He blushed and said, "Hey, did I say anything?"

Suzanne smiled and stood to go. "No, it's just a theme today." She paused at the end of the couch to watch Janice breathe. The cat looked up as she approached, then squeezed her eyes shut again, the perfect furry counterpart to Janice's deep stillness. Suzanne wasn't sure sleep was the correct term for Janice's state, maybe something more like stasis. The longer Suzanne watched, the smaller and paler Janice seemed, as if she were watching a Polaroid photograph developing in reverse. Suzanne took a deep breath and let it out slowly, then she went upstairs, changed into jeans and a short-sleeved shirt, and went outside with her phone.

The day was oddly warm and humid in sharp contrast to the chill wind of the night before. The big cumulus clouds had stopped hurtling across the sky and now hung, tinged with gray, like a painted backdrop. If it weren't October, she would say it was tornado weather. She strolled through the pseudo-cemetery front yard as she dialed, careful not to step on the wires and track for the mobile rats along the way.

"Suzanne?"

Suzanne silently cursed caller ID. "Yes, Laura. Don't hang up."

"Why would I hang up?"

Suzanne smiled at Laura's genuinely perplexed tone. "Thank you for that." She hesitated, paced the sidewalk between the headstones, then said, "I need to talk to Will. Is he there?"

"But . . . ."

"I know what I'm doing. It's important."

There was no response for so long, Suzanne finally said, "Hello?"

"I'm getting him. I just . . . I don't want . . ." Laura clearly knew the risk Suzanne was taking, knew she would have a part in it if she gave Will the phone.

"If you want, I'll call back so you don't have to answer the phone."

Laura burst out laughing. "Okay, you're right. This isn't eighth grade. I'm getting Will now. And Suzanne? It's really good to hear your voice."

Suzanne felt a wave of warmth wash over her, the sort of virtual hug that comes from only those few people who truly know you. She heard all the questions and sympathy and support without any of the words. By the time Will came on the line, she was almost smiling.

"I thought you were the one who wanted a restraining order."

She strained to hear nuances in his voice that might guide her words, but the tone was even and controlled. "I know this is a violation of the restraining order against me, and if you want to press charges, you would be well within your rights, but as soon as I get off the phone, I am going to e-mail my lawyer to drop the restraining order against you. I'll copy you on it so you know it's done. I'm also going to call her and send a notarized hard copy."

"What are you trying to do?"

This time there was no mistaking the suspicion in his voice.

Suzanne stopped pacing and looked up at the crows in the tree. "Carlos is in the hospital, and I can't come back. You need to supervise the rest of press."

"Carlos is in the hospital?" Will asked. "Wait, you want me at the vineyard? You want *me* in charge?"

"You're the only one who cares about it as much as I do." Suzanne took a deep breath. "It's your wine, too." After she said it, she knew she meant it, at least a little, and smiled.

Will was silent for a long time.

"Janice is much worse. She may have only . . ." Suzanne's voice caught. "It may not be long, but the wine has its own timeline."

"I'm sorry, Suzanne."

She could hear the decision in his voice, knew he would go. "Ricardo knows what he's doing, but the pressure of being in charge is too much for him. Carlos told him not to bother me."

Will laughed. "That sounds like him. I'll drive down right away. And I will call you if anything seems off. I'll contact my attorney about the restraining order, too."

Suzanne followed the path through the headstones to the front porch and sat down. She felt a little twinge when Will said he would call, but resisted the urge to say she'd heard that before. She needed him to finish press, and she needed him to do it right. "I read your proposal."

"I wish you had done that a year ago." His voice was quiet.

"Yeah. Me, too." Suzanne watched dark clouds gathering on the horizon like an angry mob. She could smell the ozone of the coming storm and it felt like August instead of October. "Will, I have to tell you something." She hesitated, then launched into the story before she could change her mind. "Constantine came to see me. He offered to buy you out."

"What are you talking about? Is this some kind of joke? I just saw him yesterday."

The intensity in his voice gave Suzanne a moment of panic. "I'm not kidding. And I'm not trying to screw up your investor plan. He wants my answer tomorrow."

"Then why are you telling me now?"

Will's voice sounded like it was coming through clenched teeth. *Why indeed*, Suzanne thought. "Because I just crossed a legal line and asked you to violate the same order. Because when I don't call Constantine tomorrow he's going to tell you exactly how to get even more than what you want."

Suzanne sighed and ran her free hand through her hair. She looked across the cemetery to the grave under the tree. The giant vase of flowers she'd added yesterday stood like a beacon. She could almost smell the gardenias she'd scattered from where she was sitting. It had seemed like the perfect use of Constantine's delivery. "I can't fight about this now. I'm not sure I want to fight at all anymore."

After a long pause, Will finally asked, "Trevor offered to cut me out?"

"I'm sorry, Will."

"Why are you turning him down?"

His voice was still tight, but the anger had drained away. There was an edge of something, though, maybe caution or calculation, she couldn't quite tell. Suzanne knew she was walking a fine line. "I can't say it wasn't tempting . . . but the easiest thing isn't always the best. I know you don't see him the same way I do, but I don't trust him."

"And you do trust me?" Will asked.

"I told you because I want you to trust me."

Will blew out his breath. "I don't know what I think right now. I don't know what I'm going to think. I'll head down to the winery and focus on getting all the wine into barrel."

"Maybe remind Ricardo about topping off last year's barrels?" Suzanne said.

"Sure," Will said. "And Suzanne? Thanks for telling me about Trevor. I have a meeting with him tomorrow."

Suzanne left messages for both of her lawyers as soon as she ended the call with Will, then went inside to type up the confirmation letter and send it out. She wasn't really sure if that was all it took, but it would have to do until the legal experts weighed in. She also felt a pang of buyer's remorse at tipping her hand to Will and giving up her one chance of resolving the property dissolution quickly and cleanly. But what she had told Will about Constantine was true. She didn't trust him, and she wasn't going to invite him into the winery.

Even though she knew her life was still in chaos, her divorce was nowhere near resolved, she'd started a romance she was going to abandon in a matter of weeks if not days, and her only sister wouldn't last even that long, Suzanne felt more certain than she had in quite awhile. She wished she could say the calm descended after she'd been with Mark, but she knew the reality was that it was the flower delivery that started the cascade of her decision making, maybe even just the choice to go back to Iowa.

Suzanne walked into the living room and perched on the arm of the couch watching Janice sleep. There was so little left of her, the cat seemed more substantial. Molly opened her eyes to small slits, yawned and stretched, then curled back into a ball with one white paw over her mustache. With each decision Suzanne made, each step down a path—any path, really—she regained her balance. She had been drowning in her own inertia, stuck like a fermentation ended too soon, and it felt good to be back in control. For as long as she could remember, Suzanne had been able to spin the worst case scenario for any situation, and by imagining and preparing for it, avoid it. On those few occasions where the worst case actually happened, well, at least she was prepared.

Looking down at Janice, Suzanne had a flash of their father looking nearly as frail lying in a hospital bed, surrounded not with purring cats and lavender lotion and hand-knit afghans, but tubes and beeping monitors and the stench of disinfected death. Donnie had said Janice's memory of those last weeks in the hospital was so vivid she would do anything to avoid ending up the same way. Suzanne had to wonder if her own vague memories were the source of her gift for preparing.

"What about the motorized rats? Take them in or just cover the electronics?" Suzanne yelled across the yard to where Donnie was storing the fog machine under the front porch. The muggy calm of the afternoon had taken a dramatic turn at sunset as the threatening clouds blew into a full-fledged storm with lightning flashing and the thunder getting closer. The rain hadn't started, but the wind had knocked over the vase of Constantine's flowers and scattered many of the tribute stems all over the yard. Suzanne was weighting down the corners of the garbage bag she had draped over Janice's headstone as she kept a stash of bags for the other pieces clamped under her arm.

"I don't know . . . just cover them!" Donnie yelled back.

As they rushed to protect the decorations, a crow flew out of the tree and smashed into the window of the front door. There didn't seem to be any damage, but the crack of impact was like a clap of thunder. With the next flash, Suzanne involuntarily counted the seconds until the following crack as the bolt made contact. She barely made it to two.

"Let's go!"

They ran to the kitchen door, not quite making it before the torrential downpour began without any preliminary sprinkles. Suzanne shoved Donnie through the door and nearly took off his shoe in the rush to get inside.

"Well, that wasn't so bad," Donnie said, wiping water off his face.

"Did you hear that?" Suzanne said. She walked into the living room and Donnie followed.

"Mom? Did you say something?"

Both Suzanne and Donnie leaned close to Janice to hear her.

"I said, if you two idiots are through throwing rocks at the house I could use some water."

Donnie looked at Suzanne. "I'll get it."

"We weren't throwing rocks;" Suzanne said, raising her voice over the din of the rain on the roof, "that was a crow. We were covering the graveyard with plastic."

Janice smiled wanly and shook her head. "Plastic-coated Styrofoam."

"We just don't want to have to set all that crap up again," Suzanne said. "You're such a prima donna."

Janice laughed until she wheezed softly. Even her volume had been reduced.

The lightning flashes and bangs of thunder were coming so fast as the storm passed directly over them, it felt like they were surrounded by exploding strobe lights. Donnie held out a glass of water with a straw just as the power cut off. The eerie silence of mute appliances filled the spaces between thunder bombs. Donnie groped his way to the kitchen and came back with a lighted candle on a big base which he settled on the coffee table between the lavender pot and the morphine. He wedged himself between the couch and the coffee table sitting on the floor, and Suzanne sat down at the other corner so it looked like the three of them were huddled around a campfire.

"Remember the time Mom was at work and we sat in the basement during the tornado?" Suzanne asked.

A slow smile spread across Janice's face. "I was just thinking the same thing."

"We tried to play 'I Spy' even though we couldn't see anything and Donnie cried when you wouldn't let him touch the candle flame."

"Now you can't stop me!" Donnie held his hand over the candle flame and Suzanne slapped it.

"Infant!"

"And you pretended not to be scared so he wouldn't be." Janice continued softly to herself, ignoring the interruption.

Suzanne reached over and took her hand. "And you pretended not to be scared for me."

"That's a lot of pretending," Donnie said. "Sounds like I was the only one with an appropriate emotional response; clearly crying was the right thing to do."

They all laughed softly, then sat listening to the slowing rain as the thunder rumbled away into the distance. Janice gestured for the morphine and Donnie gave her a dose. The back door slamming open made both Suzanne and Donnie jump.

"Hello!" Mark called.

There were wild circles of a flashlight as he opened and closed the door, then the spot moved toward them through the dining room. Suzanne's eyes had adjusted to the dark enough that she could see him even across the room. She jumped up to embrace him as he approached.

"This looks cozy," he said. He bent to brush back Janice's hair and stroke the back of her hand. "I just wanted to be sure you have lights, but I can see everything's under control."

Janice smiled, but closed her eyes again, sinking back into the heavy sleep that was her usual state now.

The house shuddered and a low hum rose like a mechanical Gregorian chant as all the lights and appliances kicked back into operating mode. For an instant the noise was incredibly loud, then it faded back into the white background that surrounded them every day, unheard. Mark,

Suzanne, and Donnie walked out to the kitchen together as if by mutual agreement.

"How much time was she awake today?" Mark asked.

Donnie shook his head and looked at Suzanne. "What, maybe two or three hours in little chunks?"

She nodded. "That sounds about right." The next question should have been "why?" but she didn't want to know.

Mark pulled Suzanne to him and talked over her head toward Donnie. "Did she eat or drink anything today?"

"Just water and a little broth. Very little."

Suzanne could feel Mark nodding, but didn't look up.

"You should prepare yourselves." Mark's voice was low and soothing, not heavy with emotion but strangely light.

Suzanne pushed back off his chest and looked at his face. There was pain in his eyes, and something else, but he was smiling. "But it's almost Halloween."

Mark brushed her hair behind her ear and left his hand resting on her shoulder. "What comes next is going to be a gift. Not just for Janice, but for you, too, if you let it."

Donnie was nearly purple, tears spilling down his cheeks, but when his eyes met Suzanne's, she didn't see panic. Something had shifted for him, or maybe it was just hearing the voice of experience. She turned to Mark, "Will you stay with us?"

"I would be honored," he said.

Chapter 18

Racking:
siphoning the wine off the lees into a new, clean barrel
to allow clarification and aid in stabilization

Suzanne squinted against the bright morning sun and watched Janice closely for movement. Her breath was so shallow, her respiration so soft, it was several minutes before Suzanne was certain her sister was still alive. She yawned and stretched, then stood to work the kinks out of her neck and back from sleeping in a chair. Donnie was snoring softly beside the couch, and the sound of running water in the kitchen had to be Mark.

They hadn't really discussed sleeping in the living room or sitting vigil in shifts or made any plans at all. Donnie had simply gone upstairs and brought down a stack of blankets and pillows and offered them around. Mark told them about his mother's final hours, shared a few stories from the cancer group, and then they sat quietly watchful, dozing and waking, dozing and waking with little more said for the night.

Suzanne walked to the front door to look out at the yard. The porch blocked some of the view, but she could see they had their work cut out for them reconstructing the graves and accessories. It was Monday. Monday of the deadline she'd decided to blow off. Monday forty-eight hours before Halloween. Monday with a quarter of her best pinot noir still fermenting, going through press with Will in charge. Monday,

Monday, definitely a day she couldn't trust no matter how strangely calm she felt. She smelled coffee and went to join Mark in the kitchen.

"Good morning, gorgeous!"

The expression in his eyes, delight with a hint of longing, made Suzanne almost believe he meant the greeting. "I slept in a chair, haven't brushed my teeth, and haven't seen a mirror any time recently. I think you're biased."

"Maybe I am." Mark pulled her to him and kissed her, softly at first, then with increasing passion. He started to pull away, but Suzanne pulled him in closer, felt him begin to grow hard against her before they separated.

The thought crossed her mind that Donnie was still asleep, but she said, "I guess this isn't really the time. I'll try to resist temptation."

Mark smiled and poured coffee for both of them. Suzanne looked at the clock and saw it was too early to call anyone but the winery. She didn't want to call Ricardo so early it seemed alarmist, though, and she was pretty sure Hannah Jackson would call as soon as she saw the e-mail or heard the voicemail about the restraining order.

"What's wrong?" Mark asked.

Suzanne looked away from the clock and raised her eyebrows. "You mean besides the obvious?" They both smiled. "I'm just . . . waiting. Waiting for what happens next."

"You mean in California?"

She nodded. "I asked Will to manage the winery until I get back or Carlos gets better."

Mark's eyebrows shot up.

"I know." Suzanne rested her chin on one palm. "I know it seems . . . unexpected . . . but it really was the best solution."

Mark covered her hand with his. "I have no doubt."

They were smiling at each other when Donnie walked in from the other room.

"Get a room."

Suzanne shrugged. "This is a room."

Donnie snorted a laugh and poured himself some coffee. "The front yard is a mess. I thought I'd make a doughnut run before we started."

"Comfort food and sugar, the perfect combination," Suzanne said. She looked past Donnie to the dining room. "I'll go sit with Janice while you're gone."

"I need to run over to my office for a few minutes," Mark said, "and maybe shower. Would you like me to wait?"

"No, go now. Clean up will go faster if we can work on the decorations two at a time."

Mark rose, then bent to kiss Suzanne's upturned face, and the two men walked out together. Suzanne refilled her coffee and carried it into the living room. She sat in the chair by the window, the chair that had become hers during her visits, and watched Janice. Once in awhile her breath would catch in a sort of gurgle, but when she was far under the influence of the morphine, it never developed into a full-fledged choking cough.

The box of trinkets and photographs Janice had saved for her still sat on the floor beside the chair. Suzanne reached down and opened the small box, took out the feather clip and stuck it in her hair holding up the left side. She didn't need to be able to see it to know it probably looked goofy, but she smiled and left it in. She studied each of the photos in the small album, the serious boy with the enormous cat, the girl with the piercing stare, children she never knew who grew up to become the parents she hardly knew, either. Strange how with other people you wanted to know all about their past, but when you're a child, you think your parents' lives began with you.

The photo of Suzanne as the hippie baby with Janice and as the smiling graduate standing beside her mother. She hadn't noticed before, but they both seemed to be looking past the camera to something else. Janice must have taken the picture; she was the tether that always bound them.

One night when she was sixteen or seventeen, Suzanne had had a screaming argument with her mother, the kind of emotionally over-wrought escalation from nothing that occurs only between parents and teenagers. Suzanne had stormed out of the house after shouting that "setting a curfew wouldn't make her a 'real' mother." She ran to Janice's house where Janice let her rant as Donnie pretended to do his home-work while taking it all in. When Suzanne wound down, Janice had said, "You know what Mom used to sing to you when you were a baby? 'I Got You Babe.' I would pretend to gag every time, but she would say 'babe' really loud and it would make you giggle."

Suzanne remembered how irritated she had been that night that Janice did not seem to be taking her seriously . . . until Janice started talking about what their mom was like before and how she changed after their dad died. "All the way through his sickness, every hospital visit up to the end, she was cheerful and positive. As soon as he was gone, she just collapsed. People think of hope as light, like a helium balloon, but hope can be a burden, too. Sometimes it gets heavier the longer you carry it." When Suzanne had complained that that didn't explain her reserve, Janice had shrugged. "I think it's like some weird self-defense mechanism. The more important someone is to her, the more distance she has to keep. She can't afford to lose anyone else."

That insight had helped Suzanne better understand her mother's detachment, but it hadn't been enough to erase the resentment for all the attention lavished on other people with so little left for her. Suzanne examined the photo again before turning the page. She and her mother shared not just a distant look, but a similar stance: chin uplifted, shoulders squared, smiles not really for the camera at all. Suzanne had always thought of herself as self-sufficient, but perhaps some of what she thought of as resilient independence was really a reflection of her mother's refusal to let people get too close.

Janice sighed but did not shift. Suzanne waited until she heard an intake of breath before returning to the final photograph.

Tom, Tommy, Donnie's father. It was so strange to see her younger self looking so happy with someone she remembered not at all. Suzanne reached up to adjust the feather clip to more closely mirror the picture. Where had he gone? Why had they never seen him again? Why hadn't Janice even talked about him?

Before she could follow those thoughts very far, the phone started ringing. Suzanne jumped and ran to grab the phone on the stand by the kitchen.

"Good morning, Suzanne. Did you get my flowers?"

Suzanne clenched her teeth so hard her jaw hurt. She tried to relax and get control of her ability to speak as she turned back toward the living room to be able to watch Janice. And then all the tension fell away. She took a deep breath and smiled. "Trevor. If you can call me, the sun must not have risen in California."

There was a long pause and then laughter from the other end of the line.

"Is that a vampire joke? Good one! I like a partner with a sense of humor. But you should've said, 'Money never sleeps.'"

Suzanne walked closer to the couch to see the slight rise and fall of her rib cage. "Really? I thought that was rust." Constantine laughed again, more heartily than Suzanne thought was justified.

"But you got the flowers?"

Her mouth tasted sour, and Suzanne shook her head in disbelief. "Oh, yeah. I got the flowers. And I got the point. You can find me anywhere. You know where I am. But what you don't know is that I am not your partner."

Constantine let out a low whistle. "I think that's a decision you'll come to regret."

Suzanne caught the shift in tone and felt gratified. "Maybe. But I doubt it. I'll work with you if I have to, but I'm not handing you half my winery. You know what I realized? Whether or not it made the divorce easier for me, the one person it made things easier for is you. Go work your deal with Will. Do what you need to."

"You know he's going to take you to the cleaners. I'm going to explain to him what this vintage represents to you and how far you'll go to keep it."

Suzanne laughed. "Go ahead. I already told him about your offer to me behind his back. I'm pretty sure you'll have to talk about that first." She hung up without waiting for his response.

She walked back into the living room, sat down and put the photo album back in the box. Donnie had called his father "Tom," Janice had said "Tommy." Decades had passed since they had been in contact, but maybe he deserved to know, anyway. She was willing to bet that Donnie had Googled the man as soon as Janice started talking about him, as soon as he had a name and a timeframe. She decided to ask him about it when he got home, ask him if he thought they should call his father. If they could find him.

There was a commotion outside, voices and car doors slamming and footsteps on the back stairs. Suzanne went to meet Donnie and Mark in the kitchen.

"Definitely Spiderman," Donnie was saying to Mark as they walked in.

"How can you say that? Superman has x-ray vision, superhuman strength, and he can fly. Who wouldn't want to fly?" Mark responded.

Suzanne refilled her coffee and inspected the collection of doughnuts Donnie put down on the table. "Are you guys seriously having the superhero debate?"

Mark looked sheepish. Donnie shrugged and ate half of a cake doughnut with black and orange sprinkles in one bite. "'Tis the season."

"Well, you're both wrong." Suzanne chose a cinnamon twist. "It's clearly Batman."

"Phfff!" Donnie said. "He doesn't even have any superpowers."

"Who needs superpowers when you've got chutzpah?" Suzanne said.

"Yeah, that and a billion dollars," Donnie added.

A metallic jangling followed by a loud thump in the living room sent them all running. Suzanne swallowed the partially chewed dough in her mouth too fast and almost choked, but didn't slow down. They surrounded the couch, startling the cat sitting on the coffee table who crouched down with wide eyes.

"Molly!" Donnie shouted.

The cat darted up the stairs, knocking off the bottle of morphine with her tail in the process. The lavender lotion and a water glass were already on the floor nearby. Suzanne's pulse was pounding in her ears, and her throat felt like there was still a lump of dough stuck halfway down. She held her breath until she could see Janice's and then let out a long slow sigh.

"Who wants living room and who wants cemetery?" she asked.

"The fog machine is good, but I can't get the rats to move," Mark said.

Suzanne finished organizing the plants and flowers around Janice's headstone without looking up. "Leave it for Donnie. I already tried once." She rose and stretched and surveyed the yard. The storm had blown most of the leaves off the trees, which actually added to the ambiance. They had replanted the fake headstones and fixed the strings of bats pretty quickly, but there were still crows scattered across three yards that needed to be collected and distributed to the trees and graves. It looked as if some bird plague had struck or poison been set out, and the image made Suzanne shiver as much as the brisk wind.

Mark walked over and wrapped his arms around her. "Someone just walked over your grave."

"What?"

He smiled and moved as if to brush hair off her face but left his hand on her cheek. "That's what Mom used to say whenever people shivered suddenly."

Suzanne frowned. "But that doesn't make any sense. Is it supposed to be some premonition of a future when you're dead?"

Mark laughed and shook his head, pulling her close. "You know, not everything makes perfect sense. Old sayings are more about poetry than reality. At least to other people."

Suzanne inhaled the scent of musk and spice from Mark's neck and smiled. "Yeah, well, you did just walk over a bunch of graves to get to me. I just wanted to be sure it wasn't a threat."

They both laughed, then remained embracing without speaking in the middle of the front yard cemetery. Clouds blew past overhead, trailing the storm system like groupies, but the worst of it was over. Parts of the county were still without power, and a tornado had touched down about fifty miles to the east, but no more rain was expected. Suzanne could smell winter in the air the way she used to be able to tell it had snowed when she woke up in the morning before she even opened her eyes.

"Suzanne," Donnie called from the kitchen door. "Phone for you. It's your lawyer."

Mark released her with an expression of concern.

"I'm expecting it. Don't worry," Suzanne said.

She accepted the phone from Donnie and walked inside as he walked out. "Rats and crows," she said to him as they passed.

He nodded and said, "Still sleeping." It sounded like spies exchanging coded greetings, but they both understood the shorthand.

"Are you certain this is what you want to do, Suzanne?" Hannah Jackson's voice was crisp and direct. "You realize this will undermine our position by eliminating the most powerful negotiating point we had."

"If the most powerful point we had came out of a random incident, maybe we need a better strategy." Suzanne listened to the silence, then continued. "Yes. I know what I'm doing. And I know it means the . . ." she couldn't bring herself to say "domestic violence," ". . . argument can't be used as an example if I dismiss the restraining order. This is what I need to do to take care of my wine."

"All right. I will take care of it, but with the stipulation that I have expressly counseled you against it."

"Fine." Suzanne had anticipated her attorney's objection to dropping the restraining order, but she hadn't expected Hannah to be quite so adamant about distancing herself from the decision.

"I'll have things for you to sign when you get back. I'll be in touch."

Suzanne opened her mouth and closed it again. She ended the call and went in to sit with Janice. The cat had resettled at Janice's feet, purring loudly. It stopped when Suzanne sat down and narrowed its eyes.

"Don't glare at me," Suzanne said. "I didn't knock the stuff on the floor."

She had been half joking when she'd offered to put her rejection of Hannah's advice in writing, but finding out the lawyer expected it made Suzanne feel like she had just done something so foolish Hannah was protecting herself. Janice coughed, then moaned softly. Suzanne wondered if the pain was worse or if Janice was dreaming. The paper beneath her pillow crackled as she shifted, and Suzanne slid the DNR form out from under Janice's head and laid it on the table.

Donnie and Mark came in through the kitchen, talking in low voices. Mark paused to rest his hand on Janice's forehead, then walked over to sit beside Suzanne.

"What happened?" he asked.

"I think my divorce lawyer questions her decision to represent me."

"Why?" Donnie asked.

"I dropped the restraining order and told her I asked Will to supervise until I get back."

Donnie dropped his jaw and said, "What?"

Mark just smiled.

Suzanne slowly returned his smile. "You don't think I'm crazy?"

"Oh, I didn't say that," Mark said, dodging her backhand, "I just know you would never put your vineyard in jeopardy. If you're doing it, it must be the right thing to do."

Suzanne marveled at Mark's confidence in her, at how well he knew her, as if decades had not passed with half a continent between them. "Thanks."

"But what about the divorce?" Donnie seemed less convinced Suzanne knew what she was doing. "Aren't you opening yourself up to all sorts of trouble?"

Suzanne shrugged. "Maybe. But what I'm trying to open myself up to is amicable negotiation. And trust. Trust has to start somewhere, and I decided to go first."

Their voices in conversation never rose to normal speaking tones, but hovered somewhere in the range just above a whisper. Janice's breathing had become louder as they talked, and she shifted on the couch as if waking. She opened her eyes and blinked twice in slow motion.

"Donnie . . ." Janice's voice was more wheeze than croak. She reached out toward the table and her wheezing became choking, like the smoker's hack she'd always had without the oxygen to power it. As they watched, she stopped breathing entirely, unable to get control, and started turning blue, her mouth frozen open, waiting. Donnie jumped to the end of the couch to her to elevate her back, then looked at Suzanne and shouted, "I'm calling 911."

An insistent pressure on his wrist stopped him. Janice's eyes were closed, but her grip was strong enough to get his attention. She gasped, began breathing rapidly, then slowed to the shallow respiration that had become her norm.

"No."

Donnie's face flushed and he dropped to his knees beside the couch. "Sorry, Mom. I . . . I panicked. Sorry."

"Wimp." Janice's lips lifted at the corners. "Hallow . . . een?"

"Two more days, Mom," Donnie said.

She was still for a long time, then she sighed softly. "Candy . . ."

Donnie leaned close. "Candy?" He frowned, then turned to Suzanne with a stricken look.

Suzanne felt her throat close up, fought to control her breathing even though she couldn't see through the tears welling up. "We'll give out the candy."

Hearing Suzanne's voice, Janice opened one eye and then the other, lifted her hand just enough off her chest to point to Suzanne. "Viking . . ."

Suzanne stepped closer and leaned down. "Viking . . . funeral?"

Janice managed a weak smile along with the slight nod. Her eyes were unfocused and did not meet Suzanne's. "Swear."

"Goddammit," Suzanne said.

Janice shuddered as if with silent laughter and then was still.

Suzanne abandoned all efforts to suppress her emotions and burst into great wracking sobs. Mark offered his arms, but she shook her head and stepped into the dining room. She stood beside the Kleenex box wiping her face and blowing her nose and waiting to feel normal again.

Chapter 19

Unfiltered:
wine that has not had sediment removed, believed to help
retain aroma and flavor

Suzanne felt as bad as Donnie looked, and he looked like hell. His hair tufted at odd angles, and the smudges under his eyes were so pronounced they looked painted on. Suzanne's thoughts were all askew and her emotions were right on the surface. They made quite a pair.

When Janice's body was taken away just before sunrise, Donnie, Mark, and Suzanne had gathered in the kitchen for coffee. Even sleep-deprived as they were, Suzanne knew she couldn't sleep. When she and Donnie started talking about the arrangements, Mark had rinsed out his cup, kissed her on the palm of her hand then the nape of her neck, and gone home.

Eight hours later, Suzanne and Donnie were back in the same chairs at the kitchen table, but with glasses of wine instead of cups of coffee. They had spent the whole day talking to strangers with professionally soothing voices and filling out paperwork. No physical exertion was involved, but every conversation was so emotionally draining that Suzanne felt as if she had been picking grapes for twelve hours. She rested her chin on the same hand Mark had kissed. She had pressed that palm into her cheek intermittently throughout the day just to feel him with her.

Suzanne squinted at Donnie and raised her glass. The afternoon had seemed too bright, the sky that autumn blue so intense it hurts, and Suzanne's eyes felt dry and itchy. Donnie clinked his glass to hers and waited expectantly for a toast.

Finally she said, "Dia de los Muertos."

Donnie looked confused.

"Day of the Dead. This year it came early."

They both drank. Donnie looked past Suzanne toward the living room. "It all feels so . . ." He shook his head.

"Surreal?" Suzanne finished.

"Yeah. Or unreal." He shook his head again. "And bureaucratic. Sign this, notarize that. And the cremation. Why would you buy an expensive casket if it's going to be sent immediately into an incinerator?"

"I don't know." Suzanne shook her head. "It's like the dress."

Donnie touched his glass to Suzanne's again. "Thanks for that, by the way. I was so caught up in their checklist I was ready to run home and pick out clothes until you spoke up."

Suzanne accepted his thanks with a nod. "Anything of hers we want to burn, we can save for the Viking funeral."

He froze, glass halfway to his lips. "Are you serious?"

"I am. I swore." Suzanne gave Donnie a mock serious look and they both cracked up. She thought about the postcard with the beach sunset, about the teenaged Janice honoring her father all alone. "And you know what? I think even if we aren't going to send her actual body out to sea, we can still give her ashes the send-off she deserves."

She was crying before she finished speaking. Her tears set Donnie off in the ragged tag-team grieving they had been doing all day. They would be fine for long dry conversations about assets and estate distribution, memorials and obituaries. They would laugh together at the absurd details of death's aftermath. Then suddenly, a simple phrase that sounded like Janice would catch in the throat, and one of them would fall apart, followed closely by the other.

Donnie reached behind him for the box of Kleenex on the counter and put it on the table between them. They snuffled and blew and dabbed together until they were relatively dry inside and out. Suzanne refilled their glasses from one of the bottles she had brought up from the cellar. "I think we're drinking your inheritance."

He frowned. "Didn't the wine go to you?"

Suzanne frowned, too. "I thought everything had to be sold off first to cover medical debts."

Donnie scratched his head and drank. "I wasn't paying very close attention, but if that's the case, we'd better drink as much as we can before it gets auctioned off to the heathens." He winked.

Suzanne smiled. "We can drink as much as you want, but this stuff will not go to heathens. Now that I know it's been cellared properly, we could not only sell it on eBay, we might even be able to list it in a private auction."

Donnie froze mid-sip again. "It's just wine."

"*Just* wine?" Suzanne laughed. "I know, but there are a thousand little worlds within the real one. Some people pay hundreds of dollars for sneakers; some people pay thousands for baseball cards. Passion has no logic," she lifted her glass, "and no price. People get caught up in their own obsessions, and if your thing is pinot noir, some of these bottles are worth a lot of money."

Donnie held his glass out and up to the light of the window. "I may be unworthy."

"Well, that's for sure!"

Donnie swatted Suzanne's arm with the back of his hand. They drank in silence as the early sunset dimmed the light.

"What is . . . was it with your mom and Halloween, anyway?" Suzanne caught her error, then bit the insides of her cheeks to keep from crying again. "It wasn't this big a deal when we were little."

"I know. It started a long time ago and got bigger and bigger—or worse and worse, depending on how you look at it—every year. One year I came home from school and was all embarrassed about the front yard." Donnie frowned and tilted his head to the side. "You know, I think it was the year after Gramma died." He looked lost in thought for a few seconds, then continued. "Anyway, after I finished grousing, Mom told me that Halloween was the real Independence Day. She thought Halloween costumes weren't about becoming someone else but about having the freedom to be yourself."

"That sounds like Janice."

"Mom said the scary thing wasn't what people wore for Halloween, it was that they were afraid to wear anything they wanted to the rest of the year."

Suzanne smiled a little half smile. "Or be anything they wanted, right?"

Donnie raised his glass. "Right."

"Do we even have any candy for tomorrow?"

"Are you kidding me?" Donnie said. "Mom bought candy as soon as the displays went up in the grocery store."

The back stairs creaked under the weight of someone walking up them, then Mark walked into the kitchen.

Suzanne smiled. "I think I'm adjusting to the open-door policy around here."

Mark bent down to hug her, holding her long enough to convey comfort and support and longing all together. He stood and embraced Donnie for a moment, too.

"Grab a glass," Donnie said, "we're trying to drink up all the assets before the estate is settled."

Suzanne poured the last of the open bottle into Mark's glass, then chose another from the assortment of bottles on the counter and opened it to let it breathe.

"How was your conversation with Will today?" Mark asked after tasting his wine.

Suzanne sighed. "Short. I think he wanted to tell me about his meeting with Constantine, but when I told him Janice died . . ." she hesitated and took a deep breath, "he just said he was sorry and that everything was going fine at the winery and he would talk to me later."

"That seems really . . . thoughtful," Mark said.

"I know." Suzanne shook her head, a little worried about Will's restraint but grateful not to have to deal with one more thing.

They sat together without speaking for half a glass of wine, spinning private internal memorials.

"Well," Mark said finally, "if you aren't too tired, I have something for you." He reached inside his jacket and pulled out two envelopes, glanced at the names, and handed them out. "Janice gave these to me at one of our dinners after Mom died. She asked me to give them to you."

Donnie and Suzanne looked at their envelopes, then at each other. As if by spoken agreement, they opened their letters at the same time and read silently. Suzanne frowned, turned her sheet over and back again. "Was there something else with it?"

"No," Mark said, "but she did ask that you read them together."

Donnie said, "Mine sounds like a fortune cookie: 'Go where no man has gone before.'"

Suzanne's face cleared and a smile spread. "I get it. Mine says, 'Season three, Disc two.' Get the DVDs!"

Mark and Donnie followed Suzanne into the living room and Mark watched as she pulled the red plastic case out of the box of things Janice had given her. Donnie took a detour out onto the porch and the grave-yard burst into life.

"What is it?" Donnie asked as he came back in and closed the door behind him.

Suzanne started to laugh, but her throat closed off. She handed the DVD to Mark to read. "It says 'She's Dead, Jim' in Sharpie."

"Unbelievable." Donnie shook his head. To Suzanne he said, "You and Mom and your lame Trekkie stuff. It's a wonder I made it out of elementary school alive." To Mark he added, "You'd better put it in."

Janice appeared on the screen, the image cut, and she reappeared. "Sorry, had to check the camera angle." She opened her eyes wide and extended one arm as she delivered the Gloria Swanson impression. "Mr. DeMille, I'm ready for my close-up." She settled herself onto the couch, picked up her cigarette and took a long drag, exhaling toward the camera. Her hair was just below shoulder length, tousled in a manner that suggested neglect not style. It was a faded reddish-brown threaded with white. In the back there was a swatch of what looked like turquoise.

"It's kind of weird to see her with hair," Suzanne said.

"Yeah," Donnie said, "I'd gotten used to the peach fuzz and scarves."

"The sixteen-year-old cheerleader masquerading as a counselor for our support group told us all to make a tape even if we decided not to give it to anybody. I was going to blow it off . . . I mean, I'm not really known for leaving things left unsaid, but if you're watching this, I guess I decided it was worth keeping. Or maybe I forgot about it and you're watching this years later in the middle of a late-night Star Trek marathon." Janice leaned close and looked as if she were scanning the room through the television screen. "If that's what the future looks like, guess I didn't miss much."

Janice stubbed out her cigarette and reached for something off-camera, then drank from a silver can. "Donnie. This was probably hardest on you, and if what I've heard is even remotely true, the last couple weeks weren't very much fun." Her face grew large as she pushed her face close toward the camera. "But if I spent so much as one minute in the hospital," Janice shook her finger, "you had better not count on ever sleeping again, because I will haunt you for the rest of your life." She leaned back and took another drink. "On the other hand, if you were a good boy and did what I told you, then you'll be fine." Her expression shifted from mock anger to self-amusement to a slight wistful smile. "There is one thing." Janice looked away from the camera as if avoiding eye contact, then leaned forward to collect her cigarettes and lighter from the table. She exhaled a plume of smoke and ran her hand through her hair before finally looking back at the camera. "Maybe I was wrong about telling you not to look for your dad. Don't get all excited," she narrowed her eyes, "I said 'maybe.'"

The image went black, then came back on again. Suzanne and Donnie exchanged a look.

"Station break," Janice said. "Anyway, I had good reasons for keeping Tommy away from you. At least they seemed good at the time. Even if they were selfish. Later it didn't matter because I didn't know where he was." Janice smoked without speaking for a while, stubbed out her cigarette and lit another. "Turns out I was an 'if you have to look any further than your own backyard' sort of person, and that would have killed Tommy. I didn't want you idolizing him between visits that were going to be stretched longer and longer." She looked away, looked around the room, looked back at the camera with moist eyes. "I didn't want you to run off until it was because that was what *you* wanted, not what he did."

Suzanne glanced over at Donnie. His cheeks were wet, but he was almost smiling. She put her hand over his and squeezed.

Janice inhaled deeply and blew out a big cloud of smoke. "Well. Enough of that. I'm dead now so it doesn't matter. I think I found him, but I decided not to contact him. There's a file on my computer called 'Robinson.' If you want to know anything else, that's the place to start."

Suzanne shared a smile with Donnie and Mark. "That was worth the price of admission." She realized the full implication of what she had said and froze.

Donnie shoved her gently. "Maybe it wasn't that good, but it was close."

On the screen, Janice was draining her can of beer. "Suzanne. You're probably all mad that I didn't tell you." She shrugged. "Don't take it personally. If I thought I could get away with not telling Donnie, I would."

Suzanne felt Mark's hand on hers, and she gave him a tight smile.

"I keep thinking if I sit here long enough, something profound will come to me, but the longer I sit here, the more clearly I see what a crock that is." Janice brushed ashes off her lap. "The diagnosis didn't bring me any epiphanies. So I'm dying—who isn't? Is it worse that I know when? Or that it's . . ." she made air quotes and changed her tone to a derisive nasal, "too soon? Would it be more tragic if I got creamed by a drunk driver as I crossed the street or if I was ninety and sitting alone staring at the wall in some dementia center? And if one more person tells me how 'brave' I am, I swear I'll hit 'em in the head with a dictionary. Like just getting treatment or not killing yourself is suddenly an act of heroism. Well you know what? Cancer is *not* a battle, and we are *not* fighting—I am so fucking sick of the war analogies!"

Suzanne realized her mouth was open, and she closed it as she fumbled for the remote to pause the video. She couldn't remember Janice ever being angry quite like that. She looked from Donnie, whose eyes were so wide it was as if someone were squeezing him, to Mark, who didn't look surprised at all. She tried to turn her jumbled thoughts and feelings into words, then gave up and unpaused the video.

Janice smoked furiously, then sighed. "I guess I can't escape the clichés. This must be anger." Her face twisted in annoyed disgust. "That Keebler-Ross chick should've stuck to baking cookies with elves." After a pause, she said, "You know what really sucks? I didn't think I was done, but I guess I am." Janice's face started to crumple, then she pressed her lips together and wiped her eyes. "The good news is, I don't have a lot of stuff I didn't get done." She looks around the room. "Well, besides cleaning. I'm starting that right now, though. I'll collect a box of crap for you to remember me by so you don't whine about not getting to see me. Trust me when I tell you that's better than being stuck with the memory of what I'll be like in a few weeks. You never needed much from anybody, but that's one thing I can spare you." Janice put out her cigarette and reached for another as she stood up. "Good enough," she said as her seemingly decapitated body loomed over the camera. "*Jeopardy's* on." The video cut to black.

The three sat in silence until Mark took the remote from Suzanne and turned off the TV.

"Thank you for calling me, Donnie. I'm glad I was here," Suzanne said.

"I'm glad you were, too," he told her.

Mark slid closer and wrapped his arm around her. "And you know Janice changed her mind, right?"

Suzanne's face was wet, but she smiled up at Mark and then at Donnie. "Let's watch it again."

Suzanne was leaning against a wooden rail drinking champagne as a massive sail burned above her. The sheet of flame billowed and popped in the wind like fireworks; the scent of ash surrounded her, though she didn't feel the heat. The ships bell rang and rang and then the ship vanished.

The doorbell stopped ringing before Suzanne was fully awake. She yawned and stretched, trying to reorient from dream to the almost equally disorienting reality. She had spent the night on the couch so Donnie could have the guest room. Neither one of them had wanted to sleep in Janice's room that night, even though they realized that made no sense, considering her final days were spent in the living room. Suzanne sniffed her pajamas then the cushion she had used as a pillow. She smelled like an ashtray. It finally sank in that she had not heard the doorbell ring before. Everyone walked in through the kitchen. She looked around for a clock and then grabbed her cell phone. Could she have slept through the whole day? Were the trick-or-treaters already arriving?

It was not much after seven, a.m. not p.m., and her panic shifted to annoyance. Who shows up at your house that early in the morning? Suzanne walked over to the door and looked out the window through the porch. She couldn't see anyone, but she walked out onto the porch to check, anyway. On the steps was a pan of cinnamon rolls, steaming in the morning chill, with a note resting on top. Suzanne looked up and down the street but couldn't see who had left them. She smiled and carried them into the kitchen. The name on the card didn't mean anything to her, probably one of the neighbors. She made coffee and pulled one of the rolls out of the pan and started eating it with her fingers.

After they watched Janice's video, Suzanne had spent the evening sorting and cataloging the wine in the basement. Mark had helped with the stacking and note-taking, and he had invited her to spend the night at his house. She had declined, opting to stay with Donnie in the house she would probably never see again.

Suzanne licked the icing off her fingers and picked up the phone. "I know how early you get up, so don't even pretend I woke you."

"The real question is why *you're* up so early."

"The doorbell woke me. A reverse trick-or-treater left a batch of warm cinnamon rolls. I was thinking maybe you'd like to come over and have breakfast with me."

"We could have had breakfast at my house this morning." The timbre of Mark's voice shifted. "We still could."

The invitation behind the words made her want to run to his house right then. Her breath quickened and she swallowed. She closed her eyes, picturing all the ways that "breakfast" might go, then smiled and said, "You come here. There is a great deal of . . . sticky frosting that should be shared. We can have breakfast at your house next time."

There was silence on the line, and Suzanne imagined Mark spinning scenes much like the ones she had just watched.

"I'm going to hold you to that," he said finally.

Suzanne ran a finger across the top of her roll and licked it. "You can hold me to anything you like."

Mark laughed and said, "I'll be right over."

When the kitchen door opened, Suzanne was just pouring her second cup of coffee. "That was fast." She smiled. "Help yourself to a roll and I'll get you some coffee."

Marked popped the last bite of her roll into his mouth. "Mmm . . .

I think I know who made these." He walked over to Suzanne, took the coffee cup from her hands and put it down on the table and pulled her into an embrace. His kiss was all cinnamon and vanilla. She guided one of his hands up under her top, and he slid the other down inside the elastic of her pajamas. She shuddered.

"Sorry. Cold hands?" he murmured into her neck.

"No . . . I just . . . I want . . ." Suzanne gave up trying to find words and went back to kissing Mark while she undid his belt and pants and reached inside with both hands. A creaking sounded overhead, and they both froze.

"Should we stop?" Mark whispered into her neck, setting off another shiver.

"No. Hurry."

Suzanne stepped out of her pajama bottoms and wrapped one leg around Mark, leaning against the counter and standing on tiptoe to adjust the angle. He gasped as she pulled him deep inside. The ceiling popped and groaned as Donnie walked to the bathroom, which elevated both the urgency and the excitement. Suzanne had to bite Mark's shoulder to muffle her climax, and as they heard Donnie's tread on the stairs, they separated. Suzanne pulled on her pajamas while Mark fastened his pants, and they both grabbed their coffee just as Donnie walked into the room.

"Well you're certainly up early," Donnie said as he walked in.

Suzanne and Mark burst out laughing.

Donnie frowned. "What?" He shook his head and grabbed a cup for coffee. "Never mind. I don't want to know." He gestured to the cinnamon rolls. "Has it started?"

Mark nodded. "Apparently."

Suzanne understood they were talking about the inescapable postmortem spontaneous buffet. "They won't wait until the memorial?"

"Some will. Some will come by today, and some will do both."

Something in Suzanne's expression must have betrayed her horror at the thought of having an endless parade of strangers and barely remembered acquaintances occupying the kitchen all day, because Mark reached over and squeezed her arm. "You don't have to entertain them," he said. "Just keep the coffee on and the back door open."

Mark was right. Patsy and Muriel showed up a little after nine with coffee cake and a pie. A steady stream of Janice's friends arrived in ones and twos and joined the revolving cast at the table regaling each other with well-remembered tales of Janice's practical jokes, caustic tongue, and big heart. At first it was fascinating to see her sister through the eyes of the people who had really shared her life, but after the third retelling of the incident with the hamster ball, Suzanne went upstairs.

She lay on the bed in the guest room in a lethargic limbo, intermittently dozing and weaving the bits of conversation from below into her free associations. Molly hadn't been seen since Janice's body had been taken, but Donnie didn't seem worried. Suzanne wondered if Donnie would take the cat back to Minneapolis or if he would try to get the new owners to keep her. Maybe Mark would take her so she could at least be nearby. Molly had lived in the house almost as long as Suzanne had, and for the cat it had been her whole life.

The voices faded to silence as the light began to dim, and Suzanne went back downstairs.

"Here." Donnie handed her a witch hat as she walked into the kitchen.

"Are you trying to tell me something?"

"No, this is way too subtle." He smiled. Mom always dressed up to give out candy, but I figured we could get away with hats.

"What are you going to be?" Suzanne asked.

Donnie put on a straw boater and held his hands out wide.

"That's pretty lame," Suzanne said.

"I'm one quarter of a barbershop quartet."

Suzanne winced. "That might be even more lame than the hat

without the explanation." She dodged the blow as Donnie swung the hat at her and was saved by the doorbell.

"I'll get this one," he said, grabbing a giant bowl of miniature candy bars from the table, "you get a bottle of wine and meet me in the living room."

The time between rings of the doorbell got to be so short that they eventually pulled chairs right up beside the door to the porch to cut their response time. They shared an assortment of tidbits from the smorgasbord dropped off during the day and drank a bottle of cabernet from one of Suzanne's earlier jobs. By nine o'clock, the throng of trick-or-treaters slowed to a trickle. Half an hour later, Mark walked in the back door.

"Bring a glass!" Suzanne called.

"Want me to turn out the porch light and turn off the decorations?" Mark offered as he joined them in the living room.

Donnie looked at Suzanne, then shook his head. "Nah. Let's give it a little longer."

"A lot of people asked about the memorial tomorrow," Mark said. "It's probably a good thing you decided to hold the lunch at the VFW instead of here."

Suzanne nodded. "Yeah, then I don't have to listen to Donnie whine about how I left him with all the cleaning up."

Both men turned to her with nearly identical quizzical expressions.

"I have to check in really early the next morning." she prompted.

"You're leaving already?" A flush crept up Donnie's neck to his cheeks.

"Well . . . yes." It was Suzanne's turn to be perplexed. "I came to be with Janice. There's no reason for me to stay."

"No reason?" Mark asked with a teasing lilt that didn't quite mask the hurt.

Suzanne brushed his hand with her fingers. "You know what I mean." She looked from one to the other, unable to believe that either of them would even imagine she might be staying longer let alone expect it. They knew what she had had to give up to be there for Janice's final days. How could they not know she would go home as soon as she could? She divided the last of the bottle among their glasses and raised hers. "To Janice. And Halloween."

"Trick-or-treat." Donnie added.

They all drank, and Suzanne responded to the sullen note in Donnie's voice. "It's not like I'm leaving right now. It's not like you'll never see me again."

Donnie raised his eyebrows. "Really? When was the last time you came to visit before I called you about Mom?"

"The planes fly both directions, you know." She drained her glass then got up to turn off the porch light and decorations.

"Do you have a ride to the airport?" Mark asked. "If not, I'd like to take you."

"I need to be at the airport by seven," Suzanne started to decline, then thought better of it. "That would be really nice."

Chapter 20

Sur Lie:
(on the lees) allowing the wine to have extended lees contact,
adding depth, palate weight, and complexity

"I'm stopping here for gas, if you need anything," Mark said as he exited the freeway at the Iowa/Minnesota border.

Suzanne bit her tongue to keep from telling him to just keep driving. She was almost jittery with that peculiar travel impatience—every delay is painful because while you're still here physically, the rest of you is already gone. "Maybe I'll get coffee. And use the restroom."

The trip so far had been mostly silent, but it was a comfortable silence. Suzanne rested her hand on Mark's leg as he drove in a subconscious gesture so familiar she had been doing it for an hour before she noticed. When they were together, it didn't feel like they had picked up where they left off twenty years ago, it felt like they had never left off.

Standing at the register paying for her coffee, Suzanne could see Mark removing the nozzle from the car and replacing it on the pump. He was wearing a beat-up bomber jacket, leather gloves, and a dark plaid wool scarf, and his visible breath made it look like he was talking in cartoon balloons. Though she squinted to read his thoughts, she couldn't see anything but ice crystals.

"Do you want anything?" she called from the doorway.

Mark looked up and smiled. "You mean besides the obvious?"

Suzanne laughed. "Yes. Besides that."

"No, thanks."

Back in the car, Suzanne could not reclaim the ease they had shared since leaving Donnie asleep in the house and driving north. What hung between them felt tangible, but she had to wonder if it was her own projection. She wished she could say she felt conflicted about leaving, but that wasn't really true. There was a pang of something behind her eagerness to be home, maybe it was sorrow, maybe even a little regret, but it wasn't a desire to stay.

"Mark?"

"Wait." He stopped her with a touch to her thigh. "We don't have to do this now." He looked over at her and then back at the road. "I mean . . . I am going to see you again, right?"

"Of course you are." Maybe their time together had been short, but Suzanne was certain that it was not just a nostalgic fling born out of convenience. "Donnie wants me to come at Christmas; so if that works, I could see you then. Or if he comes to California for Christmas, you could come, too . . . unless you go east to see Julie." Suzanne frowned. "Well, there's Janice's Viking funeral . . . but that's not until next Halloween . . . which is way too long." She paused, and Mark remained silent. "Maybe after the legal issues are sorted out and bottling is finished, I could come for the weekend. You did save Molly a trip halfway across the country in a cat carrier. That ought to be worth at least one visit . . ." Her voice trailed off to nothing. The certainty of her enthusiastic response was hard to sustain in the face of the logistical difficulties.

They exchanged a look and drove a long way without speaking. Suzanne thought about the memorial service and how Donnie had kept his distance afterwards, surrounding himself with neighbors and other mourners. Part of it came with the territory of being the survivor receiving condolences, but part of it looked intentional to Suzanne. When they got home where he couldn't escape her, Suzanne had cornered him in the kitchen.

"Talk to me. We don't have a lot of time, and I don't want to leave like this."

"Then don't. Leave, I mean." Donnie was close to tears.

"I am not leaving you, I'm going back to try to dissolve my marriage amicably and hold onto my vineyard. I can't be in two places at once. It's just time for me to go."

Donnie rubbed his head with both hands.

"Where's Katie?" Suzanne asked.

"I . . . asked her not to come."

Suzanne just raised her eyebrows.

"This . . . these last weeks, made me realize that she isn't . . . we aren't . . ."

Suzanne pulled him into a fierce hug.

In the end, Donnie couldn't sustain his sense of abandonment in the face of Suzanne's genuine need to be back in California. She finished sorting and labeling all the wine for sale and agreed to take Janice's ashes so Donnie wouldn't have to. He hatched the plan to spend the holidays together, and Suzanne suggested that Donnie invite his father to Christmas, too, if he found him by then. The variations on what might happen to her home, her vineyard, her life, were unlikely to be an issue before the end of the year. She hadn't said anything about what might happen after that, and he hadn't asked.

Civilization began filling in around them as they approached Minneapolis, houses and buildings grew taller and more densely packed as the overhead signs started to include directions to the airport. Suzanne brushed her foot against the bag on the floor that held the box of Janice's ashes, then turned sideways in her seat to face Mark.

"I do need to say something now. Who I am may not be what I do, but what I do matters *because* of who I am." Suzanne shook her head at Mark's quizzical expression. "Last summer I heard a TV producer say that women define themselves by their relationships, and I was tempted to see if I had a penis I didn't know about."

Mark snorted.

"If your relationships define you, then what are you without them? I don't know how you can even have a relationship with someone else unless you're already someone, something else whole and separate."

Mark reached over and folded her hand into his. "Not everyone works that way." He smiled. "Maybe not everyone needs to."

"I do, though. I need to," Suzanne said, running her thumb across the top of his hand. "Being with Janice brought back a lot of things I had forgotten—or maybe blocked out, and she told me things I never knew in the first place. Maybe all the studying and the prizes and the work were just ways to get my mom to finally see me, but maybe it was her distance that freed me to be a better version of who I already was."

Mark angled his hand to clasp hers. "It's funny, but I never saw the thing with your mom until you told me about it. It seemed like you were just . . . driven. And you always knew what you wanted. I think that's what attracted me the most."

Suzanne shrugged. "I don't know, I'm not a therapist, but I do know what makes me happy: creating something, having a purpose . . ."

"Changing the world?" Mark squeezed her hand.

She smiled. "Not the whole world, just a little piece of it. And living every day—really living. I had forgotten that part, but Janice reminded me. We got to do pretty much anything we wanted, be anything we wanted, that's the beauty of growing up in a small, safe place. She may not have made the same choices I did, but she had the life *she* wanted. And she definitely had more fun than most people wherever she was."

Suzanne thought about the pirate scarf and shook her head, then blinked as her eyes filled. Mark let go of her hand and brushed the side of her face. She searched for a Kleenex and blew her nose, then tried to pick up her train of thought.

"It's not that people don't matter to me, but relationships should be bonds, not bondage."

"Maybe a tether?" Mark asked.

"Or a set of shared electrons." Suzanne offered a half smile and shrugged.

"Where does that leave us?"

"I love you." She smiled. "And it's pretty obvious I want you. I don't know what kind of mess my life is going to be for a while, but there's no reason we can't find some time somewhere to be together, even if it's only for a long weekend here and there. And you can come stay with me for as long as you like." Suzanne hesitated. "Well, assuming I have a place to live."

Mark stopped the car at a red light, took both her hands in his, and looked into her eyes. "What if I want to be with you forever?"

Suzanne opened her mouth and closed it again before responding. "Then you know where to find me." She bit her lip and smiled.

California smelled like spring. Suzanne felt disoriented, anyway. Her parting kiss with Mark had made her long for an extra hour she couldn't have, and her intermittent dozing on the flight left her with no sense of how much time had passed. Somewhere over the Sierra Nevada Suzanne had dreamed of the ocean in a lucid state somewhere between sleeping and wakefulness. She was back on the burning ship drinking champagne as the flaming sails overhead became exploding fireworks against a black sky.

Suzanne felt like the plane had passed through some sort of time warp. She inhaled deeply. It must have rained while she had been gone. She paused outside the new terminal trying to remember where the taxi stand was now. Taking a taxi to the vineyard would be expensive, but she couldn't think of anyone she wanted to ask to pick her up. Asking one of the guys to do it would have let Will know when she was arriving, and though she wasn't entirely sure why, she didn't want to do that. That left Laura out, too, even if Suzanne wanted to extend that olive branch. Teri didn't want to be in the middle of things, and Suzanne had asked too much of Craig already, so she told him not to come. She sighed. *You pay for all your choices*, she thought as she wheeled her bags toward the crosswalk, *and sometimes it's with actual cash.*

Waiting for the light to change, Suzanne felt the man behind her standing just a little too close and shifted her weight away from him. He shifted, too, leaning in close enough to touch her. If there had been the crush of a crowd, it wouldn't have seemed strange, but there was plenty of room. She turned to tell the guy to back off just as he grabbed her ass.

"Hey, baby, need a lift?" Craig said.

Suzanne burst out laughing. "I hope you're referring to a ride and not plastic surgery."

He squeezed gently several times as if he were testing fruit. "I don't know, maybe both."

"I told you not to come." She threw her arms around him. "But I'm glad you did, anyway. It's so good to be home." Then she burst into tears. She clung to him, and he returned the hug as the crossing signal beeped through the walk sign countdown.

"Um, I think that's our cue," Craig said without moving.

Suzanne let go and wiped her face. Craig grabbed her arm as she started to cross. "Kidding. I'm parked over this way." As they walked to the car, Craig said, "You're like a trip to the amusement park." He moved his hand up and down in a wave motion.

"Yeah, welcome to my emotional roller coaster." Suzanne lifted her bags into the trunk and got into the passenger seat.

"Fasten your seatbelt," Craig said in his best Bette Davis impression, "it's going to be a bumpy ride."

"Hah! No kidding," Suzanne ran her hands through her hair and leaned back in the seat. Craig pointed to the cup holders. "I brought coffee." He took a sip from his after they pulled out into traffic. "Does Will know you're back?"

"I told him I would be coming back right after the service, but I didn't give him any details."

Craig shot her a look and she sighed.

"I know, I know. The restraining orders are gone and my paranoia should be dialed way back, but Will had a meeting with Trevor Constantine at the beginning of the week."

"And?" Craig asked.

"Exactly," Suzanne said. "Then Janice died. Will has given me brief updates on the last of the press, and I told him when the memorial was, but that's as far as we've talked." She turned to Craig. "He and Laura sent a nice basket of flowers. Janice would have hated it, but it was still thoughtful."

"What about Constantine? Did he send something, too?"

Suzanne snorted. "Yeah. He sent an ostentatious wreath on a stand. They probably had to send to the next county to get enough flowers. The message was 'My deepest sympathy for your loss,' which would sound normal coming from someone else but made me feel like it was *my* funeral."

"Okay, but your lawyer hasn't called you, right? Like nothing new turned up on her desk after that meeting?"

"No . . . ."

"So whatever they're up to, they haven't taken any legal steps, right?"

"That's right." Suzanne sighed. "You know, for a few days there, everything was so simple. What mattered was clear, and everything else just faded away. It felt like . . ." she smiled. "I was back to normal."

Craig looked at her over his sunglasses. "Honey, normal is something you are never going to be, so just let go of that little fantasy."

Suzanne smacked him on the arm. "Doctors say normal is what's normal for you. I just feel like for most of October I was somebody I don't even recognize. I don't want to go back there."

"Believe me when I tell you that none of the rest of us do, either."

As they got closer to the vineyard, Suzanne had butterflies. Her building sense of anticipation and homecoming and something else she couldn't even name was so great, she almost asked Craig to let her out on the road so she could walk the long drive up to the house.

"What are you grinning about?" Craig asked.

"Look at the color."

The canopy of trees lining the drive had turned brilliant shades of marigold and tangerine. The sun shining through them illuminated everything in a warm golden glow.

Craig picked up her coffee cup, sniffed it and put it back. "You must have gotten better drugs than I did."

Suzanne laughed. She had her seatbelt off and the door open before the engine stopped ticking. Craig pulled her two small bags from the trunk and met her at the front door.

"I know you're going to run off to the barn immediately, so just let me in so I can use the bathroom, please."

Craig carried the bags in and left them beside the door. Suzanne didn't even bother walking in. He knew her so well. She walked to the corner of the house and surveyed the property, her eyes following the chorus line of now bare vines dancing up the hillside. She couldn't wait to walk the blocks and climb to the top where the sea's perfume sometimes lingered. Suzanne took a deep breath and let it out slowly. The air tasted of both fall and spring, wood fire and moss. It was an unexpected combination, but good, like mole. She heard Will's voice and turned.

He was walking around the corning of the barn holding a wine thief and talking to Ricardo. They were both smiling, and Will was animated, describing something with his hands and gesturing with the angled tube. They stepped out of the shadow, and the sun caught the glass with a flash. Will threw back his head, laughing, and in that moment Suzanne saw the man she had fallen in love with. It was his joy she had responded to, his sense of pleasure and delight in ordinary things. And the way he thought she was extraordinary. Now she could see how irresistible that must have been to her. Maybe she hadn't loved him quite the same way she loved Mark, but Will's devotion had been exactly what she needed when she met him.

Both men saw her at the same time, and Will waved. Suzanne waved back and hurried to meet them. Without hesitating, she threw her arms around Will, and he embraced her in return.

"I'm so sorry about Janice," he said.

"Me, too," Suzanne said. "About everything." She stepped back and turned to Ricardo. "We're going to the barrel room for a few minutes. Would you let Craig know when he comes out?"

"Si, Miss Suzanne."

Suzanne didn't say anything as they had entered the cool quiet. The scent of the wine-soaked wood and yeasty fruit filled her, and she blinked back tears. She walked down the second row and held out her hand for the wine thief. As she pulled the stopper on the barrel she had chosen and inserted the thief, Will walked away and came back with two glasses. Suzanne squeezed wine into both glasses, then touched hers to Will's. There were raspberries and vanilla on the nose, cassis and cedar and lavender on the palate, and the finish was long and silky. Suzanne closed her eyes and smiled.

"It's ready." Her tone was like the "amen" at the end of a sacred rite.

Will clinked her glass again and drank eagerly. "Wait till you taste the block next to this one. It has cranberries and something earthy. I can't wait to see what you do with that. Maybe you'll do a new blend."

"If you think last year's wine is good, just wait for the wine you just put into barrels. I predict something beyond any of my Mermaid Tears."

"Really?" Will's eyes lit up. They looked at each other with shared excitement. Then recent history washed over them, and they both looked away.

Suzanne swirled the wine in the glass and held it up, though the light was dim. She took another sip, held it in her mouth for all the nuance, then swallowed.

"Will?"

"Yes?"

All the things she wanted to ask Will, all the things about Trevor Constantine, about Laura, about that one night she threatened him with a fireplace poker, all of it flashed through her mind. Then she thought about Janice and about Mark and about the wine.

"You can only make your own choices, not control everything," Suzanne said to herself.

"What?" Will asked.

"I want to keep the winery."

Will stiffened. "*You* want, right? It's always about what *you want*."

"No, wait," Suzanne felt the conversation veering away and rushed to finish. "I mean, I want *us* to keep it. I was wrong to ignore your proposal. Even if it wasn't my idea, I should have looked at it. We should keep SMW as partners. Equal partners."

"What does that mean?" Will's expression wavered between hope and suspicion.

Suzanne put down her glass and held out her right hand. "Our marriage is over, we both know that. But I don't want our business relationship to end."

Will looked at her hand and back at her face.

"You . . . want to keep working with me?"

"I do." Her mouth twitched, but she let go of the temptation to make a wedding wisecrack. "This is our winery. We built this place together, and I think we did a pretty great job. If you really think we need to bring in investors, I'm ready to talk about it." She turned her hand palm up but did not break eye contact. "Not Trevor Constantine, though. He can't be trusted."

Something shifted in Will's expression, like a fleeting wince, that told her more about his last meeting with Constantine than a full report. "I know," he said as he took her hand. He returned her squeeze with his right hand, then threw his glass against the wall and covered her hand with his left. Suzanne started, then laughed and pulled him into a hug.

"You're cleaning that up."

They separated, wiping their eyes, and Will said, "How do I know . . ." but looked ashamed and didn't finish his question.

Suzanne held up her hands. "We could fire our lawyers and hire a mediator?" She shrugged. "We'll have to find a way to rebuild the trust. I'm not saying it's going to be easy, but I think it will be worth it."

Will took her hands in his. "I would never ever stop you from making wine. All that was . . ."

"The 'strategy'?" Suzanne shook her head. "The restraining order, too. Things just got . . ."

". . . out of hand." Will finished.

"Hello? Did I hear breaking glass?" Craig called from the doorway. "If there's any blood, I'm backing out now and driving away."

"It's safe; we're over here," Suzanne yelled back. "Grab a glass and come taste the new vintage. I think it's going to be a very good year."

Epilogue

__Canciones de la Sirena (Song of the Siren):__
a dramatic wine with suppressed exuberance, it opens with aromas of
wild strawberry and pastry, offers plum and ripe red berries with a dust-
ing of exotic spices and beautifully balanced, age-worthy tannins. Like a
melody you can't forget, the finish lingers on

"I think we're ready," Suzanne said in the lull between crashing waves. A bonfire sputtered and snapped nearby as Carlos fed it driftwood.

Donnie waded into the surf with the remote-control boat carrying Janice's ashes, lifting it up above the crests until he could get past the big breaks. Suzanne tested the controller one more time as Mark, Craig, Laura, Will, Teri, and Carlos looked on. Mark was wearing a Zorro mask and cape, Craig wore a green sequined witch hat, Will was a vampire, Laura had fang marks on her neck, Teri wore all black with an orange scarf, and Carlos had painted his face like a skull. Donnie had Frankenstein bolts on his neck, which he kept trying to shield from the spray. Suzanne tugged at the hem of her Star Trek uniform and waved Donnie further out.

The air tasted of salt and the lush decay of the sea. Donnie waved and gestured, pointing down the beach. As Suzanne turned, she spotted something in the distance. It was a tall figure walking along the shoreline carrying a guitar. Tommy had said he might be late, but he had made it in time.

Donnie's dad grinned as he drew near. His silver-white hair streaked with ginger and big beard usually made him look like Santa in middle age, but today he was wearing an eye patch, gold earring, and bandana. Suzanne couldn't help but grin back. He took in the group as he approached, narrowed in on Suzanne and pulled her into a hug.

"I'm glad you made it, Tommy," Suzanne said.

"Wouldn't miss it," Donnie's father said, lifting her off her feet. "Thank you for including me."

Suzanne buried her face in his neck, surprised at how strongly she responded to a man who was still practically a stranger, but it was a good surprise. She was reluctant to let go, breathing in his sweat and musk mixed with the scent of the ocean. She had no memories like this of her own father, and Donnie was just beginning to build some. She pulled back and smiled to herself. At least one good thing came out of Janice's death. Suzanne turned away from Tommy and waved her arm in the air. Donnie set the boat down after a swell passed, then lit the flare that formed the mast for the ship. Suzanne immediately started to drive it further out to sea as Donnie waded quickly to shore, where Teri wrapped him in towels and a blanket.

The group watched the boat's progress in silence, the whine of the boat intermittently audible over the respiration of the surf. The sputtering flare dimmed, then flames shot upward as a dozen shards of light arched into the sky and exploded into stars and chrysanthemums of red and blue and gold. Suzanne heard someone let out an involuntary "ahhh" the way people always do at fireworks. She was so lost in her own thoughts, Tommy had to ask her twice before she heard him.

"Do you want me to play now?" He was holding up his guitar in both hands like an offering.

Suzanne blinked, then nodded without relinquishing the haze of memory and history that surrounded her. Donnie's father began slowly, plucking notes more like rainfall than melody, until they gathered into a song and he began to sing softly.

"Now I've heard there was a secret chord that David played and it pleased the Lord . . ."

Suzanne laughed and wept at the same time. The song was perfect. It had been so overexposed Leonard Cohen had actually asked people to stop recording it, but no one ever really got it right, anyway. Janice would have loved it. Tommy's voice was low, and he sang almost as if talking to himself, picking up volume as the fireworks died.

"I did my best but it wasn't much, I couldn't feel, so I tried to touch, I've told the truth, I didn't come to fool you; and even though it all went wrong, I'll stand before the Lord of Song with nothing on my tongue but Hallelujah . . ."

And the group joined in at the end, singing "hallelujah" until the bright sparks all dropped into the sea. In the gloom following the sunset, they were drawn to the warmth and glow of the fire, circling it. There were canvas bags and folding chairs and a big log that had been pulled close for seating, but they all remained standing. Donnie stood close to the fire to dry off while Carlos passed a box of sugar skulls around. Laura leaned against Will, and Mark squeezed Suzanne's hand. Donnie looked at Suzanne and nodded.

"A year ago," Suzanne began, "my sister died the same way she lived— on her own terms." She paused, images of Janice flashing through her mind: smoking in the kitchen, wearing the pirate scarf, hanging the Halloween decorations, lying motionless on the couch. "Janice wasn't what most people would consider a role model . . . but she was there when I needed her." She reached over and took Mark's hand. "And a lot of other people, too. Janice didn't suffer fools, gladly or otherwise, but she accepted people, embraced them, really, in a way no one else I've ever known did. She wanted a Viking funeral, and I promised to give her one," she gestured toward the sea and shrugged, "of sorts. But this is also a tribute." Suzanne knelt on the sand to open the canvas bag at her feet. She pulled out two unlabeled bottles and a box of wine glasses which she handed to Will and Laura to pour and pass. "I used to think the past wasn't important," she looked at Mark, "or maybe I just wanted that to be true. But those last days with Janice, I learned more about my family than in all the decades before. Even though you choose your path, create your own future, how you started, shapes everything. I know that now." She gestured to her wine glass. "You'd think I might have known that already," everyone laughed, "but I was a little slow to make the connection." Suzanne lifted her glass to her nose to breathe in the wild strawberries and shortbread and ocean, then she raised it in toast. "To Janice."

"Janice!" The group echoed. They all drank.

"Oh my god, what is this?" Craig asked. "It's fabulous!"

Will and Suzanne grinned and Will said, "Wild yeast, mostly whole cluster from the blocks at the top of the ridge."

"With grapes from the block with the fire mixed in," Suzanne added. Craig choked on his wine and Carlos patted his back.

"This is yours?" Tommy asked. "Nice." He sat down on a log with his glass beside him and began picking out a tune.

As soon as Donnie recognized it, he leaned over to touch his glass to Suzanne's. Mark smiled, and the rest of the group exchanged questioning looks.

"Janice named me after this song. She named Donnie after a song, too." Suzanne smiled.

"And now I'm repaying her gift, all her gifts. This wine," she held up her glass, "is a sister to Mermaid Tears, but it's something different, too." She drank the last of her wine, savoring the caress of its finish. "We're going to give it two more months in the barrel, and Craig is designing a label for it."

Will refilled everyone's glasses as Craig dug into one of the bags to pull out a portfolio. He lifted his glass toward Suzanne. "Your finest effort."

She bowed her head to acknowledge the compliment, then returned the gesture. "*Our* finest effort." They both smiled. Suzanne raised her glass as if it were a torch. "Canciones de la Sirena!"

"This isn't the finished painting," Craig said holding up a large sheet of watercolor paper as they savored the wine, "but you get the idea."

The foreground was the same rocky outcropping as on the Mermaid

Tears label, but the mermaid sitting on it had iridescent wings in shades of gold and peacock and teal and seafoam. Her head was back, eyes closed and mouth open in song. She had no tear. Rays of light in the same green-gold as the siren's scales fanned out from the lighthouse in the distance to pierce the fog.

"It's beautiful," Laura said.

Suzanne ran her fingertips lightly over the painting. "The siren is irresistible passion . . ." Suzanne smiled to herself then winked at Mark, "because this wine is dangerously seductive. The canciones are all the songs Janice loved and gave to us." She touched her glass to Donnie's and nodded to Tommy.

Suzanne looked at the characters gathered around the fire, gold light and shadows dancing on their faces as the fog seeped in around them. These people were as much a part of her as her vines and the wine she made. Each of them added flavor and nuance to her days and years that combined in perfect balance. If the years of her life had been bottled, this vintage was unexpectedly one of the best. A year ago she would never have predicted that, and the thought both humbled and delighted her. She found Mark watching her intently and leaned into him, angling her face up to meet his lips as he bent to kiss her.

"The final piece to a great vintage is the company that shares it. These grapes had nearly perfect growing conditions, and yet . . ." Suzanne swirled the wine in her glass and shook her head, "we could have ruined everything." She paused, and the silence filled with the ghosts of the battles and strife of the previous October. "Janice's death was a loss, but it also turned out to be," she offered Mark a tiny smile, "a gift. Last Halloween it would have been hard to imagine all of us here together," Craig *snorked* and Will nudged him, "but like Janice's favorite Star Trek captain," Suzanne raised her glass in final toast, "I like to think there always are . . . possibilities."

The End

Acknowledgements

Writing a novel is not so far removed from making wine as you might imagine: years of growth before anything is produced, fluctuation in quality from environmental causes, the desire to bring delight and inspiration to your consumers. And of course, the many hands involved from harvest to consumption.

Thank you to John Banning for making possible everything I do, and to Alex and Max for treating all my projects and passions as (mostly) normal. Thanks to John Billheimer, Mark Coggins, and Ann Hillesland for the monthly critique and support, and to the Unabridged Book Club: Jan Austin, Alexia Gilmore, Teri Hessel, Barrie Moore, and Jeanese Snyder for their laughter, love, and helpful feedback.

Mary Evers was an early reader on the Iowa front, and additional Midwestern support came from The Stinson Prairie Arts Council, Tracy Harmon at Train Wreck Winery, Katie Aguado, Dale Boone, Colleen Devine, and Joan Skogstrom along with residents and locations in Algona, Iowa, too numerous to name, which provided a real structure on which to build my fictional town.

I have much gratitude for the wine makers and wine connoisseurs who gave me guidance and direction whether they knew it or not: Therese and Dan Martin (Martin Ranch Winery), Andy Peay (Peay Vineyard), Jim and Judy Schultz (Windy Oaks), the folks at Sea Smoke Cellars, Lee Berger, Jackie Starkovitch, and Andres Velasquez. Any dramatic errors in the representation of viticulture are my fault, not theirs.

My exceptional editor, James Logan, saved you all from my over-zealous use of exclamation points, and Jessica Kristie provided support and guidance from the moment she accepted the manuscript—she gives publishing a good name.

Finally, special thanks to my sisters, Patty Bristow, Mary Evers, Judy Van Brunt, and Sally Winters—may you live long and prosper.

This is a work of fiction. That means I made it all up. The infusion of authentic detail helps breathe life into fiction, but don't confuse that with autobiography. If you insist on looking for something in the book that really happened, pick the sex scenes.

About the Author

Leaving Iowa for Stanford University, Sheila Scobba Banning remained in California where she lives with her husband, sons, and menagerie of pets. When not writing, Sheila creates fascinators and outlandish hats, often with a glass of wine in hand. She throws fabulous parties, wears vintage dresses, and laughs until she cries every day. Her superpower is catalysis.

CPSIA information can be obtained at www.ICGtesting.com
Printed in the USA
BVOW04s0415210813

329020BV00005B/42/P